Of El...

Story by
J. R. Knoll

Artwork by
Sandi Johnson

Dedication

This one is for my folks
Clifton and Joyce Knoll
I am what I am thanks to my parents

CHAPTER 1

Late summer, 988 seasons

The deepest regions of the Abtont Forest are where the trees have always grown the tallest. None of this forest has been disturbed by man as he is afraid to go there. This is an area where packs of wolves and dreads stalk the forest floor, where carnivorous tree-leapers pounce on unsuspecting travelers and tear them apart in moments and begin eating their victims as they ascend into the canopy with their meal still alive. Unicorns frequent this forest as trails between the tall pines and hearty hardwoods give way to little meadows where grasses and fruit bearing bushes flourish. Squirrels and rabbits and deer are unusually thick here and forest predators really have no trouble finding food, though catching it is an entirely different matter.

Because of the denseness of the trees, dragons simply do not hunt here. One can land among the trees, but that means a cumbersome climb back into the canopy to find the wind and enough room to outstretch one's wings, and larger game like grawrdox are not to be found.

Deep in this forest is a huge lake, one that keeps the ground moist for many leagues around it and is fed by three rivers that simply run out of room in the gently rolling hills of Central Abtont. Eventually, the rivers, now joined as one, exit on the other end of the lake and continue their flow toward the sea, but at one point they encounter a cliff that is fifty human's heights tall where the land seems to have just fallen away many eons ago. Much of the stone remains bare and crystals and many kinds of metals shimmer in the sunlight all over it. Among these crystals are an abundance of emeralds, jade, and many other elements that simply don't belong together, though there they are. This cliff forms a semi-circle that is more than a league wide and the river careens into a deep pool right in the middle, then it continues its lazy course to the southwest.

And in the middle of this semi-circle is a castle that has been at the center of many human legends since man could speak.

This castle was formed more than two thousand seasons ago and its construction is also something of legend. With six turrets rising above the tall treetops, the castle at the center of the Elf Kingdom is an ancient structure that predates anything that men occupy to date. Nobody is sure of its true age, but legend has it that it was constructed by a mix of elvan magic and the stonework of an army of gnomes to cut the jade and emeralds that decorated it. This is a powerful structure, green in color that blends in with the surrounding forest. Powerful sorcerers were said to have raised up and formed the stone for the palace and its battlements directly from the bedrock below and its rounded features and arched bridges between high walls and towers are more of a flow as if the stone was formed of liquid and allowed to become solid again. This is plausible, as many sorcerers still retain this ability to make stone a thick liquid, form it by their will, and return it to the stone it was, though none of the sorcerers who formed this castle were of human descent. The castle is, in fact, a part of the forest. Green things grow all over it. Fruit bearing vines cover the walls and to a great extent provide much of the food for the inhabitants. Trees grow atop the castle walls as they have for many generations. The conical peaks of the towers are covered with thick grasses and small green things that flower from spring to fall. Though hollow within, the mountainous structure looks a solid one that can support the weight of the largest dragons without fear of crack or fracture. The rooftops are emerald and clear crystal, very thick and sunlight pours through to illuminate the interior without the need of torches or lamps. Some say that the castle itself is a living entity and remains so as long as it is inhabited by the elves. It repairs itself and has, on occasion, grown to meet the needs of its expanding population of elves and a few gnomes.

Only a league from this enchanting castle, a camp was broken down and three travelers made ready for their journey to their second home. This was a small family: An elf man, his lovely wife and little daughter of fifteen seasons.

Leumas Brebor was a very tall elf, almost the height of an average human man and was built accordingly. Long arms and legs were thick with muscle and some speculated that he was part human himself, though it was well known that he came from an ancient and noble elvan family. He seemed fearless and was well trained and skilled with sword and axe and bow and many other weapons. His black beard was worn short and was perfectly groomed as was his black hair, which was cut very short at the sides of his head and just a little longer over the top. Elf men, especially those of noble blood, usually wore their hair very long, but Leumas found this to be too much of a hindrance to what he did. Grooming was something he considered very important and in this respect he was something of a rebel, even in how he dressed. This day he still wore light battle armor of polished plate over his shoulders, upper arms and thighs. Chain mail was more comfortable under his forest green tunic and the plate he wore over it was hung over his saddlebags. Black trousers were worn beneath the armor on his legs and heavy black boots reached to his calves.

As he extinguished the last coals of the fire, located in the center of the clearing they had camped in that was well within eyeshot of the main road, his wife rolled the last of their blankets and began to stuff it in one of the saddle bags of the smallest horse. She was a lovely woman with chestnut brown hair that was worn very long. Elf women of status generally dressed in long gowns or ornate dresses of light fabrics in the heat of summer, but Werhess was one who knew to dress for the environment and this day wore green tights over her shapely legs and one of Leumas' old white swordsman's shirts, belted at her waist. Since she was a head height shorter than her husband and nowhere near as heavily built the shirt fit her very long, dropping to the middle of her thighs almost like a dress. It was very light, very airy, and she had the sleeves rolled up just past her elbows for comfort. She was a well made elf who still had a girlish, flirty smile for her husband even after sixteen seasons of marriage, and the affection she had for him was clear in her eyes as she turned and looked to him, and a little smile touched her lips as she watched her daughter crouch down beside him.

Teek was an elf girl of only fifteen seasons but she was as learned as one twice her age. This was a slight girl, perhaps two thirds a human man's height as she stood straight and tall. Very long black hair was restrained behind her in a pony tail as she turned her big, emerald green eyes down to what her father was doing. Though well muscled, she was a lightly built girl and her dainty frame was not what one would expect to see camping in the wilderness. Dressed in emerald green leggings and a loosely fitting white shirt similar to what her mother wore, she also wore a green jerkin that was not buttoned and hung open as she crouched down.

Leumas looked to her with a proud smile, and when she met his gaze he asked, "Do you remember what I told you about campfires?" When she eagerly nodded, he continued, "It is very important to leave the land as we found it, and especially make certain that our fire is completely extinguished. We are the wards of the forest here."

She nodded to him again, then reached behind her and produced a leather water bladder. Pulling the stopper, she held it over the fire and poured the contents onto the coals in a circular motion as her father stirred it in. Steam rose and in short order the bladder was empty.

"Looks good," he commended in his gruff voice. "We'll just pack some earth over it to be sure." His eyes found the girl again as she began to scoop up handfuls of loose soil, and he watched as she dumped them into the fire pit one after the other. He patted her dainty shoulder, then stood and turned toward his horse, barking, "Woman! How fares my horse this day?"

Werhess strode toward him with sultry steps and replied, "Nearly as strong as you, my Lord."

Reaching her, he took her waist and brutally pulled her into him, then he wrapped his arms around her and crushed her to him. "Perhaps your Lord will show you just how strong, my pretty young damsel."

Teek cringed and shook her head, sticking her tongue out as if she was about to gag on the words she was hearing.

"Why Lord Brebor!" Werhess declared. "One would think thee a letch!"

Venting a deep breath, Teek rubbed her eyes, a little smile on her lips as she shook her head. She could not very well fault her parents for loving one another so, and since she was their only child they lavished attention and affection on her. Perhaps their love patter was a tolerable exchange for this.

When they were suddenly silent, she looked over her shoulder, her brow arching as she saw them seven paces behind her engaging in yet another passionate kiss. This was something she did not need to see. In another seasons she would be sixteen, marrying age in the Elf Kingdom, but she intended to stave that off as long as she could. She had taken notice of a few elf boys and knew that she had the attention of a great number of them, and not because of who her father was. Sure there were elf girls her age with far more generous curves, some whom she thought were prettier, but something about Teek had their attention nonetheless, and she really did not mind.

With the fire pit in order, she stood and brushed herself off before setting her hands on her hips to give the pit one more good look before reluctantly turning to her parents. She slung the water bladder over her shoulder and walked toward her small horse, trying not to look at her parents as she strode past them, but she did swing the water bottle and hit her father on the back with it as she passed.

Raising his brow, Leumas drew away from his wife and looked to his little daughter as she approached the smallest horse, one that was a deep brown with white above his hooves and a white mark down his nose. Turning his eyes to his wife, he whispered, "I think she says it's time to go."

Werhess giggled and nodded to him. "In her own subtle way."

In short order they were mounted and on their way to the palace. The road here was wide enough for them to ride three abreast and the small horses bred by the elves for generations had plenty of room. The largest horse, ridden by Leumas himself, was not one bred by the Elf Kingdom.

Two seasons prior, feeling the need for a larger mount for his sizeable frame, he had traded with one of the human kingdoms to the Northeast for a horse more fitting of his size, and it was far larger than those ridden by his family. As always, Teek rode between her mother and father, and as always her attention was on her father.

As they made their way at a slow pace to their destination, Leumas entertained his family with yet another story of his exploits across the land, and as always he had his daughter's full attention.

"One would think," he went on, "that they would have learned after our first encounter, but I suppose short memory is a condition of the slow witted. They wanted to fight again and naturally I obliged, but this time they had me outnumbered ten to one!"

Teek's brow shot up.

His eyes shifted to her. "Lined up across the field, they were, and in a full charge, coming right at me! And that, my dear, is why we train on the bow the way we do. A hundred paces apart and I began to plink at them and by the time the distance between us was gone I'd downed all but three, and I was out of arrows." He looked ahead again, drawing a deep breath before he spoke again. "It was hand to hand after that, and on horseback that is no easy task. Larger and stronger, they were, so the odds would have to be shifted yet again. Had my big battle axe on my saddle behind me, my shield hanging on my left and my sword beneath it. Stands to reason that I would go for them right away, but no. It was time they knew my intentions were to win this fight, not be a martyr, so I went right for that axe. About ten paces away, with one coming on my right and two on my left, I pulled my axe and let it fly with a haphazard aim, trusting that it would find its way, and find its way it did. The fellow on my right barely had time to respond before my axe buried itself in his chest. As he was rolling off I had time to get my shield on my am and raise it against the blade that was thrust at me."

Teek's eyes widened.

"They turned right away as we passed," he went on, "but I needed some distance. Got my sword out before turning my steed hard toward them, and when I faced them I let go a mighty battle cry. I knew they'd try and flank me again, and flank me they did, but I cut my horse hard to the left only a few paces before we met, and when he tried to raise his shield to repel my blade I sent it into his thigh instead, right outside of the plate armor he wore. Couldn't waste time, though, so I turned back hard on the other and it was sword against sword from that point. His wounded companion was not so quick to join the fight so it was finally one on one. Many seasons of training had merged within me that day and what I did was more instinct than thought. That's what the training is all about, my dear, and it was that training that led to my ultimate victory. But I didn't vanquish all my enemies that day." His eyes cut to her again.

Her brow lowered over her eyes and she raised her chin.

Leumas smiled. "Victory does not always mean your foe has to die. Sometimes mercy is a far better end. I took their swords, bandaged their wounds and sent them on their way to tell their leaders that they could come back in friendship or they'd meet my steel once again. The fellow I dueled even shook my hand before they departed. Not easy to find one who is gracious in defeat and I was proud to know him. A treaty was signed the following spring and those two soldiers and I enjoyed getting drunk together."

Werhess loudly cleared her throat as she cut her eyes to him.

With a jolly laugh, Leumas shook his head and assured, "The girl's fifteen, my Love, and more worldly wise than I know you are comfortable with."

"Still," Werhess began.

"Still nothing," he scoffed. Looking back to Teek, he smiled again and went on, "Nothing brings out a man's passion like battle, and after that battle he's looking for a stout drink and a lovely woman to defile."

"Leumas!"

Teek covered her mouth as a hushed giggle erupted from her and she enjoyed a good laugh with her father

Leumas winked at his wife, smiling broader as she blushed and looked away from him. When he turned his attention forward again, his smile went flat and he raised his head, his eyes widening as he saw smoke over the treetops, lots of smoke! He reined in and stopped his horse, then quickly pulled the tunic from him and laid it across his lap. Reaching behind him, he was quick to get his plate armor over his chest and back and buckled each side with one hand.

Teek and Werhess had stopped their horses just beyond him and turned, looking back at him with the same concern they had many times.

Looking to them in turn, his was an expression of focus and determination as he ordered, "Keep your weapons handy, but if something happens you are to get to the forest and wait for me." The roar of some horrible beast drew his attention and his eyes narrowed. "This could get messy. Teek, remember everything I taught you." He looked to his wife. "Werhess, I go with you and our daughter in my heart."

She bravely raised her chin and said, "Come back to me in victory, my Love."

Without another word he kicked his horse's flanks and launched himself into battle against yet another unknown enemy.

Werhess and Teek watched after him with fearful eyes even after he had disappeared down the road. A moment later they looked to each other, and Werhess could see the distress in her daughter's eyes. "He'll be fine," she assured. "He always is. He's the Elf Kingdom's greatest hero, after all."

Teek nodded and looked back down the road.

Heaving a heavy breath, Werhess looked that way too. "He has commanded us to wait in the shadows of the forest until it is safe, but he always forgets that we have had ample training in battle, too." Her eyes shifted to her daughter and she smiled ever so slightly. "String your bow, little girl. We'll hide in the forest closer to the castle."

Normally, the last couple of leagues to the castle would have taken the better part of the day. That ride is when Leumas spent his best time with his two favorite girls, but today the forest blurred by as horses were pushed as hard as they would go and galloped on fleet hooves toward the battle ahead.

Finally, they could see where the road would open into the grassy field that surrounded the castle and closed the circle started by the cliff wall behind it. This was a huge, wide open space of many hundreds of acres where horses and other animals were taken to graze in safety, but this day it was the scene of a horrific battle.

Werhess pulled her reins and stopped her horse right at the tree line and Teek stopped beside her. Out in the field was a creature they had never seen before, never imagined.

This was a dragon, but not one that was native to the Abtont Forest. Very lean, this dragon had the neck of a serpent, the orange eyes of a serpent, and the long, thin tail of a serpent. It was black for the most part with the sunlight reflecting dark reds and purples as the sunlight hit its scales just right. The dorsal scales that ran from between its long, black horns all the way to the end of its tail each ended in a long spine and these scales stood erect as the dragon turned on the castle again. Its limbs were relatively thin but clearly very powerful. Long fingers on its hands ended in sharp claws that curled inward. The armor of its belly was a very dark red and in transverse scales from its jaw to the end of its tail. Orange eyes with vertical pupils were wide as its long, narrow jaws gaped in a roar that would remind one of an angry forest cat, though far louder and somewhat deeper. Its many teeth were very long, very thin and all pointed and directed backward and as it roared two fangs that were nearly the length of a human's forearm rocked down from the roof of its mouth.

With its scaly brow held low, the dragon turned its attention to the palace wall where archers were doing their best to repel it, and it gaped its jaws wider. Fire exploded from between its teeth and the flames were sent in a long, boiling strike that burned those on the perimeter wall to ash in seconds.

As Werhess and her daughter looked about, there were soldiers and horses lying everywhere around the dragon and some of the grass of the field was on fire. Fear found them both as they looked for Leumas.

Teek's eyes widened and she pointed toward the palace which was directly across the field from them.

Leumas had emerged from a concealed place about two hundred paces to the left of the main gate on the perimeter wall. Even from this distance they could see that he had gone for his heavy helmet and longbow and his ornately decorated metal shield hung from the side of his saddle. He was circling around the dragon's flank while its attention was still on the palace archers. With his bow in his hand and a crystal tipped arrow ready to shoot, he controlled his horse with his heels as he raised the bow and took a quick aim.

The dragon saw the elf hero and turned toward him with wide steps, spreading its wings as its jaws swung open in another horrible roar, but its reaction came too late and the arrow streaked toward it in a blur, striking the dragon in the belly, and as the crystal tip shattered the magics within were released in a terrible explosion that finally breached heavy dragon scales. An ear splitting shriek sounded from the dragon as it stumbled backward and fell, and this was the elf hero's time to strike.

Throwing his bow from him, Leumas reached behind him and pulled his axe from its place there, then he reached behind his shield and slipped his arms into place, lifting it to shoulder height as he turned his horse to charge the dragon. When he was nearly in striking range the dragon lifted its head and swung its tail, tripping the horse. As the horse stumbled and fell, Leumas dove from his saddle. He hit the ground shield-first and rolled expertly to his feet, never losing his grip on his axe.

The dragon had all the time it needed to get back to its feet and it turned to square off with its puny opponent with its wings half spread and its arms open, its claws ready for battle. The left side of its belly was burnt and bleeding and the dragon turned slightly to guard its injury.

Elf warrior and dragon studied each other for a moment, and each knew that the dragon held all of the advantages.

And so did Werhess. As her husband and the beast slowly circled she removed her bow from its place behind her saddle and reached for the quiver that was tied to her saddlebag. Looking to the elf girl beside her, she ordered, "Wait right here, Teek. No matter what happens or what you see stay close to the forest and hide if you need to until it's safe again.

The girl hesitantly nodded and watched with wide, fearful eyes as her mother kicked her horse forward at a fast pace and into the fight.

Leumas raised his shield to repel a blast of fire and kept his axe ready for the dragon to come into range. His sword still hung on his side and he had already planned out how it would come into play. He also knew that this fight would have to end quickly.

The dragon had clearly faced such an opponent before and circled a couple more steps, baring its teeth to hiss as it did. It seemed to know that the axe could bring it harm and appeared to be plotting a way around it.

Behind the dragon, Werhess slowed her horse and took careful aim with her bow. The barbed steel tip would not penetrate the beast's scales, but when it turned its head down those scales opened from one another and perhaps her arrow would pierce the skin between the scales. As the dragon lowered its head, she found the opening she was looking for as two scales separated where its neck turned the sharpest and at only about forty paces away she loosed the arrow with a true aim.

The steel arrowhead did in fact penetrate the blue-gray skin between the dragon's scales and it shrieked as it was stung, swinging half around to see what had gotten it. By the time it saw the elf woman she had another arrow ready and loosed it at the dragon's face, and it shied away as the arrow glanced off of the scales of its snout.

Leumas took full advantage of the dragon's distraction and held his axe over his head shouting, "Awaken spirits in the blade!" With those words an emerald fire exploded from the blades of the axe and with all of his strength and a mighty yell he threw it with his best aim toward the dragon, aiming for its already wounded belly, but the dragon swung around and began to crouch as the fire trailing axe was in flight and took the impact square on the chest.

A horrific explosion blew the dragon off of his feet and he slammed onto the ground flat on his back, his wings and limbs sprawled and his head striking last. A wave of air could be seen across the tops of the tall grasses and in a moment all was silent.

His eyes narrow and locked on his downed foe, Leumas' hand slowly found his sword and gripped it tightly. This was not over. With steps hesitant at first, he strode toward the dragon, his shield ready and he slowly pulled his blade from its sheath. Nearly there, he paused and looked down to the smoking axe which lay at his feet that still glowed emerald at the edges of the blades. Sliding his sword back into its place, he reached down to pick the axe up and nearly did not hear the dragon's tail cutting through the air in time, and barely got his shield up as the spiny scales of the end of the dragon's tail reached him. The impact was a hard one and he rolled to a stop some distance from where he had been. The dragon's scales had cut through his shield and as he rose up on his knees he gingerly pulled what was left of it from an arm he knew was broken. Cradling his arm with the other, he glared at the dragon as it turned over and got to all fours to face him. He looked down at his arm to see it bleeding as well. With a quick glance around, he found his axe and picked it up, holding his broken arm to him as he slowly stood.

The dragon also stood, revealing another burnt wound, this time to the right part of his chest. Some of the scales had been blasted away and the wound that was left bled slowly from cracks and splits in burnt skin. Growling with each breath, the dragon bared its teeth again, opening its jaws only slightly as it hissed at its challenger. The flanks of its neck swelled, its eyes locked on the big elf man before it.

Leumas knew this meant fire and with no shield and no way to hold one he was openly vulnerable to such an attack. "Spirits of the blade," he shouted. "Release your fury against this beast!" With another mighty yell he held the axe over his shoulder, then back, then he threw it toward the dragon's head with all of the strength he could muster.

Fire exploded from the dragon's gaping jaws and met the axe nearly to its head, and as the fire and axe met there was another horrific explosion, one that knocked both combatants to their backs.

The fire did not reach Leumas, but the shockwave left him stunned and he lay on the ground for long seconds trying to regain his wits.

Recovering quickly, the dragon rolled to all fours again, turning to face its downed enemy. This was the moment the beast needed to strike its death blow and it would not hesitate, nor would it reach its intended victim in time.

Another arrow slammed into its head near its eye and it flinched away again as the arrow glanced away, then turned with bared teeth on the new threat.

Still atop her horse, Werhess already had another arrow in place and was taking aim when the dragon wheeled around to charge her. She loosed this one with a quick aim and kicked her horse's flanks, yelling, "Yah!"

As she watched the dragon charge her mother and her mother retreat, Teek swung down from her horse and took her bow from the saddle. Slinging the quiver over her shoulder, she trotted forward as she readied her first arrow, her eyes locked on the battle before her. She was terrified and knew that she was not even close to a match for this beast, but she also could not leave her parents to be killed. With Werhess retreating and the dragon turning to pursue her, Teek found herself running as fast as she could with her bow ready but not aimed, her eyes locked on the black beast before her.

Still, this horrible creature seemed a little clumsy on the ground and Werhess' horse was able to turn sharply and outmaneuver it, though it did not give up its pursuit.

Having regained his wits and his enchanted axe, Leumas readied his weapon again as it pursued his wife, his eyes widening as he saw the throat of the dragon swell, and he knew it meant to belch fire at the woman he loved. With another mighty yell, he brought the axe over his shoulder and commanded, "Spirits of the blade, fell the enemy of the elves!" He threw the axe with a true aim and all his might and the emerald fire burned in a spiral toward the dragon's neck, this time hitting the heavier armor near its back. The power exploded as before, but this time did not penetrate the scales, though it did draw the beast's attention.

Leumas noticed that his axe had ricocheted away and disappeared into the grass some distance behind the dragon and at once drew his sword, holding his shield ready on his broken arm as the dragon stalked toward him. The pain from his broken arm was evident on his face, though a defiant snarl was on his mouth as he squared off against his foe again.

Werhess and Teek both knew that when the dragon charged it meant to finish the big elf hero and that it likely could before Leumas could strike his death blow, and both of them acted quickly with arrows. Teek's glanced off of the dorsal scales between its shoulders while her mother's found a place where the scales were raised and wedged itself between them. This clearly stung and the dragon barked a short roar before turning on her.

Teek knew that her father would need his axe to finish this fight. She had seen the area where it had settled into the tall grass and ran as fast as she could to retrieve it. Suddenly, she felt the weight of the battle fully on her shoulders. Her big green eyes were wide as she looked about in the grass ahead of her. She *had* to get that axe to her father! Finally seeing where the grass had been flattened out ahead of her, she dropped her bow and ran as hard as she could that way. Still, the weapon was elusive and she dropped down and groped for it.

The loud scream of her mother drew her attention and she stood, looking to the battle. Cold air rushed into her as she watched the dragon stand and fling its head over, opening its jaws as it did.

And the body of her mother tumbled through the air and disappeared into the grass.

Leumas yelled and charged the dragon, raising his weapon as the beast turned on him.

Teek's foot hit something and she looked down, finally seeing the axe there and she was quick to reach down and grasp it with both hands to pick it up. It was very heavy and she held it close to herself as she darted toward her father. Her father was yelling in a voice she had never heard before and was swinging his sword like a mad-elf, hacking away at whatever the dragon would present to him and missing often. His was pure emotion, pure rage and grief and everything else that spilled from his heart. Always he had taught his little daughter that victory meant a clear mind and controlling one's emotions, making every strike count, but he was nothing but pure, suicidal rage.

When Teek was thirty paces away she held the axe ready.

Gaping jaws were thrust at Leumas again and he responded with his sword. The blade opened a scaly lip and the dragon withdrew with a shriek. Bleeding from that stuck lip, the dragon opened its jaws and bared its teeth, this time responding with fire. Leumas backed away, raising his shield against the thin jet of flame that was sent against him and not realizing that this was merely a diversion.

Teek froze, her eyes wide as events unfolded in front of her. The dragon slammed its hand onto Leumas' shield and flattened him to the ground, and as the elf hero struggled under the beast's weight, the dragon opened its jaws once again. Narrow fangs as long as swords swung down from the roof of its mouth and it ripped the shield away and lunged downward. Leumas let out a cry as the fangs plunged through his armor and into his body, bringing his sword up one last time to ram into the dragon's throat, but his strength had already abandoned him and his arm fell.

The dragon slowly raised its head, its orange, serpentine eyes locked on its unmoving foe.

Even thirty paces away, Teek could see that her father was still breathing, and she poised the axe to attack the dragon herself as she trotted forward.

Its jaws opening once again, the dragon's head descended to its enemy and its smaller teeth grabbed on.

Teek drew a gasp and stopped where she was, her wide eyes following the dragon's head as it lifted her father from the ground. Those teeth were sunk into his chest and his head and one shoulder were inside the beast's mouth! With the last of his strength, the elf hero hacked away at the dragon as he shouted defiantly from within its jaws.

Lifting its head, the dragon opened its jaws and lunged, taking the big elf further into its mouth, then again until only his kicking legs could be seen. One more time and it finally swallowed, and the muffled screams of its meal grew more and more faint until they could not be heard. The dragon's throat bulged as it swallowed this greatest of the elf heroes and more bulges appeared as it moved down toward his belly.

Leumas Brebor was still alive!

Finally, and with a deep growl, the dragon lowered its head, looking around it and finally locking its eyes on Teek's unmoving mother. With two strides it was there, and it ate her in the same manner.

Teek dropped the axe and sank to her knees, watching in horror as it swallowed her mother whole as it had her father.

Turning its attention to the castle, the dragon roared, almost a scream, and it strode toward the sealed gate of the castle. No archers shot at it and the entire elf kingdom stood by in stunned silence.

It scanned the battlements for a moment, baring its teeth, and finally demanded in a gravely voice that sounded almost like an old woman, "Bringing out Elf King." Even though its voice was more old woman than dragon, it was quite clearly male.

As King Arlo appeared at the battlement right above the main gate, which was easily five heights above the dragon's head, the dragon's eyes narrowed and its spiny scales stood erect as he backed off a step to see the Elf King a little better.

Teek could not see the King well from this distance, only a small silhouette atop the first wall.

Long, tense seconds followed.

With a toothy snarl, the dragon said, "Vultross has conquered Elf Kingdom. Vultross will have tributes or Elf Kingdom will suffer more. Not opposing Vultross and live." He took a few steps back and opened his wings, warning, "Vultross returns tomorrow. Having tributes for Vultross and leaving in peace. No tributes and many elves perish."

Teek watched as the dragon turned toward her. She was frozen there and could not even get off of her knees as the beast strode toward her and her wide eyes followed him as he swept his wings and easily lifted himself into the air—with her parents in his belly. Slowly, her gaze sank to the ground before her. She could feel nothing, not her thoughts or emotions, not grief or sadness, not her own body. Her vision closed to a pinpoint and her long lashes slowly descended over her eyes as she fell forward.

CHAPTER 2
Late Summer, 989 seasons

Sixteen. Marrying age. Still, only one suitor really appealed to her, though a great number vied for her elusive attentions, and that one suitor had to be the very one who was forbidden to her.

The palace suite of Leumas Brebor was very big, very spacious for elves and was divided into two bedrooms and a larger living area. Decorated with many trophies from his exploits, it was well furnished with deep cushioned chairs and a special made love seat with plush pillows in forest green and tan. Many of the decorations were clearly his wife's doing and many vases were about, but there were no flowers in them. It was one of the most comfortable places in the palace, but for the last season or so. This was where the Brebor family stayed, a room given to the Elf Kingdom's greatest hero by King Arlo himself. Leumas had an estate in the forest, but he had spent much of his time at the castle, in part to stay close to the King and Council should some important issue arise and in part for the comfort of his family. With him gone, his estate could be lost as Teek was too young to maintain it and was not married. A woman, especially one so young, was not often left in control of such properties unless she had a husband or a large family to assist with it. Teek had neither.

A large, oak dining table was on one end of the family room. It was oval and had been the scene of many wonderful meals and gatherings with her family, and she would listen to her father with her full attention as he told her stories of his many adventures.

This day, with the frilly, decorative cloth that usually covered it wadded up in one of the chairs, her armor and arming undergarments were laid out in their places as they would be worn.

Furniture had been pushed to the walls of the spacious room, leaving only the huge carpet there in the middle.

Teek was lightly dressed in tight fitting white undergarments. Though the lower piece hugged her hips tightly, it offered her tremendous freedom of movement and left her legs completely bare. The top piece only covered the top half of her chest and plunged between her breasts where it was only held together by a single strap. Two straps over her shoulders held the small piece up. In the last season, womanhood had taken her with a vengeance and she found disguising her curves more and more of a chore seemingly every day. Her hips were broader, her bosom far larger and more pronounce and her shoulders had broadened. Relentless training, the same training that had her winded and sweating this day, had almost doubled the muscle in her arms and especially her legs. Her waist was still a tiny one despite the extra weight in muscle she had added over the last season. Her obsidian black hair was restrained in a long pony tail behind her and swayed with her movements.

With a sword that was a little longer than her arm, she practiced moves taught to her by her father, the greatest elf warrior who had ever lived. A timber stand was in the middle of the room with arm length pegs protruding from four sides of it. The weapon she brandished was in a wooden sheath that was weighted at the blade for training purposes.

She had backed away, her eyes on the training target in an unblinking stare. Cutting her blade through the air with quick, fluid motions, she advanced again, ducking down as if to spin away from a thrust, then she wheeled around and cut her blade across the middle of it, then brought it up into one of the thick pegs, then parried against another. Spinning the other way, she crouched and thrust her sword hard right into the middle of the timber, nearly knocking it over, then she spun back around and kicked it with the flat of her foot and this time the bottom-heavy stand fell hard.

Winded, Teek struggled to catch her breath and rubbed some sweat from her eyes. Fatigue was picking at her again, but she was refusing to succumb to it. Something within drove her to train harder, way past the point of exhaustion when her body begged her to stop.

Near the large oak dining table, a chair was pulled out with a white towel laid over the back of it, and she turned and strode the three paces to it, taking it in her free hand and blotting the sweat from her face with it. Pressing it against her eyes, she found some comfort in the softness, just as she had found comfort in the arms of her parents. Perhaps she did this to remember, or simply for the comfort it offered. She could not be sure.

Teek threw one end of the towel over her shoulder and laid her sword in its place on the table next to her armor. A cup of water waited beside a pitcher and her hand found it next, raising it to her mouth, she emptied it quickly.

A knock on the door roused a little of her anger and she cut her eyes toward it. She did not want to be disturbed, often staying alone as long as she could, sometimes for days. Though exhausted, she was not through training and did not want company. Another single knock sounded, then another a second later, and another a second after that.

Anger was pushed aside and a little smile found her lips. She set her cup down and blotted her face once more as she strode to the door.

The handle was a simple mechanism that unlatched the door with a simple pull of the ornate, brass ring that hung on the left side, and when she pulled it a series of clicks and a piston slide freed the door and she pulled it open, forcing the smile from her lips before she revealed herself there.

The young man on the other side of the door was a very tall, very handsome elf. More than three quarters the size of a human man, he was broad shouldered and well made. Very young in the face, he had dark blue eyes that were almost black. His dark blonde hair was worn long, past his shoulders, and it was thick and well groomed. He was only two seasons older than Teek, eighteen and in his prime, and in her eyes he was the most dashing and handsome elf in the kingdom.

Folding his hands behind him, he asked in a voice befitting his age, "Am I disturbing you?"

That little smile found her again and she nodded in slight motions.

"Oh," he drawled with a little nod himself. "I should go then."

As he turned, she grabbed onto his sleeve and pulled him inside, closing the door behind him. He was more than a head height taller than she was, but still she pushed him against the door and wrapped her arms around his neck, locking him in her embrace with her elbows as she rose up on her toes to bring her mouth close to his. When his hands found her tiny waist and pulled her in closer, their lips finally met and she closed her eyes to relish one of the few pleasurable moments her life offered.

Slowly, his hands slipped around her back, sliding along her sweat beaded bare skin. Teek pulled herself closer to him and kissed him harder, then she pulled away from his mouth and nuzzled into his neck, and she began to relentlessly kiss him there.

"You little temptress," he breathed.

A hushed giggle escaped her and she nodded, then she turned her head and kissed him under his ear, and nibbled gently with her teeth.

"I can't stay that long," he whispered, turning his head to give his mouth a chance at her neck.

Her breaths came hard once again, but this time it was all raw passion. No suitors appealed to her, but this young elf-man did.

"Teek," he summoned in a low voice. "We can't right now. You're already late."

She pulled away enough to look up at him with questioning eyes.

He raised his brow. "My father went to great lengths to get you employment the way he did. You're already supposed to be in the kitchen of the banquet hall."

She rolled her eyes up and released a deep breath, finally remembering an obligation that had slipped her mind.

"It's okay," he assured. "The King is usually late himself and he won't have anyone pouring his wine but you."

Teek looked down and nodded.

"It is more than that," he went on, drawing her eyes to his. "Councilwoman Gisan is back on your father's estate."

Releasing a breath drawn in frustration, Teek looked aside, her brow low over her eyes as she snarled just a little. This issue had been a thorn in her side since her parents had passed and there were a few elves of status, especially Councilwoman Gisan, who were trying to seize the Brebor lands and holdings in the name of the state, but really for their own greed. She despised them and made no secret of it.

The young man took her chin and raised her face and eyes. "Look. I can continue to stall them and King Arlo has assured me he is in no hurry to see Leumas' estate taken so." When her lips tightened and she nodded ever so gently in his hand, he went on, "You are forbidden to me and we can't... Okay, after the issues of the dragon and the states talking secession have been resolved then we can approach the King about us and that will lay to rest any more talk about seizing your rightful lands. But we can't now and you know why."

She lowered her eyes and nodded again.

"I wish it could be different," he whispered. "I don't want some spoiled brat princess or uppity noble's uppity daughter, I only want you, so I'll simply continue the ruse that I have a while longer."

Her eyes returned to him with a blink.

He huffed a hard breath. "I know you don't like it, but if I'm not out there sewing my wild oats then he will become suspicious. He has to stay on my back about choosing a wife until I know he will be receptive to the idea of you and me. Believe me, continuing on like this with woman after woman is not something I greatly enjoy."

Teek raised her brow.

"I said greatly," he defended. When she cocked one eyebrow up he conceded, "Fine. I've had worse tasks, but please believe that I'd rather be with you each time and I always imagine that I am." He gently stroked her hair. "I'd like to be with you right now."

She smiled.

Leaning toward her, he kissed her neck and whispered, "Perhaps tonight. I'll sneak over to this part of the castle as usual."

Her body quaked in a little laugh and she hugged his neck tightly and nodded.

"Okay, I should go, and you should bathe. Looks like you worked up quite a sweat doing whatever you..." He pushed her away and held her at arm's length. "Teek, what were you doing?"

Her lips tightened, her wide eyes locked on his as she shook her head.

He set his jaw and looked beyond her, then he moved her aside and stormed into the suite, stopping halfway as he saw the toppled practice timber, the armor on the table, and the sword with the wooden training sheath on it.

When he turned, Teek lowered her eyes and slowly wrapped her arms around her belly.

"We've been over this!" he scolded. "King Arlo himself told you to stop this battle training. He's forbidden you..." Setting his hands on his hips, he looked away and shook his head. "I know that you are planning to go after Vultross and as the King himself has forbidden it, I do also." His eyes snapped back to her with a blink. "Do you hear me? I forbid you to throw yourself against this monster or even to think of it further!"

She backed up against the door and would not look at him.

He stormed to her and took her shoulders, pulling her small frame brutally toward him. "Teek, listen to me! This kingdom lost its greatest hero and I lost a dear friend and mentor. I'll not lose my dearest love, too!"

Her mouth tightened to a thin slit and she turned her eyes down again, and reluctantly she nodded.

Slowly, gently, he reached up and stroked her hair. "You need to understand if anything were to happen to you my heart would tear itself from my chest and throw itself on my sword. And I'm sure the King feels just as I do. Leumas was his dear friend as well and his Majesty would give his own life to protect you." He cupped her chin and raised her eyes to his. "And so would I."

Teek could only stare back into his eyes for long seconds. She always craved such affection and such pretty words but she had no way to express this and no way to return such words. Her lips tightened again and she slowly nodded.

Tenderly combing his fingers through her hair, he offered a warm little smile and whispered, "That's my girl. I need to get going. Much to do before the council meets and you'll need to get yourself ready." Bending to her, he tenderly kissed her lips before he reached behind her and pulled the door open.

As it closed behind him, Teek gently pressed her hand against it and her eyes closed as she bowed her head. It was nearly time indeed.

***

King Arlo of the elves limped through the cavernous and elaborately decorated center hall of the castle on his way to meet with his advisors and the Elf Council yet again. He was a plump elf with dark hair that was thinning at the top and turning white around his pointed ears, as happens with older elves. He wore a white shirt with an ornately embroidered forest green vest over it, forest green trousers and polished black boots. An overcoat was usually called for when the council was convened but the day was growing hot and he opted for comfort over the formality of the council chamber dress. He was, in fact, the first elf king to do so in a long line.

Much was on his mind and he stared at the floor with very dark blue eyes that showed strain. The only thing he really had to look forward to in there was a good drink of wine, or two, or however many it took to get through this session.

Light footfalls behind him approached at a running pace but he did not break stride as he looked over his shoulder, and a smile finally found its way to his mouth as he saw the slight girl who was running to catch up to him.

Teek had changed into an emerald green top that left her belly bare, a short skirt of the same color and lighter green leggings that one would expect to see on an archer in fall or early spring when a chill lingered in the air, and they conformed to her legs like a second skin. Pointed toe boots, worn ankle high, were the style of the elves, but she found them cumbersome and uncomfortable and opted for light slippers that better conformed to her small feet.

The King slowed his pace slightly, allowing her to catch up to him, and he extended his arm as she reached him, pulling her in close to him and hugging her tightly as she wrapped her arms around his thick trunk.

"And how fairs my little Teek today?" he asked with a jolly smile.

Looking up at him, she beamed a big smile back and nodded.

"Very good," he chuckled. "I see you're late, too." When she nodded again, he assured, "Well, if they feel the need to speak to you about it then they can just take it up with me."

Teek hugged him tighter and laid her head against his shoulder.

And this is how they approached the council chamber at the end of the long hallway.

At the end of this center hall was a set of ancient and well maintained timber doors. Each door was meticulously carved with the image of the outside of the castle and polished to a glossy finish. They were flanked by two burly guards, each nearly a human's height tall and adorned with forest green tunics over their well polished dress armor plate. As the King approached with the girl under his arm, the two guards reached to the doors and opened them ahead of him and he never broke stride as he strode between them. At this point Teek knew to pull away and slow her pace to walk in behind him. Everyone knew that she was very special to him, but they did not want to flaunt.

The council chamber was just what one would expect. Three other doors sealed the other three walls of the yellow and green room and a long wooden table that was ten paces long and two wide was in the center of the room. Only two seats were empty, and one was his. Seated at the table were the ten members of the Elf Council and the Gnome representative, a stout, bearded fellow who wore a heavy gray shirt and a white jerkin over it. His white hair was cut short and his bushy eyebrows were as well groomed as his long white beard. Pale blue eyes were locked on the dark blue eyes of the Elf King and Arlo offered him a long look in response as he took his chair. The other elves were very well dressed and all but a few wore elaborately embroidered overcoats.

Wine and snacks were served by elf women and girls and a few young men who were dressed in light attire to allow them freedom of movement. Most of the elf women in attendance, those without husbands, wore cropped tops and short skirts, this to attract the eye of an elf man who would appeal to them.

As the King settled himself, Teek went right to work, darting to a kitchen door on one side of the room and emerging a moment later with a large bottle of gold colored wine which she hugged to her chest as she strode with quick steps to the King's chair. A crystal goblet was in front of him and she set the bottle down and pulled it to her, then slowly, carefully filled it with wine. As she did so, her eyes strayed to King Arlo, her brow arching as she saw the strained look on his face. His glass filled, she set the bottle down and picked up the goblet, offering it to him with both hands.

He took the goblet absently, but still offered her a little smile as he always did, strained as it was. Leaning back in his chair, he stared down into the goblet for a moment, swirling it around as he collected his thoughts. Finally, he raised the goblet to his mouth and took a sip, and his brow lowered. Looking to the slight girl who still stood beside him, he asked, "Peach? No white grape?"

She shook her head, holding the bottle of wine close to her that she had retrieved when he had taken his goblet.

"I thought we had ten cases left. What happened to it all?"

Raising her brow, the girl set the bottle down, then raised her hands before her, curling her fingers as she bared her teeth and widened her eyes, then she held her fists out as if holding something and made a motion like she was breaking it.

Arlo released a deep breath. "In the last attack?"

She nodded.

He growled a sigh and looked back to his goblet. "Well, I like this one too."

The King took another long drink, then he cradled his goblet with both hands and stared down into it for long seconds before he spoke again. When he did, it was to the council. "My fellow elves and esteemed representative of the gnomes, we have a problem ahead of us." He shook his head. "And I am at a loss. For all of this power controlled by the Elf Kingdom, we have not the means to wield it in our own defense."

An older elf with long gray sideburns and dressed very formally with gold embroidery adorning his royal blue overcoat leaned forward and folded his hands on the table. "What of the weapons forged for Leumas to be used against this beast? Perhaps they could be wielded by several warriors and that way he could be overwhelmed and killed."

"And if they fail?" a woman directly across countered. She was also formally dressed in a scarlet red jacket with black and gold embroidery around the cuffs and the lapels. Her long black hair was restrained behind her with bejeweled barrettes worn just behind her pointed ears. They were joined by a gold chain to keep her hair in check. Her amber eyes were piercing, commanding eyes, and this day showed determination and fear.

Many of the elves present exchanged nervous looks and did not respond.

King Arlo looked to the gnome representative who sat to his right and raised a brow. "Your thoughts, Hes?"

The gnome stared back for long seconds, then his eyes darted away and he shook his head. "My people have been plagued by such beasts since the dawn of our kind. We've no means to fight back or defend ourselves, and it has always been thought best to just placate them."

Another elf, a younger fellow with short red hair and wearing a white jacket and red shirt, leaned forward and announced, "I don't think giving him sacrifices of our people will make him leave! I've been saying for many seasons that the Elf Kingdom is woefully unprepared to defend itself and we've relied on too few for too long!"

The older fellow nodded and agreed, "I heard your words and always agreed, but in times of prosperity it is difficult to justify preparing for war."

Arlo added, "This is the first time in our history we have been attacked so. Perhaps a thousand seasons ago our ancestors were better prepared, but so much knowledge of the Heart of Abtont was lost or forgotten…" He shook his head and finished his goblet of wine, then he offered it to the girl beside him. "If you would, my dear."

She carefully poured him another goblet, then set the bottle down on the table as he took a few swallows.

Shaking his head, the Elf King stared down into his goblet for a time, then finally grumbled, "We've already the issue of two states of our people talking secession, and now there is this to worry over. How do we keep our people united under such threat?"

The doors opened and a very handsome and strapping young elf man strode into the council chamber. Like the King, he was dressed for comfort and wearing no overcoat, but he did wear a green satin cape. His white shirt and black trousers looked almost like they had been slept in and his dark blond hair had clearly been attended to with great haste. He wore the hint of a smile on his young, hairless face and blue eyes that looked much like the King's showed not a care in the world as he strode to the one vacant seat at the table, the chair that sat on King Arlo's left.

Teek's eyes never strayed from him from the door to his chair and she hugged the wine bottle to her as she slowly pivoted to watch him. She got but a glance, but that glance and the subtle smile he flashed at her sent her heart racing and she struggled to breathe. He had been in her room and her in his arms just an hour before but every time she saw him and knew she could not feel his arms around her the wanting was even greater. He seemed to know this and he seemed to feel it as well, but he played his part flawlessly as he lounged in his chair and picked up his crystal goblet.

"Well," the King announced, his eyes on the strapping young man who sat beside him, "thank you for taking the time to join us, Prince Wazend. We are honored that you would clear your schedule enough to attend to a few matters of the kingdom, inconvenient as that is for you."

The Prince held his glass toward Teek and defended, "Come now, Father. I do have the issue of boosting the morale of the people in these troubled times. Must keep spirits high." He turned his eyes to his goblet as Teek filled it and his eyes flitted to her a couple of times.

The younger councilman laughed and said to the Prince, "One barmaid at a time, Highness?"

A few snickers erupted, but most in the room were not amused.

His glass full, Prince Wazend held it before him, staring into it with his brow held high. "It was long, hard work, but I think spirits were raised."

More snickers rippled among the council.

Teek held the bottle to her again and walked behind the Prince's chair and nobody noticed when she jabbed her finger hard into the back of his shoulder, and he tactfully turned a painful wince into a clearing of his throat before looking back to his father. "So. No resolution to our lizard problem, I assume?" When no one answered and the King simply looked away, he nodded and confirmed, "I thought not. Well, I'm still all for killing the thing and having done with it."

"Are you volunteering?" the councilwoman asked straightly.

"No, I am not," was Wazend's reply. "However, we have an army, and I am under the impression that Leumas left some of those enchanted weapons behind." He glanced at the servant girl as her lips tightened. "He was the greatest warrior of the Elf Kingdom, the greatest hero in our history and in his honor I think we should finish his work."

The girl looked down and nodded.

Leaning forward on the table, the councilwoman looked to the Prince and folded her hands before her, asking, "And how many will die this time?"

"How many will die if we don't?" he countered. "Councilwoman Gisan, the notion of sacrificing our people to placate this beast does not sit well with me or most of the kingdom. If he is to kill our people then they should die trying to kill him."

"The army is still reeling from the last time they met him," Gisan pointed out.

"Then they will have to be rallied," the Prince said in a loud voice. "I'll ride out there myself with them if that's what it takes!"

King Arlo slammed his fist down and shouted, "I forbid it!" He looked to his son. "You'll not ride to your death against this monster!" The King drew a calming breath and leaned back in his chair, reaching out to tap the rim of his goblet as he thought, and Teek refilled it for him yet again. "How many in the dungeons?" he finally asked.

The older councilman replied, "Twelve, I think. What are you proposing?"

"Give the beast the worst of us," the King replied "those with life sentences, those who cannot be rehabilitated. It will buy us some time."

"I'm sure their families will understand," Prince Wazend grumbled.

"I don't like it either," Arlo assured, "but we have little choice at the moment." He took a long drink from his goblet and emptied it, then slammed it back down and tapped the rim.

Teek looked to the bottle, and poured the last few drops into the King's goblet, then she raised her brow and turned her eyes to him. Turning toward the kitchen door, she waved her hand to get someone's attention, and when she did she held up the empty bottle and pointed to it.

Another councilwoman, this one wearing a blue jacket and a white shirt, raised her chin and observed, "It was one hero who almost rid us of him and in the ancient writings it is always one hero who stands against such threats. Perhaps that is the course we need."

Councilwoman Gisan pointed out, "We don't exactly have a hoard of volunteers beating down our doors."

"Then perhaps they need incentive," the Prince suggested.

"Like?" Gisan prodded. "What amount of gold is worth one's life?"

She shook her head and insisted, "I believe the best course is to just give the dragon what it wants."

Prince Wazend turned a very cold look to her, asking, "And what if what it wants is to eat you? Will giving this monster what it wants sound like such a splendid idea then?"

She sighed an impatient sigh and would not look back at him. "Highness, we have lesser citizens here who—"

"Lesser citizens?" the Prince roared as he sprang to his feet. "We're talking about our elf brethren, not a herd of goats and I don't think a single life here is any less important than any other! How dare you even suggest that?"

Approaching the King again, Teek smiled ever so slightly. She always loved when the Prince asserted his position, but more than that she hated Councilwoman Gisan and loved to see her put in her place.

Gisan's eyes again would not fix on the Prince, but she did look to King Arlo and raise her brow, looking for his intervention.

Arlo loosed a deep breath through his nose, then he raised his glass to his mouth and gulped down the last of his wine.

Just as Teek knew he would, and she was right there to refill it.

The King watched the little elf girl slowly fill his goblet, and finally he ordered in a low voice, "Wazend, sit down." When the Prince complied, he continued, "These are tense times for us all and we do not need to be fighting amongst ourselves." His eyes found Gisan in a deadly stare. "Nor will there be talk of *any* elf being regarded as a lesser citizen and expendable to our population as a whole." Picking his goblet up, he took a few swallows before setting it down on the table again, and this time he considered for long seconds before he spoke again, his eyes never straying from his glass. "I wish we had a way to kill the beast. That would greatly simplify our lives." His eyes shifted to the Gnome Representative. "Hes, surely your people had some way to respond that did not involve simply placating the beast."

The Gnome's gaze found his own wine goblet, and slowly he shook his head. "None, King Arlo."

Slamming his fist onto the table, the Elf King shouted, "By the Gods there has to be some way to kill the beast! There has to be!"

Teek set the bottle down and patted his shoulder to draw his attention. Once she had it she tapped her fingernail on his crystal goblet, then she pointed to the end of her finger, then her chest.

The King's brow lowered and he raised his chin to her. "What are you trying to say, Lass?"

She picked up his wine glass again and this time thumped the rim, and the ring reverberated loudly. Glancing about, she raised her brow, waiting for responses.

"Wine?" someone guessed, and she shook her head.

"Glass," Prince Wazend said, and when she beckoned him on he corrected, "Crystal."

She pointed to him and touched her nose, then set the glass down and pointed to the end of her finger again.

The Gnome representative squinted slightly and guessed, "Finger. Fingernail."

"Tip," the Elf King announced, and when she turned and held her arms as if holding a bow and pulling the bowstring back, his eyes narrowed and he finished, "Crystal tip arrows. Leumas' crystal tip arrows, the enchanted weapons he nearly killed the beast with last summer."

Teek pointed to him and nodded, then tapped on the middle of her chest with her fingertips.

"His heart," Prince Wazend said almost absently. "That's what Leumas was trying to hit when he fought the beast."

Nodding again, Teek pointed to him and then patted her chest.

"How many remain?" the Prince demanded.

Teek held up three fingers.

Looking down to his empty wine glass again, King Arlo drew a breath and grumbled, "Three chances to kill the beast."

Councilwoman Gisan reminded, "Leumas took those chances a season ago and failed. His arrows wounded the beast but did not stop him. Your Majesty, I say we dare not even try! Provoke him further and there is no telling what he will do to the people of this kingdom! He could double the demands of elf blood he wants should we fail!"

Mumblings of discord rippled among the elves as they looked to each other, and most were shaking their heads.

Arlo's eyes finally shifted to her and he grumbled, "We are reputed to be the best archers in the world and you would have us sit idly by while that monster rapes this kingdom and devours her people every few days."

"What if this attempt fails?" she pressed.

"What if it succeeds?" Wazend countered. "This beast is demanding elvan sacrifices. Our people are dying and we are having to give him what we can just to make him leave. How many of our people will die over the seasons if we don't try?"

An older elf down the table from Gisan asked grimly, "How many will die tomorrow if we do?"

Teek clenched her teeth. With the council divided so, it would be impossible to convince them to kill the beast. With a fresh bottle of wine, she carefully refilled the King's goblet, then her eyes cut to Prince Wazend as he spoke.

"When did elves become so timid?" he grumbled. "We spent too many seasons relying on Leumas, and now we've no answer to one dragon."

The older elf leaned on the table and folded his hands, his eyes on the Prince as he countered, "That one dragon killed Leumas."

Wazend clenched his jaw and slowly looked to the older councilman. "And we've done nothing to avenge that, either. I don't recall the King or Council declaring that we've surrendered to this beast, and if it comes to that then I'll be the first to cast a nay vote."

The younger councilman across the table slammed his fist down and cried, "And seconded!"

Gisan leaned forward, shaking her head as she declared, "You'll condemn this kingdom for sure with such actions! How many elves must die before you realize—"

"Enough!" King Arlo shouted. His outburst drew the attention of all, including all of the servants present, and for a moment he was silent and seemed lost in thought as he stared down at his wine goblet. Finally drawing a deep breath, he shook his head and said almost absently, "We've shed so much blood over this issue already, and now we'll shed more if we act or not. Now, even my advisors and the Elf Council are equally divided. War against this beast has proven futile, but sacrificing our people is just as unacceptable."

"Then make the decision," Prince Wazend demanded. "I am ready to lead my garrison against this beast and fight to the last elf, and other commanders feel the same. We may lose scores or even hundreds but we'll end this thing once and for all!"

Another old elf, sitting on the same side of the table as the Prince and wearing light blue with silver embroidery on the ornate vest he wore, leaned forward and folded his hands on the table. From the look of him he had a history in the elvan military and his white beard was perfectly groomed, as was his short hair and the sideburns that grew long. Clearing his throat, he drew the attention of the council, the King, and the Prince before he spoke. "You'll find problems there, my Prince. With two of your states talking secession we may find ourselves in need of the bulk of our forces in the event of civil war."

Gisan rubbed her forehead. "How do we negotiate with those states under such a threat? Next thing we know they'll involve humans and other creatures."

Someone else added, "How do we know these other states did not bring this dragon down upon us?"

Mumbling rippled through the room again.

Teek grasped the Prince's shoulder, then she patted her chest and jabbed her thumb in over her heart.

He shook his head and whispered, "No!"

Her lips tightening, she looked to the King and set the wine bottle down rather hard. When he looked up at her she patted her chest again and jabbed her thumb into her chest over her heart.

Arlo set his jaw and slowly shook his head.

Clenching her teeth, she patted her chest harder, then pointed toward the door, finishing by making the gesture of drawing back a bowstring.

The room was suddenly silent.

"Isn't this charming?" an older elf councilman said, almost laughing. "The bravest of us turns out to be one of the smallest."

When many of the elves present laughed softly, Teek glanced around with venomous eyes and her jaw clenched tightly. Looking back to the King, she patted her chest again with such annoyance and determination in her eyes as was rarely seen there.

Arlo shook his head again, replying, "No. I lost my closest friend to this beast and I'll not allow it to take his only daughter as well."

The rage in Teek's eyes was all too apparent and she set her hands on her hips and stomped her foot, her eyes never leaving the King's.

His eyes narrowed and he said with a growl in his words, "I said no, Teek, and that is final. Do not press the issue further."

Not deterred, she made the motion of pulling a bowstring again, and with her hands clenched into tight fists she stomped her foot again and patted her chest very hard.

Arlo slammed his palm onto the table and shouted, "I said no! The discussion is over!"

Her breaths coming forced and deep into her, she spun around to storm out, and when the Prince grabbed her arm she jerked free and continued on toward one of the doors to the kitchen, her hands held in tight, shaking fists as she disappeared through it.

Everyone watched her depart, and the Prince finally met his father's eyes and he hissed, "*Now* you show some backbone." Before the King could respond he sprang from his chair and pursued the little elf girl.

The room was left in stunned silence, and a moment passed before the King finally announced, "We'll recess and reconvene this afternoon." As all watched, he rose from his chair and limped stiffly toward the door he had entered through.

**

Despite many oil lamps, the wine cellar that was beneath the kitchen was a dark place. The floor was the stone of the bedrock the castle sat on, smoothed and somewhat polished by hundreds of generations of elves who walked there. Rows of wine racks went on seemingly as far as the eye could see. The cavernous cellar seemed huge with arched ceilings that were a human's height and a half tall. Stone pillars three paces across connected the floor to the ceiling and added strength to the castle and stone floor above. The air was very cool here year round and about the same temperature in summer or winter, and here is where Teek often retreated to when she needed solitude.

Past all of the racks that held thousands of bottles was a stack of barrels that formed its own wall nearly all the way to the ceiling, and all of these barrels were full of wine. The Elf Kingdom consumed a lot of wine and produced huge quantities every season.

One of these bottles was open and held tightly by a hurt and angry elf girl who was huddled at the base of a wall of barrels. Her knees were drawn to her and she had an arm wrapped around them. Her other hand clenched the neck of the bottle that sat beside her. She did not cry, would not cry, though inside she really wanted to, so she just stared into the broken darkness, her brow low over her eyes as she considered the day's events, and considered more how to finally get around the King's orders to her. She did not know how long she was down there; she only knew she did not want to be disturbed.

Hearing footsteps coming up on her, she raised the bottle to her mouth and took another long pull from it, then she turned her eyes away from the Prince as he stopped only a couple of paces away.

He just stared down at her for a long moment, and finally shattered the silence with soft words. "I tried to tell you."

She did not respond.

"He loves you dearly," Wazend went on, "and he does not wish to see your life thrown away any more than I do." When she still would not even look at him, he took another step toward her. "Teek, I need you to listen. Will you at least acknowledge me?"

Very reluctantly, she finally turned her eyes to him, then behind him.

Seeing her eyes shift from him, Wazend turned, raising his chin as he found himself facing his father.

King Arlo had approached quietly and unnoticed and did not have a pleased look for his son. With features of stone, he ordered, "Get back to the council chamber. We'll talk there."

Wazend clenched his jaw, knowing that another heated argument with his father was imminent, and with one more look down at Teek he spun around and strode toward the steps back to the upper level without another word.

Arlo watched until he knew the Prince was out of the cellar, then he looked down at Teek again. When she turned her eyes away from him, he closed the last paces with three steps, then turned and sat down beside her.

She looked down to the dirty stone floor.

The King took the wine bottle from her and took a few gulps from it before he spoke. "I don't enjoy being cross with you so, but I won't apologize for it. You were out of line and you know it." When he looked to her, she finally looked back at him. "And you're far too young to be down here drinking wine." He finished with a wink, took another drink from the bottle and offered it to her.

She took the bottle from him and took a drink, too, then she bumped him with her shoulder.

Something more solemn took his face as he said, "I love you like you are my own, little girl, and this castle would be a big and lonely place without you."

Her mouth tightened as she just stared up at him.

He slipped his arm around her shoulders and pulled her tightly to him. "Call me a selfish old man if you will, but I could not stand life here without you. Believe me when I say I've felt the pain of your parent's loss every day since it happened. I know it is not such a deep wound as yours, but I do feel it, and I feel for you every day you must be without them." He took the bottle from her and took a long drink from it before speaking again. "You should know, little girl, that I know about you and my son." When she tensed up he continued, "I've known for a while now. Since I think of you as a daughter I'm not sure how to feel about it, but I suppose no harm's done." Looking down at her, he met her eyes and smiled. "He thinks I'm easily fooled, but age and wisdom have their place. Just don't let on that I know. I rather enjoy watching him slink about as he thinks I'm oblivious to his activities."

Her brow arched and she nodded in slight motions.

Arlo squeezed her to him. "Not to worry, little girl. Rest assured that when the time comes and my son finds his own wisdom and the courage to approach me about you, you'll have my blessing, and you'll finally, truly be a member of my family."

A little smile was pulled from her.

"All the more reason I don't want you throwing yourself against that beast," he insisted. "You'll be kept here and kept safe so that my son will finally settle himself down and take a bride, and I will hope that he will be worthy of you."

A silent giggle escaped her and she butted her head into his shoulder.

Arlo pulled her closer to him, tenderly kissing the top of her head. "Just stay safe, little girl. Just stay safe."

CHAPTER 3

Morning had found tensions high in the Elf Kingdom, but this was to be expected with the dragon due before high sun. Archers clad in ceremonial armor and feathered hats took their positions on the perimeter wall but they were clearly there for appearances. The only soldiers present were also in dress uniforms with polished armor and feathered hats. Most people had fled the castle or sought refuge in the basements and catacombs. But for those who would be presenting sacrifices, those six who were sacrifices and the soldiers who served only a ceremonial purpose, the entire castle seemed deserted.

Unnoticed behind the vines that grew all over the perimeter wall was one elf who did not intend to serve a ceremonial purpose. Dressed in a forest green archer's shirt that was cuffed at the sleeves, Teek watched and waited as the six prisoners were led out into the field in chains. Seeing the trampled down grass and grains stirred her ire further. Since the dragon visited every few days, most grazing animals did not. She had loved to see unicorns graze out there early in the morning and would watch the sparkling forms as they moved about without fear so close to the castle. Held sacred by the elves, no one would dare approach them and all elves kept their distance while the unicorns grazed for fear of violating the law. Teek always watched from a distance, but for the last season. The unicorns were not coming anymore and it had to be that dragon's fault!

Her dark green leggings conformed to her like a second skin and her black, ankle high boots were not polished but rather made to be dull to make her more difficult to notice. The shirt she wore was belted at the waist and wore like a short dress, dropping halfway to her knees. With her long black hair restrained behind her in a pony tail, she had excellent vision from her vantage point among the thick and ancient vines. Fruit hung on the vines in places and she took advantage of the extra cover as well as a snack while she waited.

On her side hung the sword her father had commissioned for her, but in her hand was the bow he had used, held vertically before her with one end resting on the ground. On her back was her quiver with one of the three crystal tipped arrows waiting to be shot. The second of these arrows was in her grip with the bow. Her right hand slowly stroked the bowstring. When the dragon came for his sacrifices and while he was distracted would be her best shot at him, and should the first arrow fail to kill him then the second would be loosed close behind it. She figured she would only get the two chances, so the third arrow remained safely in the Brebor suite of the palace, and it would await the next elf who was brave enough to wield it in battle against this dragon should she fail.

Looking to the prisoners, she saw that all were dressed in white, all had their heads down and two wept. They knew what awaited them. It had happened before and Teek was determined that it would not happen again.

Her hiding place was only five paces to the left of the castle's gate and she could see everyone who came and went, but she paid little attention beyond making sure she was not noticed.

Then she heard a familiar voice, one that she had hoped she would not hear. Looking to her left, her eyes widened as she saw Prince Wazend, dressed in his polished ceremonial armor, his green and yellow tunic and his two point hat with the long white feather, as he strode out of the castle with two guards at his sides, and he was rather anxious about something.

"I don't care what you have to do. Arrest her and lock her away if you must, but she is not to be allowed on this side of the castle!"

One of the guards nodded. "I understand, Highness. I have almost a garrison looking for her and you'll be alerted as soon as she's found."

Teek swallowed hard, knowing it was her that he was talking about.

"See that you do," he ordered. "I don't want anything to happen to her, anything at all."

The guard bowed and hurried back toward the palace.

Setting his hands on his hips, the Prince growled, "Where have you gone?"

Someone on the perimeter wall shouted, "Dragon!"

Teek looked to see the black, winged form soar over the treetops and fly toward the palace, and her eyes narrowed anew. Here was her target, her enemy. But even as she made herself to focus on what she had to do, an uneasy crawl started in the pit of her belly. Seeing the beast that had killed her parents and many others she knew shot pangs of doubt and reservation throughout her. Even as the beast landed only fifty paces away and strode toward the waiting prisoners, she found herself hesitant to step from her hiding place and attack him. He was on the ground, on foot and standing fully erect and she had a perfect shot at his heart, but hers was now thundering with fear.

Drawing deep breaths, she tried to calm herself, finally closing her eyes and resting her head back against the wall behind her. Courage was failing her and she reached to her heart within to find any that her father might have left her.

The dragon growled and took a step back, complaining, "Not to old

Vultross' liking. Not bringing those elves do not want for tribute, bringing elves of status. Bringing elves worthy of Vultross' appetite."

"Highness," a guard summoned in a low voice from her left.

Teek cut her eyes that way, drawing a gasp as she saw the Prince still standing outside the wall and only about five paces away from her.

"I know," Wazend grumbled, "but I'll not cower behind stone walls while that thing eats our people."

"We wouldn't want it to mistake you for one of its sacrifices," the guard informed. "We should get you to safety before you are seen."

"Let it see me," he snarled.

As if summoned, the dragon raised his head and looked right at the Prince, and his eyes narrowed. "Other tributes?"

The guard backed away but the Prince held his ground, folding his arms defiantly as the dragon turned toward him.

Teek's lips slid away from her clenched her teeth as the beast just stared at him and ice ran up her spine as it took a step toward the Prince she loved. Fear or no, it was time to act. Grasping the bow tightly and maneuvering the arrow into place, she pivoted and pushed through the thick vines back first, and once clear of them she wheeled around and pulled the bowstring back, raising the arrow to her eye and aiming down shaft as quickly and carefully as she could. She hesitated as the dragon's attention shifted to her and that chill lanced through her belly as her eyes found his. When he lowered his body, she changed her aim and found herself adjusting with his movements as he stalked to one side. His attention was fixed on her and he seemed curious and perplexed, rocking back and forth as he appeared to try and get a better look at her.

"Teek!" the Prince shouted from her left. She heard his footsteps as he ran up on her but she kept her eyes locked on the dragon, and when she was confident with her aim, time itself seemed to slow as she opened her fingers and released the bowstring. As the string pushed the arrow toward the curve of the bow Prince Wazend slammed into her, and her aim was thwarted ever so slightly.

The arrow streaked toward the dragon on its deadly mission with a true aim, but a shifted aim and it barely missed his chest, exploding into his shoulder. The dragon roared in a higher pitch than he usually did as he was spun around and stumbled backward, reaching for his injured shoulder.

Teek and the Prince fell to the ground, she on her back and him on top of her. She knew she would have to act quickly so she pushed the Prince off of her and rolled the other way, ending up on one knee with her bow still in her hand. Reaching back to her quiver, she grasped the other crystal tip arrow and pulled it perfectly into position, hesitating as she found herself looking down at only the back half of the shaft! Her wide eyes found the dragon again as he got his bearings and wheeled back to face her. This was now a very angry dragon and she no longer had the weapon she needed to finish him. Dropping her bow, she sprang to her feet and backed away as she reached for her sword.

Wazend seized her wrist and stepped between her and the dragon and he took her other wrist and held them tightly together between them. His eyes were pools of rage and terror as he hissed, "What are you doing? Teek..." He clenched his jaw, closing his eyes as he bowed his head.

She did not resist him, she just stared back, infuriated that he had thwarted her aim and kept her from killing the dragon and at the same time saddened by the thought of hurting him.

Palace guards in their ceremonial armor rushed from the gate and two of them ran to the Prince and the girl he held, and each of them took one of her arms.

"Be gentle with her!" he growled, his eyes to one side. Thumps on the ground betrayed the approach of the dragon and he turned and looked up, seeing the beast stop only forty paces away with a glare in his orange, serpentine eyes, a glare that was locked on the elf girl. Wazend did not know what to say, what to do, but he did hold his ground between the girl he loved and the beast that surely meant to kill her, and he held his ground even as the dragon lowered his head to bring his nose only a pace away from him.

A deep growl rolled from the dragon and he bared his teeth. His eyes were not on the prince; they were on the girl behind him.

Ever the quick thinker and diplomat, Wazend raised a hand and assured, "I know you want to kill her and I know you have the right to."

The dragon snarled, "Move or die with it then."

"I can't allow you to be deprived of what you really want," the Prince said quickly. "If you kill her now then the satisfaction you should have you will never get, and revenge will never be placated."

Drawing back slightly, the dragon growled softly again, leaning his head as he demanded, "Explaining words to Vultross."

"You are a magnificent and mighty dragon," the Prince explained, raising his chin. "Chained sacrifices are not worthy of you, nor are sheep brought to you for an easy meal. Mighty Vultross should hunt, and the Elf Kingdom shall give Mighty Vultross his hunt."

Raising a scaly eyebrow slightly, the dragon listened, and his eyes narrowed as he seemed to understand.

"You would never find her in the forest," the Prince went on, "so she would have to be banished, sent to a far away land that you can easily reach where she can be hunted at your leisure."

Teek's lips parted slowly as she watched Prince Wazend from behind. Shocked at first by this offer, she finally realized what it was he was doing and almost smiled at his cunning before she turned her attention back to the dragon.

"That is how your sacrifices should be," the Prince insisted. "Mighty Vultross should hunt his sacrifices and bring them here to show the people his strength and cunning."

The dragon considered further, his eyes narrowing, then he took a half step toward the Prince and nudged him aside with his nose.

Teek could feel the guards tense up as the dragon drew in close and as he bumped her with his nose and took a deep sniff of her they released her and backed away. Terrified, she remained perfectly still as his nose went to one side of her, then the other, and she knew he was collecting her scent.

Finally drawing away from her, he stood and arched his long neck back, those horrible, orange serpentine eyes locked on her. He snarled, then ordered, "Knowing you now, elf. Old Vultross knows you. Returning here and finding your scent then many will die. Elf Kingdom will pay in blood." He turned his attention to the Prince. "How quick getting little elf to the Hard Lands?"

"We have portals in the Temple that have been there for hundreds of generations. One will go to an abandoned ruin there in the desert near the mountains."

"Sending there," the dragon hissed. "Mighty Vultross finding treacherous elf and having hunt." He looked down to her and his scaly lips slid away from his many long teeth. "Banished from Elf Kingdom for life. Vultross finding you and killing you. Show you to other elves before I swallow you." He looked to his wounded shoulder, then back to the Prince as he stood fully. "Vultross finding elf in the Hard Lands or Vultross coming here and killing many." With that last warning, he turned and strode toward the center of the field, opened his wings and lifted himself effortlessly into the sky.

All eyes watched until he flew out of sight, then all eyes found the elf girl.

Wazend approached her with heavy steps and framed her face in his hands, saying through clenched teeth, "I told you not to throw yourself against that monster! I told you! Why, Teek? Why?"

She pushed away from him and backed away a few steps. Pointing at him, she shook her head, then pointed to the broken arrow that lay on the ground at his feet.

Looking down at it, his mouth tightened to a thin slit as his eyes returned to her. "You almost did it, didn't you? And then I came along and disrupted your aim."

She folded her arms, raised her brow and nodded.

"Then I should be going out there with you," he suggested.

Teek simply could not stay angry with him and just shook her head. Movement from the gate drew her attention and she looked that way. Everyone did.

King Arlo, dressed in his ceremonial armor and tunic, strode to them with that familiar limp and Councilwoman Gisan at his side, and they were followed by four soldiers. His eyes found Teek only briefly, then the ground in front of him. As he and the councilwoman reached them, he glanced at his son, then cleared his throat and looked past Teek, ordering, "Guards, take her into custody."

Storming toward him only two steps, Prince Wazend roared, "What do you think you're doing? You can't just—"

"Wazend!" he shouted back. He would not meet anyone's eyes and his just darted about, finally calming himself enough to order, "Take her away."

The guards who had held her before took her arms again and one of the soldiers who had followed the king out strode to her and took her sword.

Lowering her eyes, she tried to grasp what had happened. When she had risen before sunup and dressed, eaten a hearty breakfast and donned her forest clothing and bow, she expected to emerge from the fight a hero. Now, she was a common criminal, and about to be banished from her home forever.

**

The accommodations in the dungeons beneath the palace were as one might expect. Small cells were about two paces square and had little in them except for a wooden rack covered with hay and a blanket for a prisoner to sleep on. Straw covered the stone floor. The walls were also stone, one of which looked like it was carved from the bedrock the palace sat on while the other three were stone and mortar, and very thick. Two rusty old rings were mounted to the wall at the back of the small cell about half a height from the floor and chains were shackled to them.

And at the other end of those chains were Teek's wrists. The chains were less than half an arm's length and did not leave much freedom of movement. Teek sat on the cold stone floor between them with her arms suspended out away from her. The iron shackles that held her were thick and heavy with sharp edges that chafed her delicate skin. Most would have been too big for her little hands, but these had been recently fashioned to accommodate her and were just snug enough to prevent her hands from getting through them. With her legs drawn to her, she sat quietly with her arms extended to both sides and tried to sleep. The only light that got into the cell was through the small, barred window in the heavy timber and iron door directly across from her, the only way in or out. By morning she would be forced through one of the portals at the temple and into the hot and barren Hard Lands where there would be no place to hide from the horror that meant to kill her. She knew if she evaded him for too long she would die of thirst, or the heat, or starvation. While her father had taught her everything she needed to know about surviving in the forest and even the scrub country, she did not know how she would last in the desert. The only thing that was clear was that her short life was about to end, and no doubt her death would be horrible and painful.

Noise outside of the door drew her attention and she slowly raised her head, looking to it as the bolt on the outside was slid back and it was opened. To her fury she saw the well dressed Councilwoman Gisan enter the cell with a very smug and condescending look about her.

Gisan strode to the center of the cell and stopped folding her hands behind her as she looked down to the little prisoner with nothing short of contempt. Half turning her head, she said to the guard behind her, "That will be all. I will let you know when I am ready to come out."

He nodded and left the cell, leaving the Councilwoman alone with her prisoner.

Raising her brow, Gisan asked, "How are you liking your accommodations?" When the only response she got was a glare, she continued, "I made sure you would be taken care of, and you'll be here until morning when the clerics come for you. Then it's off to the Hard Lands to answer for your crimes against the Elf Kingdom."

Teek looked away from her.

Looking down at one of her rings, Gisan shook her head. "You know, it is such a shame when someone from such a noble family becomes such a threat to all we hold dear." She turned venomous eyes on the elf girl. "You've been a thorn in my side long enough, little girl, and you've quite conveniently given me the means to finally be rid of you. It is such a pity as you have just reached marrying age. A husband would most definitely be able to look after the lands you leave behind, but not to worry. I intend to see to the Brebor lands and holdings in your absence. A shame Leumas did not father a son, isn't it?"

Her brow low, Teek slid her eyes back to the Councilwoman.

"Well," Gisan sighed, "I should leave you to your thoughts. Just wanted to pop in and wish you well." As she turned, she looked over her shoulder and smiled. "So I wonder how he will finish you: Killed with a single swipe of his claws like your mother or swallowed whole and alive and screaming like your father?" She waggled her fingers and bade, "Tah tah," then strode out with a very smug look and posture.

Teek just glared after her, and as she door closed she slowly lowered her head. Memories of how that beast killed her parents were renewed in her mind and she could not rid herself of them.

She could not know how much time passed when the bolt holding the door was slid back again and she slowly raised her head as it opened again. This time, she pulled her feet under her and stood, and the light returned to her emerald eyes as she saw Prince Wazend stride in toward her. When she tried to go to him, to embrace him, the chains stopped her, but she pulled against them anyway to reach him.

He wrapped his arms around her and pulled her to him as tightly as he could, burying his face in her neck as she did the same and for a moment he just held her. When that moment passed he stepped back, took her shoulders and pushed her against the wall behind her, anger in his eyes now as he scolded, "I told you not to throw yourself against that beast! Teek, I told you! The King told you!" When she looked away from him he seized her head with both hands and forced her to look at him. "What were you thinking? Damn it, Teek, what were you thinking?"

With a hurt pout on her lips, she turned her eyes down. Slowly raising her hands to the limit of the chains, she finally was able to touch him, if only a little.

"I have a plan," he informed in a whisper. "We only have tonight to iron out the wrinkles and it may have no chance of working, but it's better than just sending you to your death."

She nodded, still looking down at his chest.

He turned his eyes down to the chains that held her wrists, then he looked over his shoulder, and called, "Guard! Get in here!"

The dungeon guard was a rather round fellow who only wore dirty trousers and a light shirt that he kept open. He strode into the cell on very old and faded boots and looked to the Prince.

"Unlock her," Wazend ordered.

The guard loosed an uneasy breath and reported, "I was ordered by Councilwoman Gisan to keep the girl chained in her cell."

Turning fully, Prince Wazend folded his arms and growled, "Now your *Prince* has ordered you to release her. If that is going to be such a difficult task for you then I'm sure you can be replaced by someone a little brighter."

Tight lipped, the guard nodded, then he reached for the ring of keys on his belt.

Teek watched as she was freed of the uncomfortable chains, then she looked up at Wazend as he took her arm and pulled her toward the door.

Not quite there, King Arlo stepped into the doorway, raising his chin as he found his son removing the prisoner he had come to see. Looking down at the keys in his own hands, the King cleared his throat and observed, "Oh, I see you already... Well then, we should just go." He turned to lead the way out of the dungeon.

Teek and Wazend looked to each other, then shrugged and followed.

**

The Brebor suite of the castle was a beehive of activity when Teek and Wazend strode into it. Many palace scribes seemed to be taking an inventory of the belongings there while other laborers were busy packing and crating Leumas' belongings—and Teek's.

While they stood there in shock at what was happening, King Arlo pushed past them and shouted, "What in Hell is going on in here!"

Everyone stopped what they were doing and spun around.

The King strode to the middle of the room and barked, "Who is in charge here?"

A woman dressed in the light green of the castle servants but with gold embroidery over her shoulders and her graying brown hair pulled up in a bun timidly approached the King with a pad and pen and reported, "I am, Majesty. We... We are acting under the orders of—"

"Councilwoman Gisan," he finished for her. Setting his hands on his hips, he looked around him and yelled, "Put it all back! Now!" As the servants sprang into action, he added, "Anything removed from this suite is to be replaced exactly where it was found or I'll find whoever took it and feed them to that dragon next!"

Two of the servants hurried from the room.

He looked around again and noticed the elf woman in charge still cringing in front of him. With a bit of a snarl on his lip, he growled, "Go find Gisan and tell her I will be in my study in a half hour, and if I do not find her there she will spend the rest of her life looking for a new place to live."

Nodding in quick motions, she hugged the paper to her and hurried around him, as wide as she could around Teek and the Prince and out the door.

Arlo pointed at a young man across the room and barked, "You! Go to the guard's station and tell them that I want a detachment of at least five men outside of this suite at all times until I say otherwise. Nobody but myself, my son or someone from the Brebor line in or out. Go!"

The young man hurried from the room.

Things were put back in their places quickly as King Arlo stood in the middle of the living area and supervised. Before the last servant left he

40

grabbed onto her arm and ordered, "Go to the kitchen and tell them to have the best meal they can prepare brought up here within the hour. And a few bottles of wine." As the servant fled, Arlo looked to his son and folded his arms.

Wazend and Teek had remained by the door while all of this had been happening and only stared back at him, and Teek looked unnerved.

The King beckoned to her with one finger.

With a glance up at the Prince, she pulled away from him and hesitantly crept to the king, her brow arched high over her eyes as she anticipated the scolding that was to come.

As the girl reached him, Arlo just loomed over her for a time with his arms folded and his narrow eyes trained in an unwavering stare on hers.

Wazend finally approached himself, and he started, "Father…"

King Arlo raised a hand to silence him, then folded his arms again, drawing a deep breath before he spoke. "My dear, what's done is done, and for all the power I wield I cannot undo it. But you will not spend your last night at my kingdom in a cell; you will spend it in the comfort of your family's home."

Her lips tightened and she nodded, then she threw herself into him and wrapped her arms tightly around his chest.

Returning her embrace, the King looked to his son and guessed, "That ploy of yours to have her banished was your idea, I assume. And I can also assume that you have more up your sleeve than buying her some time."

Wazend nodded. "I do."

Nodding, Arlo smiled ever so slightly and said, "It's good to see us finally agree. I've already had supplies assembled for her. Bring her to the Temple in the morning and we will discuss matters there." He looked down at her and stroked her hair. "We will also look at some maps I've had dug out." Taking her chin, he raised her face and looked into those big green eyes. "Your father was our greatest hero, little girl. Now, the burden is on your dainty shoulders. Enjoy your evening, for tomorrow you embark on your own adventure to save our kingdom, just as your father did so many times. Find hope for us, Teek, and bring about the fall of this monster."

Tight lipped, she nodded to him.

King Arlo pulled away and turned toward the door, informing, "You'll have a hearty dinner tonight before you do anything, and in the meantime we will set things in motion."

As his father reached him, Wazend nodded to Teek and bade, "I suppose I'll see you in the morning, then." When he turned, the King's arm was thrown across his chest and he stopped.

Still facing the door, Arlo's eyes slid to his son and he informed, "I already know about you two. Most of the kingdom knows. Don't waste this night sneaking about to try and see her, just lock the door behind me and enjoy the evening." He looked over his shoulder at Teek and shook his head.

She smiled and shrugged.

As the door closed behind the King, Prince Wazend turned and set his hands on his hips, his brow tense as he barked, "How long has he known?"

CHAPTER 4

The sun was not even up yet when Teek awakened beneath the linins and blanket of her bed. Curled up on her side, her first realization was that she was not alone there, and as she awoke fully, she smiled as she remembered the first night she could openly have an intimate time with the elf she loved. The room was dark but for the candle that burned low on her lavatory table across the room. It offered her just enough light to see Wazend sleeping peacefully on his back beside her. She shifted ever so slightly so as not to awaken him and was quickly aware that her leg was drawn up to her and lying across his thigh.

He stirred and the arm he had stretched out beneath her head curled over her. Even in sleep he was rather strong and she was pulled toward him.

Slowly, gently sliding her hand across his chest, she turned ever so slightly to bring her body against his and laid her head on the pillow next to his.

"Can't sleep?" he asked in a low, soft voice. He turned his head and looked to her as his fingers stroked her bare shoulder ever so gently.

Teek pulled herself over his chest, helped along by his arm pulling her toward him, and as she closed her eyes, her mouth found his and she kissed him as deeply and passionately as she could.

After a moment, he pushed her away and his narrow eyes met hers as he asked, "Do you intend for me to make you late getting to the Temple?"

She pursed her lips as she looked away and considered, then she met his gaze again and nodded.

"I was hoping so," he admitted. Without warning he rolled toward her and in an instant he was on top of her. His mouth took hers like some ravenous animal and his hand explored her delicate body beneath his as if for the first time.

And as before, she surrendered herself to him.

They did not know how long it was before their passions exhausted them, but at some point sunlight was illuminating many rooms of the suite and they knew it was time to go.

Dressed in her forest green leggings, dark green belted shirt that dropped to the middle of her thighs and one of her ankle high, round toe boots, she had her other foot propped up on a chair as she pulled her other boot on. Even before she got her foot on the floor Wazend seized her around the waist and pulled her up off of the floor and she smiled as a hushed laugh escaped from her. When he finally put her down, his arms enveloped her and he pulled her close to him, kissing her as he had before.

They finally parted and he ran his fingers through her long hair. The look on his face was nothing short of absolute confidence in her, as if all of his faith was poured into one thought that he knew to be true. "I'm not worried at all," he told her. "You are the daughter of the great Leumas Brebor. His blood runs through you like wildfire. In short order you will return here to save the Elf Kingdom from this threat and then I shall have you as my wife at long last."

A strained smile curled her mouth. His faith in her was absolute, and now she had to find that faith in herself. Once she was on the other side of the new world she would be on her own. How to defeat the dragon on his own terms was not something she even considered possible.

"Just think," he said dreamily as he looked toward the ceiling. "I'll be married to the Elf Kingdom's greatest living hero." Turning his eyes back to her, he went on, "I'll be famous! And this hero will bear me many strong sons! Oh, and one daughter, and I shall call her my Little Gem."

Teek's smile forced itself a little broader.

His eyes were glossy and strained and his mouth tightened as he announced, "We should get you on your way. The sooner you get out there and defeat this menace, the sooner I can have you back." He pulled her to him and crushed her little body to his. "And you'll be mine forever."

**

A huge structure even by human standards, the Temple was a building of stone that had never been completed. It was cavernous inside and actually looked something like a cavern. Columns about every ten paces looked like flow stone and were smooth to the eye and the touch. The marble they were made from hinted at emerald green and, upon a closer look, veins of emerald could be seen within the stone and seemed to give the columns more strength. The walls, also some kind of granite, were more than a pace thick and composed of this same kind of stone, though they were speckled with many different kinds of jewels that were encrusted within the semi-transparent stone. With a domed roof that was ten human's heights high in the center, the whole thing looked more like it was formed from nature rather than built by the hands of elves and gnomes, and, in fact, this was the legend about it. Far older than the palace, no records of how it was made still existed. There was only one way in, but for the hundreds of windows that were four heights above the floor and offered most of the light. The huge, ebony doors stood open as they almost always did and were polished to a high gloss. The hinges, bolt and door handles were plated in gold and were many generations old themselves.

Inside, there was nothing but open space, a few alters to forest gods, works of art such as statues and paintings and tapestries, and ancient furnishings, all of which were along the walls. It was thirty paces wide, twice that long and its floor was smooth and polished white granite.

The far end is where there was a gathering of elves and a couple of gnomes who awaited the arrival of the daughter of Leumas Brebor. What one might think were seven stone doorways built into the back wall were, in fact, the portals that could be open to seven different locations around the Abtont Forest. The next to the last one to the left was where a gathering was, and three old, white bearded elves, each of whom held a different color crystal orb, stood on a line to one side of it. They were dressed in long white robes that had sashes across both shoulders with ancient writing embroidered in gold. Each sash was the same color as the orb that was held by that cleric.

Escorted by six palace guards, two in front and four behind, Teek held the Prince's hand tightly as he walked beside her. Only when she saw the clerics, the other palace guards and King Arlo at the other end of the Temple did she begin to feel that quake in the pit of her stomach. She had once imagined herself riding off to save the kingdom all by herself, but that was when she was much younger. Now, she was expected to do it for real, but only by a few people. The rest of the kingdom was forced to banish her on the word of a beast that was their enemy.

The walk to the Wall of the Portals seemed to take forever and she was more and more unnerved with each step. She did not display this outwardly, but ten paces away she squeezed the Prince's hand a little tighter, and he squeezed back to reassure her.

King Arlo met them about four paces from the portal, stopping right in front of the girl he meant to banish. Gently stroking her hair, he whispered, "I am sorry for this."

She forced a smile and reached up to touch his bearded cheek.

"When this beast is dead," he assured in a low voice, "the Elf Kingdom will welcome you home. I will personally see to your lands and holdings until you return, no matter how long it takes."

With her gaze fixed on his, she nodded, then reached up and touched her lips and extended her hand to him.

"No need to thank me," he said with a little smile. "You are family, remember?"

She nodded again. Teek touched her chest, her heart, then she pressed her hand to his chest, over his heart.

The King whispered back, "I love you, too, little girl." He took her hand and put his fist into it.

When he opened his fingers she felt a few coins drop into her palm.

"Put those in your pocket," he whispered to her. "You may be able to trade those for a favor or two, maybe hire someone to help us with this problem."

She smiled as he winked at her, and she subtly did as he told her and slipped her hand and the coins into her pocket.

One of the clerics, holding a clear orb, approached the King from behind and said in a low voice, "It is time, my King."

Arlo nodded, his eyes still on the girl before him. He looked to one of the guards and nodded, then back to her and informed, "I have something to tell you before the council comes to witness your banishment. I'm sending you with a pack of supplies, three days worth, but also some money and a map of that area. Humans are about and in a colony that borders the desert only a day's walk east of the ruins you will emerge in. Perhaps you can barter with them. Perhaps you can lead Vultross to them and they will call upon one of their Dragonslayers to deal with him." He held a finger up. "But, a few day's travel into the forest and past a vast lake is the lair of another dragon, one known to forest folk as Falloah the Scarlet. If our dragon gets too close to her she may just emerge to do battle with him, and that could rid us of him as well. Take no unnecessary risks out there, Teek. Don't let the other dragons see you and keep yourself hidden when you can. I want you back here a hero, not another kill made by this monster."

She nodded.

Wazend raised her hand to his mouth and kissed it tenderly before he bent to her ear and whispered, "I will send help and they will have that last crystal tipped arrow. If you must do battle with him again, you won't do it alone."

Teek turned fully to him and slid her arms around him for a hug.

Well dressed as they almost always were, the Elvan Council filed into the Temple and strode with purpose to the Wall of Portals, and they did so in silence. Leading them was Councilwoman Gisan, who still had a smug look about her but it was clear that she had recently been put in her place. Her eyes were fixed on the elf girl to be banished and she made no secret of how overjoyed she was by this.

Ignoring her, Teek glanced about at the other council members and she stepped away from the Prince as one of them strode from his place among them. This was the youngest of the council, the man who had repeatedly advocated killing the dragon to save their kingdom, had repeatedly helped King Arlo strike down any disbursement of the Leumas lands, and had always been kind to her.

Dressed in a light blue jacket, white shirt and darker blue vest with trousers the same color, he stopped within arm's reach and took her shoulder. "What you do today will save the lives of hundreds. Give him a good hunt, Teek Brebor, frustrate him, and if you devise a way, kill him. I shall anxiously await the return of the Elf Kingdom's youngest hero, and I shall watch for you every day. Upon your return the Brebor name shall once again bring hope to our people and fear to the enemies of our people."

Tight lipped, Teek offered him a single nod and her eyes never left his.

The council had formed a semi-circle around the portal to the desert and he took his place among them, folding his hands before him as he gave Teek a solemn but confident look. No one else spoke.

King Arlo's duty was to pass sentence and see to it that the sentence was carried out, and it was clear that he did so with a heavy heart. He took the cumbersome two strap pack made of buckskin from the castle servant who offered it to him and turned fully to the condemned girl. Drawing a breath, he started, "Teek Brebor, you have been banished from the Elf Kingdom to be hunted by the black dragon in place of his tributes. To protect the Elf Kingdom from his wrath, you are hereby banished to the Hard Lands where your sentence will be finalized." He held the pack to her, and when she took it he continued, "You are forbidden to return here."

"Ever," Gisan added, drawing daggers from the eyes of the King and Prince and most present.

"Go now," the King ordered. He looked over his shoulder and nodded to the clerics.

The three pace wide portal was merely an arch of stone built into the wall. The clerics formed a shoulder to shoulder line right in front of it and extended their arms, holding their orbs under the arch. An unnatural glow of golden light illuminated the arch and the orbs hovered off of their hands and slowly rose toward dimples in the stone inside the top of the arch, and simultaneously they sank into their respective places, filling the dimples perfectly, and as they did they glowed brightly. The stone wall seemed to disappear and there appeared to be another room on the other side, one that was lit by the sun and made out of a different kind of stone. As the clerics stepped away, a fog fell from the top of the portal to the bottom and a hot breeze blew from it, dissipating the fog about halfway down.

Teek looked back to King Arlo once more, then to Prince Wazend, then, mercifully, she turned and walked into the portal, disappearing into the other side, and as she did, the glow that illuminated the stone arch slowly faded and the orbs began their slow descents back down where the clerics stepped forward to meet them. In seconds everything returned to what it had been and the stone went completely dark.

King Arlo set his jaw, staring at the portal that was now quiet, and he ordered, "Show that the sentence was carried out and the banishment of Teek Brebor is done." Tight lipped, he folded his hands behind him and limped toward the door.

Slowly, the council and guards turned to follow him.

Wazend found himself standing under the arch of the portal and he gently placed his hand against the stone wall, bowing his head as he whispered, "Stay safe, my love. I beg you stay safe, and come back to me."

**

Teek looked around her, finding herself in what appeared to be another temple, one made of red stone and pink granite. It had clearly been abandoned for decades. Built much like the temple at the Elf Kingdom, this one was about a quarter the size and only had the one portal against the far wall. Looking ahead of her, she noticed that all four walls were still standing, but the doors leading out were gone and some of the roof had caved in a long time ago. Drawing a deep breath, she put her arms through the straps of the pack and settled them over her shoulders, carrying the weight of the pack on her back.

She emerged from the old temple into what looked like an abandoned township of some kind. All of the buildings were made of stone; sandstone, limestone or granite, and all appeared to have been in disrepair for a long period of time. A few of them had collapsed but many stubbornly defied the elements and remained standing. This had been a town of considerable size and she took her time exploring it. A couple of merchant shops were still full of the products that were to be sold. Bakeries had the ancient remains of the goods they made. After more than an hour of exploring she finally ran across an armor smith or blacksmith that was in a rather thick walled structure that appeared to have been attacked by something. When she entered, she first noticed that anything made out of wood had been charred and the whole place had been burned at some point. A few old weapons, swords and spears and bows and a few shields, littered the floor beneath the scattered remains of the roof that had fallen in. Her brow lowered inquisitively and she turned and strode back out, looking about the street a little closer. There, where she had just come from was the outline of a sword under the soil of the street.

Teek knelt down beside the outline and brushed away some of the loose sand and soil, and sure enough there was a sword. Taking it by the hilt, she pulled it from its resting place and stood with it. It was huge, as long as she was tall and very heavy. Someone with a really good arm must have wielded this. Laying it back down, she looked about her again, this time for something more specific, and she found what she suspected. The surviving doorways were all very tall, almost twice as high as the top of her head, and they were much wider.

Scanning the area once more, the realization of where she was finally drove home and she felt that uneasy crawl deep in her belly.

This had been a human village!

Drawing a breath, she managed to calm the panic that welled up within her, reassuring herself that this place had been abandoned for some time.

Continuing her exploration, she finally realized that the air was very hot and getting hotter. She did not want to deplete her three bottles of water without a source to refill them, but thirst was a more immediate issue, and the first of them was removed from her pack. It was a simple water bladder like she was used to, like her father always carried and she sat down in the shade of a broken down building and laid the pack beside her. Pulling the stopper, she started to raise the bladder to her mouth, then hesitated, and lowered it to her lap. Something was amiss. Squeezing the bladder, it did not feel like water, it felt like…

She turned it over beside her, clenching her teeth as sand poured out. Dropping it, she reached for the next and pulled the stopper, and sand poured from it, too. The same was found with the third. With narrow eyes, she knew this was not King Arlo's doing. It was clearly Gisan trying to be sure that she would die in the desert one way or another.

Emptying all three bladders, she shoved them back into the pack with angry motions and reached for a tin of what she hoped was dried meat or bread, but when she opened it she found dried goat droppings instead. Huffing a hard breath out through her nose, she tossed that tin aside and reached back in, finding a second tin, then a third with goat droppings. She tossed the third away from her and leaned back against the wall. Turning her eyes skyward, she drew a deep breath, knowing that this conspiracy was meant to be sure she would not return.

Not one to feel sorry for herself for long, she rubbed her eyes and looked back to the tins, then dumped out the goat droppings and put them back into the pack. It could be that they would be useful at some point. She stood and slipped her arms back into the slings, shrugging the pack back into position behind her shoulders. Now it was time to call upon the many seasons of her father's wilderness teachings. No village this size could survive very long without a reliable source of water, and it had to be somewhere nearby, perhaps right in the center of the village itself. Looking around her, she saw mountains in the distance to the west, and often where there were mountains there was concealed water.

A half hour later she was standing at the west edge of the village, looking toward the mountains. She studied the scrub brush, the cacti and wandered about for some time until she finally found something that looked out of place. There were bushes out here that were larger than the rest, but not evenly distributed. They actually formed a line from the village to the mountains and one of her eyebrows cocked up as she realized this.

Her thirst was becoming more and more bothersome as she followed that line through the village as best she could, and finally she found a very large, domed structure at the village center. Stone arches a human's height and a half high were all the way around it, giving it the appearance that it was open on all sides. She could see support columns within that surrounded a wall that was perhaps half a human's height tall. Once inside, she went right for the wall which formed a nearly perfect circle right in the center of the dome. Sunlight poured in from the other side where part of the dome had collapsed into a scattering of rubble on the floor of the other side. Peering over the wall, she smiled as she discovered that it surrounded a pool of crystal clear water. The wall, it seemed, formed a bowl of sorts to contain the water, which must have been under some pressure from the rock beneath it. How deep the pool was could not be determined, but the rock at the bottom was clearly porous and many large openings made it look like a network of water filled caves were down there.

She hopped up on the wall and sat with her feet dangling over the side as she removed her pack and set it down beside her. Rummaging through, she found the three water bladders and pulled the stoppers one by one, holding them upside down to make certain that all of the sand was out. Twisting around, she held the first bladder under the water, and as she did so she reached into the water and withdrew a handful of it, raising it carefully to her mouth. Drinking what she could, she ran her wet hand over her forehead, then around her neck, closing her eyes as she rolled her head forward. In the heat of the desert this felt wonderful and she repeated it a few times while she filled that first bladder. Once it was full she lifted it from the water and took a long drink from it, allowing some of the water to spill out and run down her shirt, down her chest and belly. Feeling her thirst quenched, she returned the bladder to the water and refilled it.

Once all three were full, she loaded them back into the pack and rummaged around for something to eat, something that Gisan might have missed. Predictably, nothing was to be found and she released a deep breath through her mouth as she closed the pack and stared down at it for a while. While she was hungry, at least her thirst had been quenched.

With water taken care of, she hid her pack in the debris of the dome and ventured out west of the village with one bladder over her shoulder. Surely some of those trees still had fruit or berries on them. Or, perhaps she could catch something. Sure enough, she found a bush that had a few dark red berries on it and she set about collecting some of them, eating a few as she picked them and then stuffing the rest into her pockets.

Collecting her only source of food like this made it easy to lose track of time, and before she realized, the sun was just over the peaks of the mountains to the west. Once it was on the other side of the mountains darkness would settle in quickly and she needed to have her camp set up before then.

Returning to the water pool, she refilled her depleted bladder and retrieved her pack. Somewhere in the ruins of the village she could find a safe place to sleep for the night. Although she knew the desert would grow cold at night, she was too afraid to build a fire anywhere.

During her search, she stopped by the old blacksmith shop where she had found so many abandoned weapons. There were many to rummage through, but the one that fit her hand the best was a small dagger, no doubt one that was designed by the humans to be concealed easily. The blade was a little rusty and the hilt was wrapped in thin braded and dried out leather, but it seemed a sound weapon and she felt a little more secure having it.

Finding a house that had weathered the ravages of time very well, she crept in and found an old bed that was still intact, and she wasted no time pounding off as much dust as she could. The floor of the old house was made of smooth cut wooden planks that had turned gray over the seasons. It backed up to another building and shared walls with the two beside it and the only window was a pace to one side of the door. It was only one room with a table in the center and two overturned chairs on the sides. Within an old wardrobe, sealed shut for many, many seasons, she found a few articles of clothing still within and a few blankets on a top shelf.

She pulled off her over shirt and laid it neatly on the corner of the bed. Inside and at night, she would not have to worry about the sun burning her and she could sleep comfortably in her undershirt. She also pulled off her leggings and folded them neatly. The desert would grow cold soon and this little house provided everything she would need to get her through the night. There was a fireplace, but she did not want to draw the attention of the unknowns out there and it would remain cold. Pulling a chair from the table over to the wardrobe, she was able to reach the musty old blankets on the top shelf and retrieved them both. They were dusty and did not smell so good, but they were still soft after all of these seasons and somehow they were free of bugs and spiders, though she vigorously shook them out anyway to be sure.

Set for the night, she ate a couple of handfuls of berries from a pocket in her shirt, had a drink of water, then, as darkness fell, she curled up on the middle of the bed and wrapped herself in the old, musky smelling blankets to spend her first night away from home in a while.

Loneliness set in quickly, then thoughts of the unknowns out in the darkness. Sleep would be elusive this night. She simply did not feel safe. Every time the wind blew or something in the quaint old house creaked, her eyes darted that way. Every nerve was alert and her entire body was taut. Hours passed and her eyes grew heavier and heavier, and before she realized, she was fast asleep.

**

Sunup was still more than an hour away and the house within was almost completely dark.

The wooden floor near the front window creaked.

Teek's eyes flashed open. Though afraid to move, her hand found the hilt of the dagger she had nearby and tightly wrapped around it. Another creak on the planks of the floor and her entire body went rigid. She could not move, nor did she have a desire to. Not knowing what was there and unable to see it in the near pitch blackness of the house, she did not want to draw its attention, though she was certain it could hear her heart slamming away within her.

Whatever it was shuffled along the floor toward the other side of the room. It was testing the air, sniffing loudly for something.

To Teek's horror, it began to move closer to her, sniffing the floor as it went. She lay frozen where she was, too afraid to move, but ready with that dagger should it attack her. Her breath froze in her chest as the bed shifted, telling her that whatever it was had started climbing up on it. She heard sniffing again, then something dragging, and she was sure that it was her shirt she heard hitting the floor.

Then came the smacking sound. It was eating her berries! Moving slowly, she felt her way along the edge of the bed, toward the wall at the back of the cabin. On that back wall was the shelf with a few cooking utensils that would make wonderful projectiles. As she groped for them, she knocked something off made of thin metal and it hit the floor with a horrible sound and she cringed, covering her ears. Whatever was in there with her panicked and shuffled quickly toward the door, clumsily retreating from the house. Door hinges creaked as it bumped the door on its way out.

Teek made her way that direction, finding the door and pushing it shut again, then she groped for the bolt and pushed it into place. Breathing in deep gasps, she leaned her head against the door and closed her eyes, hoping that whatever it was would not be back.

Even with the rest of the night quiet, she could not find restful sleep and simply dozed off and on for some time, and finally a deeper sleep claimed her as an early morning glow began to illuminate the eastern horizon.

Daybreak found her up early, standing in the middle of the house with her hands on her hips as she stared down at her torn shirt and the purple stains that were all over it from her berries being eaten. Looking across the floor, she noticed that the dust that had collected on the floor over the seasons had left perfect footprints of her visitor, footprints that looked like some kind of giant rat. Her father's survival training surfaced and she was well aware of one thing: This animal was a food source, one that would be hunted if and when he returned. Judging from the size of the tracks he was about the size of her leg and would no doubt provide enough meat for a few meals at least. Survival had become a priority and she intended to do so as long as possible, and that meant she would remain where she was for a while, gather her strength and formulate a plan to deal with Vultross when he eventually found her. And big predator evasion was one of the first lessons her father had taught her.

She finally picked up her shirt and looked around her. Time to get to work.

As the morning progressed, she gathered more of those berries, filled the basin with water and cleaned the little house as best she could, especially the beddings. She also washed her shirt and hung it in the doorway to dry. Nobody was about so wandering around in her undergarments would not be an issue. It would also be much cooler this way in the desert heat. With all of this done and after another handful of those berries for breakfast, she returned to the broken down shop where she had found the weapons and poked around there for a while. To her dismay, most of the weapons were for much larger people, for humans, and all were too big for her to wield comfortably. Moving an overturned wooden shelf with great effort and the help of a spear for leverage, she found more weapons beneath it, smaller weapons including many daggers and a broken crossbow. Among them was something that caught her eye and she moved a couple of sharpening stones and a rusty sword breaker aside to get at it. Picking it up, she found the leather wrapped wooden handle still in very good shape, not cracked nor splintered. Holding it before her, she realized that the rusty head of the single sided war axe was also sound and just needed a good cleaning and sharpening. Digging further, she found a tin in the shape of a bottle that still had the lid on it and was half full of liquid. Pulling the stopper, she smelled it and nodded, finding it full of oil that would condition metal and leather nicely.

By high sun she had taken many finds back to the house, and she also found a few treasures. The humans who had abandoned this place had left almost everything behind and she even found gold and silver coins from time to time, and she collected all she could find. They may just be useful at some point, as the money King Arlo had left in her pack had been taken by someone before it was given to her.

With each little success she felt more and more triumph. She was beating Gisan at her own game and was more determined than ever to survive and return home, but it was not more out of spite for the councilwoman than revenge for the dragon killing her parents.

Having collected wood from everywhere she could, she cleaned out the fireplace of the house and stacked in small pieces and some dried grass to start a fire, which she planned to do around dark. She was sure that the dried wood from the dilapidated structures would burn quickly, but a few timbers she found had one end still solid, though dry, and hopefully they would burn longer. With the fireplace ready, she would not build one until near dark.

A midday meal consisted of those berries, which she had to venture further and further from the abandoned village for, and she sat down on the bed after to work on the war hatchet. Time was something she had in abundance and here she used as much as was offered. The urge to explore nibbled at her and she eventually jumped down and put her belt on, sliding the axe into it as she strode out of the house to look into surroundings again. Keeping her mind occupied was the best way to defeat the loneliness that constantly hovered around her.

She visited many a rundown shop or house, collecting little trinkets here and there or finding something that could be useful. In one house she found an oil lamp still hanging near the inside of the door and, though dirty, it was intact! And on a shelf on the other side of the room was a shelf that had, among many other items, a glass jar with a tin lid that was full of oil for the lamp.

Teek spent the day enjoying the slow turn in her fortunes and had nicely set up housekeeping in the little house, making it as homey as possible. She even found a painting to hang on the wall over the bed, one of a flowery field with a dense forest beyond.

Venturing out yet again, she found a wider street that ran to the north from the water pool and walked down the center of it, looking about for anything that might interest her. She found herself completely carefree, pushing feelings of loneliness aside and concentrating on her surroundings as she searched for anything that might be useful.

A larger stone structure had once stood only a hundred paces from the pool and had partially collapsed, leaving the interior exposed and visible. A stout building, it had weathered the ravages of time despite the loss of much of its front wall. It had been a place of importance from the look of things as the interior appeared to be a great hall of some kind. As she entered, she first noticed that the floor was made of marble that had been carefully cut and polished and laid in place by expert hands. It was huge within, at least forty paces deep and about half that wide. Stone benches were distributed along the walls, and the place looked much like the temple at the Elf Kingdom. Most of what had been inside appeared to have been piled up at the front door before the wall collapsed.

She wandered in, taking her time as she looked about. The rest of the building appeared to be rather solid and she felt secure entering deeper to have a look around.

On the other end of the cavernous hall she found a door that looked like it had been sealed at one time. On closer inspection in the lower light on this end she discovered that the door had been, in fact broken through, and barricaded on the other side. She pulled it open, the ancient hinges creaking horribly as the door moved. She peered inside the next room, discovering that it was but a narrow stairway that led downward. On the floor just within, just before the first steps down, was an old metal lamp. The glass chimney had been broken and it was covered with dust, but when she picked it up she could feel that there was still liquid inside, and when she opened the top it smelled of lamp oil. Fashioning a wick from a piece of her undershirt, she lit the lamp with her flint and hatchet and it lit the way as she cautiously made her way down the stairs. There was a burnt smell and the awful odor of death from long ago, though it was still pungent. The walls appeared to be covered with soot and were burnt and blackened and absorbed much of the light from her lamp.

The stairwell turned and she proceeded with caution, looking down to see a discarded sword, then a rusty helmet a few steps further down. Finally at the bottom, she shined the light about, freezing as her eyes fell upon the horror hidden in the darkness for many decades.

Piled in the corner of the basement were thousands of bones, and thousands beneath them. The remains of clothing were still tangled among them in places. Human skulls were randomly mixed with them. They were not the bleached white bones she had seen before in the forest, not of animals that had died and been scavenged until only bones remained. These bones were a dingy yellow brown and had never seen the sun. Bodies had been piled in that corner many decades ago, or perhaps they had huddled together one atop the other to escape something. Her imagination ran rampant and she slowly backed away. Turning, she found other bones strewn about, mostly those that she could identify as human, and many more skulls littered the underground room that was carved right out of the sandstone. She was barely aware of the stone columns that were evenly distributed about the room, the old furnishings, beds and tables and chairs that were stacked along the far wall. Her attention was consumed with the many bones that were seemingly everywhere.

Slowly backing away, she stumbled as her foot caught on the first step of the stairs that would take her out and she fell to her backside on the second, her wide eyes still darting about at the ancient carnage before her. Tearing her gaze away, she turned and ran hard back up the steps, and in a moment burst from the door and ran toward the sunlight.

Stopping at the pile of debris that had been the front wall, she dropped the lamp and scrambled over it, out into the sunlight. Her heart was beating very hard but she did not stop to rest until she arrived back at the house where she slammed the door and slid the bolt into place. Gasping for each breath, she still pushed against it and leaned her forehead against it as she struggled to catch her breath and slow her pounding heart.

Reason returned to her slowly, but it did return, and she finally realized that the village had been abandoned quickly, that everything had been left, and in all of her exploration she had never found the remains of the inhabitants. Now she knew what happened to them, where they had gone, and why none remained in the village. The sulfur char smell of the stairwell had permeated her senses and she could still smell it, that and the horrible stench of decades old death.

She raised her eyes. The wall torn open, the door broken inward... Something big had attacked them, something big had torn through the stone wall, through the door to that large basement and it had burned...

A dragon!

A chill ran through her and she turned and wandered to the bed, crawling up onto it to lie down. She remained there for a time as she allowed this realization to sink in. Sent away to hide, to find help, she had been sent right into the middle of the dragon's domain. It was only a matter of time before he found her now.

There was only one enchanted arrow left, and it was at least a hundred leagues away, a month's travel, and locked away in a place she could no longer go.

A while later she pushed herself up, just staring at the door for a while before she hopped down from her bed and strode out of the house. If the dragon wanted to find her in this place and could, then she would meet him on her terms, not cowering in the shadows like some kind of frightened rat.

It was time to go back to the armor smith's shop and find herself some weapons to deal with him.

The walk there was not a terribly long one and she strode down the middle of the dirt street completely lost in her thoughts and seemingly oblivious to everything except finding some way to kill Vultross. This lack of alertness was not something that was common to her but with everything happening as it was, with so many people wanting her dead… And she was not even seventeen yet!

A shadow floated by, probably a cloud.

Spears. Perhaps something could be found with metal that was hard enough…

The shadow floated by again, this time going the other direction.

And this time she stopped. There was a sound from above, one that she remembered, one burned into her memory forever. It was almost like canvas on the wind, almost like linins on a drying line at the castle, like the flags and banners that flew from the towers.

Like the wings of a dragon!

Hearing it again and behind her, she turned and looked up, and this time she met the orange, serpentine eyes of the dragon that hunted her!

Out in the middle of a street that was wide enough to accommodate his wings, she had made herself easy prey. He was less than fifty heights in the air and streaking down at her with terrifying speed.

She found herself frozen where she stood for only a few seconds before that precious moment of clarity finally burst into her and she darted off of the street and toward one of the shops. A stone building would surely not stop him, but perhaps it would slow him.

Running through the open door of the old shop, she turned quickly and slammed the door shut. The bolt was not aligning and she frantically worked with it for a few seconds, finally realizing that it would do her no good, anyway. She turned and pressed her back to the door, her eyes flitting about as her mind scrambled for her next move. There, at the back of the little shop which was littered with wooden debris, broken clay pots and what appeared to be metal cooking utensils, she saw a window and was quick to dart to it. Her palms slammed into the stone wall under it as she looked up to the window shelf which was right above her head. The sash and glass had long ago crumbled and it was just an opening and she grasped the wooden shelf and started to pull herself up, pausing to look over her shoulder as she heard the dragon finally hit the ground right outside. For more long, precious seconds her wide eyes were locked on the door and she drew deep breaths through her mouth with some difficulty.

Outside, she heard heavy footsteps, heard the dragon sniffing right outside the door.

With all of her might, she pulled herself up onto the window ledge, kicking off of the wall with one foot to propel herself up. There was another stone wall only a pace behind and she looked down to the alley between the buildings, finding dust covered broken glass, more broken pots and some scattered bones, and seeing this prompted her to carefully lower herself down where she dropped flat footed onto the ground below.

Crouching down, she listened in horror as something banged on the door and the hinges creaked as it opened. The dragon tested the air again and a soft growl rolled from him.

Teek moved slowly, carefully along the wall, trying to make it to the next building, then she noticed a hole in the wall across the alley and about four paces away, and it looked just big enough for her to slip through. As she carefully made her way to it, she recalled the training her father had put her through many seasons ago. This predator was following his nose right to her, and if she could immerse herself in water then he would lose her scent. That meant going back to the pool in the center of the village.

A horrific crash sounded through the window and she gasped, looking that way. From just on the other side of the window she heard the dragon test the air again, then he growled. More debris fell as he forced his way through the roof and into the small room.

Time to go!

She darted toward the little hole across the alley, removing her axe as she got there and tossing it through first. With a quick glance back at the window, she drew a gasp through her wide open mouth as the dragon's nose poked through the window, and tested the air again; seeing this, she dove into the hole and scrambled on through.

This was not just a hole, it was more a tunnel and she crawled through it as fast as she could with her axe in her hand. There was no time to think of spiders or any other horrors that might be laying in wait. She just crawled as fast as she could in the pitch blackness. The smell was one of char and burnt wood and she found herself crawling through something that felt like a very fine powder and bits of courser debris, some of which crunched under her hands or knees. On the far end she ran into what felt like a metal door and paused to rub her head where she had hit. Groping ahead of her, she pushed against the small metal door, grateful that it opened, yet cringing at the loud creak it made as it did.

Peering out, she looked out into the half collapsed building, noticing first that she could see one of the main streets that led right to the pool. All she had to do was make it there. This place looked like it had been a bakery of some kind, and she had emerged through the fire pit of the big stone oven. There was another crash that she heard both behind and above her and she retreated into the oven when she heard it.

A long quiet followed. Sweat rolled off of her as she listened for the dragon outside and watched the road on the other side of the wrecked bakery through the open oven door. From inside the thick stonework of the oven she could hear very little and could only see through the half open door, and not knowing the dragon's whereabouts was frightening in itself. A moment passed and still nothing. Finally, she moved silently forward, peering outside once again but careful not to touch the door, lest it move and its creaking alert the predator that hunted her. Everything was still and she looked about the broken wreckage of the bakery, noticing that the roof had caved in some time ago and the clay tiles that made it up were in a long pile in the center of the room before her and that most of the timbers that had made it up were still in their positions and looked like the ribs of some huge animal as the ends were still propped up on top of the walls.

Still gripping her axe, she slipped out of the oven and pressed her back to the wall, her eyes darting about for any sign of the dragon.

He slammed into the ground on the street right outside of the shop, right in front of her!

Frozen where she was, she pressed herself hard against the wall behind her, her wide eyes fixed on the huge predator before her as she watched him look around him. She was in the open and all he had to do was turn and look to his right through the ruin of the bakery. His brow was low over his eyes and his scaly lips were pulled half away from those deadly looking teeth. A growl escaped him as he scanned the area and at one point he turned and looked right toward her! Then his eyes swept on. His jaws gaped and he roared through bared teeth, a long roar that shook all around him.

She wanted to cover her ears but was too afraid to move.

He barked another loud roar, a quick one this time, looking around him once more after. Then, with slow, heavy strides he proceeded down the street, right toward the pool she needed to get to, and his attention strayed fully from her.

Teek finally realized she was not breathing and forced a breath into her as she watched the dragon walk out of her field of vision. She heard his wings take air a few times, then nothing. Still, she could not move and sat there with her back pressed against the stone.

Another moment passed and she could hear nothing.

Her body relaxed and she finally looked up toward the sky, seeing only a few thin clouds against the blue field. Daring to take a few hesitant steps forward, she started toward the street, then veered over to the wall on her right, ducking under the timbers that had once held the roof up. There was a thin, triangular corridor that was mostly clear of debris and only an old wooden hutch stood in her way.

The pace toward the street was kept very slow, very quiet, and when she was nearly clear of the bakery she paused to look around her again. The dragon's footprints in the middle of the street were very easy to see and they stopped abruptly thirty paces toward the pond at the center of town, and apparently he had taken flight from there. With one more quick scan of the sky, she slipped around the wall and strode very close to the buildings as she made her way toward the domed structure that covered the pond.

The huge gap in cover from where she was and where she needed to be was going to be a problem and her stomach was restless within her just at the prospect. She stood at the corner of the last building, looking that way as she tried to calm her nerves and muster the courage she needed to dart across to the water. The part of the dome that had collapsed offered a wonderful labyrinth of cover and the water itself would wash away her scent, if only for a while. She did not know how patient this dragon was, but she was willing to wait him out if she had to. At least while he searched for her he would be away from the Elf Kingdom. In this small way, she felt she held some degree of power over him, even if it was only to keep him away from her home and her people for a while.

Her eyes swept the open area between her and the pool, then the sky once more. Gripping her axe tightly and drawing a deep breath, she crouched down, then launched herself toward the dome. Halfway there her confidence surged up. The sun was behind her and she had a clear field of vision.

Then the shadow fell over her.

Warrior training sprang forth and she darted aside, throwing her shoulder down and rolling to the dirt street right before the dragon's claws swept the ground right where she had been a split second before. Rolling to her feet, she spun around just as the dragon's hand slammed into her and in an instant the breath exploded from her as she was rammed back first into the road. Her wits returned quickly and she tried to struggle up, soon realizing that the dragon was holding her down with his clawed hand across her body and his fingers and thumbs pinning her arms to the road beside her. Only her shoulders were not in his grasp and her undershirt had torn away from one. As she struggled desperately to free herself, he pressed down and crushed her to the road. Barely able to breathe, her struggles stopped and she turned her eyes to the orange eyes that had her in their gaze. They were horrible eyes, thin slits that were his pupils widening as he lowered his head to her.

Teek cringed. The axe was still in her grip, but even if she was not pinned to the ground she doubted it would be much use against him. He had her, and they both knew it.

A snarl took the dragon's snout as a growl rolled from him. He turned his head and looked to his shoulder, which still showed the scar of his last encounter with her, then his eyes found her again.

She watched in horror as he raised his other hand, and one of his clawed fingers drew close to her, finally touching her bare shoulder. It was gentle at first, just the tip of his claw touching her bare skin, then he slowly pressed down and she clenched her teeth as he brought her ever worsening pain. She tried to scream but there was no voice to call upon, only a rush of air. He let up and his claw rose from her. His intentions were all too clear now. He did not want to just hunt her. His intentions were to make her suffer, and there was nothing she could do to stop him.

A sinister breath hissed out of him, right through his teeth and he put his claw to her shoulder again, and he seemed to smile. "Little elf hurting Vultross, now Vultross hurting little elf, then swallowing little elf."

Horror filled Teek's eyes as she remembered her father being swallowed alive by this thing, and another silent scream burst from her as he pushed his claw down on her shoulder, but this time slower, deeper, and she felt her bones on the brink of breaking.

He let up again, apparently not wanting to injure her too quickly nor kill her too fast. "Vultross having revenge on treacherous elf."

Her lips sliding away from her clenched teeth, Teek glared defiantly back. This beast did not deserve revenge. Vengeance was to be hers. Her struggle resumed, this time with all of her strength and determination. If only she could free one arm, one hand… The claw pressed down against her shoulder again and she threw her head back as it nearly penetrated her skin this time.

Vultross growled, then his jaws gaped and a low shriek burst from him, one that tore painfully through her ears. "Mighty Vultross will killing all challengers, killing slowly!"

A crash on the ground behind the dragon preceded the tremors that radiated into Teek's back.

Vultross sprang up and wheeled around, his dorsal scales standing erect as he backed away a few steps.

Teek grasped her shoulder and looked, her eyes filling with the massive predator that had just arrived and was less than fifty paces away.

Though his scales were black, they reflected jade green and midnight blue as the sun hit them just right. Crouched down on all fours, the big dragon's eyes glowed red as they were locked on Vultross in a deadly stare. This beast was truly massive, at least twice Vultross' overall size and the bulk beneath his heavy armor scales betrayed muscle of unimaginable strength. Curved, pointed dorsal scales stood erect and the big dragon held his wings half open, his long, thick tail thrashing behind him. The horns that swept back from behind his eyes were also black, very glossy and sharp on the ends. Thick, scaly lips slid away from long, pointed sword sized white teeth and a thunderous growl rolled from his throat, a low growl that sent tremors through the ground. Slowly, the big black dragon stood, his head towering five human's heights in the air and two full heights higher than the other dragon. Much thicker built, the big dragon allowed Vultross to have a good look at what he was up against, then he rocked forward and brought his body almost parallel to the ground, holding his arms ready as he swung his jaws open and roared a deep and mighty challenge through bared, sword size white teeth.

Bearing his own teeth, Vultross took a similar posture and hissed back. His longer neck arched back and he swung his jaws open, his long fangs swinging down as he backed away a few more steps.

Teek found herself right between two dragons that intended to fight and this realization prompted her to scramble to her feet and back away, toward the dome and the water pool within. Her eyes shifted from one dragon to the next as they appeared to size each other up. Though much larger, the bigger dragon seemed hesitant to approach. He held his thick brow low over his eyes, the skin and scales over his slender snout wrinkling as he drew his lips away from his teeth further.

Vultross' jaws gaped and he roared and was answered instantly by the bigger dragon, but this time the bigger black one advanced with heavy, ground shaking steps. These were two apex predators squaring off for what could only be an epic battle, and an elf girl would be the only witness.

Striding toward his smaller enemy, the bigger dragon's jaws swung open, as did the smaller dragon's, but Vultross' fangs folded back slightly and he aimed his head upward, spraying a mist of venom toward the larger dragon, who shied away and retreated a step. Now it was clear why he was hesitant.

With his larger foe backing away, Vultross advanced and sprayed his venom again and the bigger dragon shied away and turned his head to the side. He backed away another few steps and predictably the smaller dragon pursued, but when he sprayed his venom this time the bigger dragon responded with fire. The venom ignited explosively and this time it was the smaller dragon who shied away. The big dragon's next burst of fire was a brutal burst that slammed into his smaller opponent and sent him stumbling away, and this time the big dragon pursued with rapid steps, and before Vultross could turn to respond, the big dragon's hand clamped around his snout and he pounced on his smaller foe. When venom could not turn the tide, the smaller dragon had little he could call upon to respond with but his quickness. He twisted away, narrowly avoiding his bigger enemy's deadly teeth. He managed to spin away and tear his snout away from the bigger dragon's grip and he barely avoided the crushing jaws and teeth a second time. With the big dragon now relentlessly pursuing, Vultross turned and fled, on foot at first, then he opened his wings and stroked them hard, lifting himself quickly skyward.

The big black dragon only pursued a couple of steps, then he stood up from his battle stance and watched the smaller dragon retire. Bearing his teeth, he loosed one more ear-splitting roar at his retreating opponent before he seemed to relax and his dorsal scales laid to his back, interlocking into a solid looking ridge from between his horns all the way to the end of his long tail. The red glow in his eyes faded until all that was left was pale blue within the white, and the small round pupil of black-red. His eyes narrowed and he grunted as he simply watched the faster dragon withdraw.

Then, to Teek's horror, he turned his bulk and looked right down at her. She dropped her axe. With her big green eyes locked helplessly on his, she knew in her heart it was over. Against Vultross she had almost no chance, barely one in a thousand of defeating him. Against this brute, not even that. Even if she'd had her father's enchanted weapons she knew nothing she could wield would even wound a brute of this size and power. So, she simply stood motionless, unable to move at all as she awaited the inevitable.

He just stared down at her for a moment with no discernable expression, only a cold, predator's stare that studied her, and a low growl rumbled from his throat. His eyes narrowed and he looked around her, around him, up and down the road they stood on, then to the pool behind her and the stone dome that covered it. He blinked, then his deep, booming voice shattered the silence with, "You weren't followed here by a little white unicorn, were you?"

Teek flinched at the sound of his voice, then she looked around her, back up to him and shook her head.

Still looking beyond her, the big dragon nodded and absently said, "Good. That's good." He finally looked back down to her and lowered his brow again, baring his teeth slightly as he informed, "This place is to be left abandoned and you should not be here." He turned and simply walked away from her, finishing, "Go back home and don't be here when I return."

She watched him open his wings and lift his bulk almost effortlessly into the sky and her eyes followed him as he flew toward the mountains, veering north where he disappeared over the tops of the buildings. Moments ago, Vultross had been the most powerful being in her experience. Now, she had watched him not just defeated but driven off by one that was far more powerful. He seemed very noble, very wise…

Very imposing! Terrifying!

Teek just watched the sky for a few moments, almost hoping that the largest creature she had ever seen would return. She loosed a breath and reached down to pick up her axe, absently slipping it into her belt as she started the walk back to the house she had been sleeping in. Despite the big dragon's warning, she would not simply walk away. Not yet. Perhaps in the morning.

Perhaps she could convince the big dragon to help her, to help the Elf Kingdom. She had nothing to lose by trying.

CHAPTER 5

The giant rat did, in fact, return, and Teek was waiting for it.

Cooking utensils were put to good use, some edible roots were found among the trees as were some dried herbs that were sealed in jars and tins around the house and a few other places she visited. It was the best meal she'd had for two days. Having eaten wild caught game with her father many times, she knew how to prepare it and cooked it all at once, some in a thick stew that she ate that night while she cooked the rest over the fire on sticks after rubbing it with some salt she had found and some of the spices left behind. Cooked and dried like this, it would last a long time and the tins she had brought from the Elf Kingdom were thoroughly cleaned and prepared to receive the strips of meat once they were done.

That night and well into the morning she slept soundly with the door closed and barred, the window also shuttered, a fire going and no more worries about visitors in the night. Not even Vultross occupied her fears, not since he had been driven away by the much bigger dragon, and it was that dragon who she found in her dreams. She found herself less afraid of him, but she could not be sure why. One thing was certain: He had ordered her to leave the village ruins, and leave she would. He clearly laired in the mountains, well within earshot of another dragon's roars. It couldn't be that far!

Morning found her curled up in the middle of the bed, burrowed into the linins and blankets she had cleaned the day before. Slowly, her eyes opened. She had cleaned all of her clothing the night before and it hung near the fireplace overnight to dry, and this is what her eyes had found first. The chill of the night still lingered, the fire had burned down and hanging over the coals was that cast iron pot she had cooked the stew in, and some of it was still in there.

Breakfast time!

Teek did not dress right away. Wrapped in a blanket, she padded over to the fireplace, found her bowl from the night before, cleaned right after her meal, and filled it with the stew from the pot. She had breakfast in the middle of the bed where she had slept, nestled in among the blankets and linins to keep warm against the still chilly desert air. While she ate, she planned her day, how to find the big dragon and, more importantly, how to convince him to help her. With nothing to offer and really no way to communicate with him, she would have to formulate a plan to make the plight of the Elf Kingdom seem so important that he would want to go to their rescue of his own accord.

As she always did, she cleaned up after herself, dressed, and made sure the fire was out. Preparing to leave was almost a sad event, but she knew she would return if she did not find the dragon. Her last stop before leaving the village was the pool, where she filled all three water bladders.

Her direction was not immediately to go in the direction the dragon had taken. Instead, she followed the line of small trees and brush to have some cover while she made her way toward the mountains. She did not know if Vultross would brave the wrath of the big black dragon again, but she did not want to risk being caught in the open a second time. Her forest green shirt would no doubt help to conceal her among the green leaves of the bushes and trees she stayed very close to.

Once at the mountains, she did not find the going very easy. Avoiding the open desert, she climbed about on the rocks, the boulders and the piles of rubbish the mountains had discarded to make sure she would not be easy to see from above. Further, she had planned ahead for this. Stripping off her shirt, she stuffed it into her pack and pulled out a bed sheet she had covered with that night, one that she had cut down to about two thirds its normal size. Laying it out in a flat area, she covered it with soil and sand, then she withdrew a jar she had filled with water and began to sprinkle the water about on top of the dirt laden sheet. Kneeling down on it, she pounded it with her palms to work the soil in. She continued the process of sprinkling water on it and pounding on it after until finally the jar was empty and she stood from her work and took one edge in her hands, picking up the dirty sheet and shaking off much of the loose soil and sand. She did not shake it hard, instead leaving much of the dirt on it. With this done, she slipped her shirt back on, put her pack back in place and threw the sheet around her shoulders, tying it at her throat. It was close to the same color as her surroundings now, a mix of many browns and reds and oranges, and she was confident that it would offer her some concealment.

Staying as close to the mountain as she could, she made her way toward what she hoped would be a friendly rendezvous with the super predator she hoped to enlist for the Elf Kingdom. Thoughts that he would eat her were quickly pushed from her mind. If he had wanted her for a meal then he would already have done so. Instead, he had simply ordered her on her way and left her alone otherwise. More troubling thoughts were how to convince him to help. She had nothing to trade but her own life, but perhaps she could barter some of the Elf Kingdom's substantial gold reserves. All of the scripts she had read about dragons agreed that they loved gold, and even her father had mentioned this a time or two.

Hours passed and her trek continued. Not wanting to exhaust her water too quickly, she waited until her thirst burned from inside of her and her legs ached before she took a drink, and even then it was done sparingly.

Hearing the unmistakable sound of huge wings from behind her, she quickly dropped to the ground and allowed her makeshift cloak to cover her, pulling it up over her head as she crouched down. Now would be a good test to see how well her camouflage really worked. Beneath the cloak she listened with wide eyes as the creature drew closer to her. She did not want to move and give away where she was and remained as still as she could, barely daring to breathe. As the whoosh of wings passed and moved on, she dared to lift her head from under the cloak and look that way, and ahead of her she caught the glint of red scales just turning to the other side of the mountain. Her brow lowered as she watched the scarlet form bank over and turn toward the mountain. As its long, slender tail disappeared behind the rock, Teek finally, slowly rose up on her knees. This was curious. Had the dragon changed color? Was this a challenger? She was slow to stand and just stood there for a moment, staring that direction as she pondered this new development. One water bladder hung over her shoulder and she absently took it, pulled the stopper and took a long drink before resuming her trek.

Teek had no way of knowing how far she had gone or how long she had walked along the stone of the mountain, but in short order a rubbish pile that had slid off of the mountain a long time ago blocked her path. About four human's heights high and two thirds that wide, much of it looked as if it had been dug in, and by something quite large. A hole that was as high as her head was at ground level and right up against the mountain and about two paces wide, and judging from the off colored soil and stone that had been kicked out, it had been dug recently. She really did not want to know what was in there, and even as she stared into the hole she found herself wanting to move on and put some distance between herself and that huge burrow.

It seemed like a good idea to just walk wide around the mound and that's what she did, and she was careful to keep three or four paces distance from it. Circling to the other side, her attention was ahead where she expected to find the dragon. Since she had seen the red one, she expected to hear the sounds of a battle erupt any time, but so far it was not to be, and this made her curiosity grow even more. Half the day was gone and she had hoped to have found the dragon by now, but the way back was not so far and she was confident she would be able to return to the village well before dark.

Something moved behind her and rocks and sand slid down part of the slope.

Teek wheeled around and had her axe in her hand and ready for battle before she realized. Her wide eyes were on the slope where a few large stones still tumbled down the side. Slowly, her eyes tracked up to where they had come from and her lips parted as she saw what had disturbed the pile.

It was still mostly concealed in the pile of sand and stone, but its boar-like head and narrow shoulders were fully out, as were the short forelegs that ended in long, thick claws. It was a dark, reddish brown for the most part and its huge flat nose wiggled as it tested the air. Two sets of long tusks protruded from its lower jaw, very sharp looking tusks. A mane of thick, course hair concealed a very blunt neck and small eyes seemed to have her in their gaze.

Staring back, Teek swallowed hard and slowly backed away.

The beast emerged slowly, and the short front legs were suddenly longer and able to reach out past its nose. As it slid from the hole that was two heights up the slope, it revealed that the course hair of its back was fused into thick, rust colored plates from its neck all the way to the end of its body. Its long tail was completely ringed with these plates, each of which ended in tufts of its thick hair. Its hind legs were thick and rather blunt and did not really protrude outside of the armor plates that covered it. Twice the size of any horse she had ever seen, it was relentlessly going after her and its snorts and grunts, much like a wild boar's but much deeper, told her that it had its next meal in its sights.

Teek backed away further, her wide eyes locked on the beast. Its back was about a human's height from the ground and it was at least as thick around the body. She had never seen one of these before and it was a frightening sight to say the least. Not knowing how fast it could go, she turned and ran as hard as she could toward where she hoped to find some place to hide from it. Looking over her shoulder, she gasped as she saw it pursuing her with alarming speed, and gaining on her!

Forty or so paces ahead she saw a boulder that had fallen from the mountain and the small space between it and the mountain wall, and she sprinted toward it with everything she had. The space between them was barely big enough for her to get into with her pack on but she quickly scrambled into it on her hands and knees, finding it about two paces to the other side. The hog creature slammed into the gap and reached in with one of its forelegs and those long claws swiped very close to her, missing by a finger width. She scrambled away, almost to the other side as she watched it over her shoulder. As it dug relentlessly to get at her, it snorted and ominous squeals sounded.

Just as abruptly, it withdrew, and in a second was out of sight.

With barely enough room to turn around, Teek squeezed her body around and crawled back that way, very slowly. Her every sense was alert and her every muscle was pulled taut and ready to spring. Half turning her head, she listened, and heard what she was listening for: The ground crunched under something very heavy—behind her!

With another loud squeal, it raked its claws into her hiding place and she dove toward the other side, looking over her shoulder to see it trying to dig its way in. It was sniffing, smelling for her, and it had her scent.

She finally felt like she held some advantage and quickly pulled the cloak over her head and off of her, then she shrugged out of the pack and finally pulled her shirt off. Turning around, she reached quickly into the pack and found a clean shirt, then she threw her other one toward the hog creature and grabbed a water bladder. Frantically, she pushed her pack and cloak closer to the beast as she backed out the other side. Pulling the stopper from the bladder, she stood and dumped it over her chest, then over her shoulder, wetting her back. Quick to throw it back into the hole, she slowly backed away more, pulling the clean shirt on as fast as she could. The creature was still trying to reach in and get at her and was digging the ground away with frightening speed to widen the hole. With its head almost all the way inside her hiding place, Teek circled around the boulder, and once to the other side she looked to the occupied creature only for a second before she sprinted away, following the mountain as she had before.

When she heard something crashing to the ground behind her, she slowed to a trot and looked over her shoulder, her eyes widening more as she saw a second one—a much larger one!—running toward her from its hiding place under the slope. Its call was an even deeper squeal that alerted the first.

Teek kicked her stride longer, tightly gripping her axe as she looked desperately for some place to get away, some place they could not follow. Ahead of her, where a canyon appeared to open into the mountain seemed to be her best option. Though her throat burned from thirst, she pushed herself as hard as she could, all the while hearing the thumping footfalls of the beasts behind her drawing relentlessly closer. She remained close to the canyon wall as she sprinted down it, each breath burning as it entered her and feeling like she simply could not get enough air.

There! Across the canyon! A crack in the red and orange stone, or a fault! It looked big enough for her to squeeze into and she changed direction, making for it with everything she had left. The crack in the sandstone was a human's height high and just barely wide enough for her to squeeze into, but she turned her little body and slid in as far as she could. It seemed very deep but narrowed as it went into the cliff side, and she was only able to get in a couple of paces. Her brow arched over her wide eyes as she looked out into the canyon, and ice felt like it was coursing through her as she saw the creatures coming right for her. Now she was cornered, and they knew it.

The smaller of the two slammed snout first into her hiding place, its nose stopped just within arm's reach. It sniffed and snorted and Teek knew it had acquired her scent once again. It squealed suddenly and backed away, grunting at the larger one as it was nudged aside. The larger, a darker rusty red, stuck its nose in and also sniffed, snorted, and it grunted in frustration. Withdrawing its snout, it reached in with those massive black claws and tore at the sandstone, widening the opening to force its way in at her.

Wedged in as she was, Teek had little chance to defend herself, but still she hacked away at its huge paw with her axe, desperately trying to drive it off. The axe did nothing, but it was all she had.

The larger creature tore away enough of the surrounding rock to reach in further and she shrank away as much as she could but still the claws reached her. Blunted from digging, they scratched but did not tear into her skin. Had it been closer it would have. It pawed at her a few more times and finally its claws snagged the neckline of her shirt. When it withdrew, it drug Teek out with it. She resisted, trying desperately to pull away, and even as her shirt tore half from her she was drug from her hiding place and fell to the ground right in front of the larger of the creatures.

Quick to roll to her back, she swung the axe hard right at the creature's nostril and it squealed as it shied away from her. She tried to stand but her shirt was still snagged in its claws, pinning her to the ground. Even as she struggled to pull away, ripping her shirt more, she found herself swinging the axe wildly as its jaws came at her again, and this time she hit its thick lower lip, right near its front tusk, and this time her blade penetrated its skin enough to draw a little blood. It shied away again, but was clearly becoming angry. While it was distracted with this she reached over and tugged at her shirt, tearing much of it from its claw. She swung the axe at its face again and this time swung downward toward its claw, severing the last shred of fabric that held her down. Rolling quickly to her feet, she swung wildly as it charged her again with its jaws open and she retreated into the rock of the canyon wall.

No longer intimidated by the axe, it moved in to kill her.

The smaller of the two squealed a higher pitch squeal than it had, drawing the larger one's attention to it, and it backed away and turned.

Teek looked, drawing a gasp as she saw the red dragon slam into the smaller of the creatures and bite at its head and neck. Only about two thirds the size of the black one she had seen, this one was well muscled, but with leaner, feminine lines. Red horns swept back from behind amber eyes and her outstretched wings flashed the same ocher as her belly and throat as she stroked them to maintain her balance. With claws ripping, her armored back and dorsal scales standing erect, the dragon attacked with her kind's legendary ferocity. She was larger than the creature but did not seem to outweigh it.

The larger of the two charged right at the dragon, calling a challenge that sounded like the huge boar it was. With this one charging, the dragon backed away, roaring at the larger as she retreated. Both creatures turned on the dragon and both bayed at her and attacked with chomping jaws as they tried to get in a critical strike with their tusks.

When it appeared that the red dragon would have to depart, the big black dragon dropped from the sky, his jaws opening wide as he went after the back of the larger creature.

Turning hard, the larger tried to strike back with its tusks, then squealed loudly as the dragon's teeth plunged through its armor plate with a sickening crunch. The dragon wrenched his massive head over, his powerful jaws driving those sword sized teeth deeper into the creature. This looked briefly like an epic fight between two titanic foes, but it was soon clear that the creature the dragon attacked really had no chance. The dragon released the boar to bite again, this time around its head and neck with a similar crunch as the heavily made, sharp teeth did their grisly work against armor and bone. The dragon planted his hand against the creature's back near where his jaws were clamped around the creature, wrenching his head one way, then the other in a horrible succession of pops and cracks from his foe's neck.

As Teek watched with wide, horrified eyes, the creature that had meant to eat her went limp and fell as the dragon wrenched its head almost completely off.

Lunging toward his vanquished foe, the black dragon opened his jaws to collect more of the creature's neck and head in his mouth. Twisting his head, he pulled the creature's head off, his teeth slicing almost easily through tough muscle, armor and bone as blood sloshed everywhere. Raising his head, he gaped and collected more of his prize in his jaws, raised his nose and repeated this, then did this a third time and the creature's head disappeared completely into his mouth as he swallowed it whole.

The scarlet dragon strode toward him, holding her head and body low as she looked up at the big black dragon almost submissively. Looking down at the smaller dragon, the black one bared his blood stained teeth and growled at the red, who responded with a soft croon.

Teek felt as if she was going to watch yet another fight with this big black one, but the scarlet walked right under his neck and chest, raising her head to stroke her snout to his throat, and the black dragon simply grunted in response. Raising her brow, Teek finally realized that the scarlet dragon was possibly the mate of the huge black one and she almost smiled as she realized she had just witnessed a tender moment between these apex predators.

The scarlet looked down at the black dragon's kill, then her eyes and her attention shifted to the tiny elf who looked on. Still holding her body low, she strode around the dead creature and lowered her head further, leaning her head as she did, and to Teek's surprise, she said in a lovely, feminine voice, "Hello."

With a deep grunt, the black dragon looked down at her as well, his brow lowering as he growled, "You again?"

Looking over her shoulder at him, the scarlet asked, "Do you know this little one?"

"I found her in the old village," he snarled, his gaze locked on the elf girl. "When I said to leave the village that was *not* an invitation to stalk toward my lair!" The black dragon glanced about again, out into the desert, and finally back to the elf girl. "Are you sure you aren't being followed by a white unicorn?"

Struggling to hold her shirt together to keep herself covered, Teek raised her brow and nodded.

"Good," the black dragon said with a nod. "That's good. Now get yourself back to the forest before she finds you."

Lowering her eyes, the elf girl shook her head as she pondered how to tell him what she needed to.

"Why are you so determined that she go?" the scarlet asked.

With a snarl, the black dragon growled, "Because when creatures like this find me my life gets complicated, and that usually means an annoying white unicorn steps into it with one of her damn crusades and I have no intention of taking another one of those on today or tomorrow."

The scarlet looked to her again and observed, "Well, she did lure the terraboars out in the open so that we could catch one."

"Where did the other one go?" the black dragon asked.

"Let it go," the scarlet sighed, looking back at him. "This one should be plenty for today."

The black dragon growled. "What makes you think I'm sharing?"

Standing fully, the scarlet raised her head up to his and stroked the bottom of his bloody jaw with her nose, answering, "Because you always do."

He growled again and looked back to the elf girl, who was pulling her torn shirt back over her as best she could. Raising an eyebrow, he said, "You aren't well suited to the desert, little elf. Return to the forest where you belong."

Shaking her head, Teek arched her brow and dared to take a step toward him, raising her hand to draw his attention. As she watched, he bent down to the dead creature and slammed his teeth into it again, this time picking the rest of it up and turning down the canyon. With the black dragon just walking away, she stepped backward as she kept her eyes on him, pressing her back to the canyon wall. Despair was in her eyes as her mind scrambled around how to communicate with him, how to plead for his help. When he disappeared down the canyon, she looked up at the scarlet dragon and rested her head back against the stone behind her.

The scarlet had also watched the black dragon's departure and looked back down to the little elf, and she appeared to smile. "He's right, you know. You aren't well suited for life in the Hard Lands. Why are you so far from the forest?"

Teek really wanted to explain things, but the first explanation would have to be why she could not. She raised her chin and patted her throat, then she touched her lips and shook her head.

With the slight raising of her brow, the scarlet seemed to understand and she asked, "How long?"

The elf girl made a cradling motion with her arms.

A dragon's grunt sounded from the scarlet's throat and she nodded. "I see. You don't seem to have any difficulty communicating, though."

A little smile touched Teek's lips and she shrugged, thinking, *It can be very difficult with people who have not known me a long time.*

The dragon looked back up the canyon and said, "Your gestures are clear enough to me, so knowing you a long time does not seem to matter."

Teek nodded, then her eyes widened and her mouth fell open.

"I'm guessing you did not know that dragons can hear thoughts," the dragon said with an amused tone.

Shaking her head, the elf girl could not erase the astonishment from her features.

"It's quite all right," the scarlet assured. "Many creatures are unaware of this, and we can only hear thoughts that are open to us and from those who wish to communicate with us." She looked back down to the elf. "Why are you way out here all alone? The desert is not a place you can wander without being prepared and you are here with no water or food."

Looking back the way she had come, Teek thought, *My pack is back that way. I left it behind when they started chasing me.* She looked up at the dragon and leaned her head. *I should be afraid of you, but I'm not, and I'm terrified of dragons.*

"You've had a revelation," the dragoness informed. "You seem to have learned that we don't kill just to kill. Dragons always kill for a purpose."

Nodding the elf girl agreed, *Yes. I've heard many stories but I see only about half of them hold much truth.*

"Stories are just that: Stories." The dragon looked back up the canyon and growled a sigh. "I wonder how much of that terraboar he's going to leave me? More importantly, you'd better find your supplies and get yourself to shelter. Night is coming and that's when most of the desert predators come out."

Teek turned nervous eyes that way, toward where she had left her pack. *It will be waiting for me there.*

The dragoness turned and assured, "I'll walk with you. It won't be so quick to come out and try to eat you with me at your side. Come along, now. Let's find that pack of yours."

Trotting to her side, the little elf girl looked up to her and thought, *My name is Teek.*

"In your tongue I am called Falloah," the dragoness countered. "How did you come to be out in the desert?"

**

When Falloah landed a hundred paces from the end of the box canyon, the black dragon lay outside of a huge cave at the very end of it. Bones were strewn around, much of the rock was burnt and hardy clumps of grasses and scrub brush grew randomly where they could take root. Beside the dragon's head was what remained of the terraboar; a hind leg, most of the pelvis and half of its rib cage. Otherwise the carcass had been finished. Trotting off the last of her speed, she approached the big black dragon and barked a roar at him.

Laying on his belly and facing toward the approaching scarlet dragon, the black dragon slowly opened his eyes, turning them up to the scarlet's, then down to the elf she held cradled in her hands. He drew and then released a deep breath, finally growling, "I thought we understood each other on this matter."

Gently setting the elf girl down, Falloah locked her gaze on the black dragon as she said, "Ralligor, you need to hear this."

"She doesn't talk," the black dragon snarled.

Ignoring him, she continued, "A dragon has invaded the forest and attacked the Elf Kingdom."

One of the black dragon's eyebrows cocked up slightly.

Falloah continued, "He has killed many elves and declared himself the ruler of the Abtont Forest."

"And?" the black dragon asked. "It sounds like Drarrexok's problem, not mine. And if he can't attend to it then Agarxus will."

"It's not that simple," she went on. "You fought this dragon yesterday."

Ralligor finally raised his head. "That vipera I drove off? *That's* the problem? Falloah, when Drarrexok finds him there he'll simply drive him off as I did or kill him. And you know Agarxus won't tolerate one of those in his domain. Just let them attend to it."

Holding her shirt closed where it had been torn, Teek dropped her pack and hesitantly approached the black dragon, stopping only five paces away. As he looked down at her, she sank to her knees and clasped her hands together, her eyes begging. *Please help my people, mighty dragon. Please.*

"Tell him the rest," Falloah ordered with stern words.

Still tightly clasping her hands together, Teek closed her eyes, bowing her head as she complied. *I was banished from the Elf Kingdom by command of the dragon, banished here so that he can hunt me and kill me like he did my parents. I can never go home.*

Ralligor looked away and growled.

Falloah's eyes found him and she snarled, "That means the *vipera* will keep coming back to the Hard Lands until he finds her."

Looking down to the elf girl, the black dragon asked, "And if he does not find you?"

Teek did not answer for long seconds and just stared at the ground before her, but finally replied, *He will kill more of my people until he does. Please! Please help me.*

The black dragon looked away and growled again, then his eyes found the scarlet. "And what would you have me do? Spend days or weeks of my time hunting down this simple minded *vipera*?"

"Isn't that your duty as Agarxus' *subordinare*?" she countered.

He raised an eyebrow and did not look pleased at her response.

Falloah leaned her head, raising her brow back as she reminded, "She did flush out those terraboars we like so much to eat, and you know as well as anyone how hard those are to catch."

He huffed another breath and looked to the mostly eaten carcass of the terraboar, then down the canyon. A moment later, still staring down the canyon, he ordered, "Take her to that human settlement on the north side of the scrub country. If the *vipera* finds her there then he'll become their problem as well. I'll consider what can be done about him in the meantime."

Teek and the scarlet dragon watched him lay his head back down and close his eyes, then they looked to each other.

"Well," Falloah sighed, "you'd best collect your belongings and let's be on our way."

**

Falloah landed right at the edge of the scrub country and stood there for a moment with Teek cradled in her hands as before as she stared ahead of her at the rooftops of a human settlement in the distance. "This is as far as I go, elf girl. It is best not to alarm them so I should not be seen." She gently set the elf down and backed away a step. "Do you have the means to trade with them and find something to eat?"

Teek looked up at her and nodded.

"Ralligor knows what he is doing," the scarlet assured. "He acts grumpy but I could tell he means to help you with this, so not to worry. Just go find a comfortable place and wait for what happens to happen."

Staring up at her, Teek nodded, then turned and strode toward the human settlement. After walking a good distance, almost to the first of the struggling trees and bushes that made up the scrub country, she looked over her shoulder to see the scarlet dragoness gone, and suddenly she felt alone.

The settlement was only about an hour into the scrub country in a place where the forest seemed to invade. Here, a small river ran right through the middle of the settlement and there was farmland and many groves of fruit trees on the outskirts of the village. This seemed like a prosperous place and many of the structures on the two main roads that led through it and parallel to the river on each side were of stone and timber construction. This looked like a place that was frequented by travelers who were passing through on their way to wherever their travels led them. Perhaps one more traveler would be welcome.

Knowing that her ripped up undershirt would not be appropriate in this human village, especially since it no longer covered her well, she traded it for the green shirt she had salvaged from her pack, one that had also been torn when she had been attacked by the boars. A little creative knotting at the neckline and she was satisfied that she would look okay. She also wore her hair down, concealing the points of her ears as best she could. Since she had never encountered the tall humans before she did not know how they would react to her kind, so it was best to try and just fit in. However, arriving in the village itself and walking down the wide, dirt road between the one and two story stone and timber buildings, she soon realized how much bigger the humans were. All of the adults were huge, larger than her father who was a rather big elf in his own right. Though warrior trained and confident that she could hold her own against almost any adversary, these humans were far more intimidating than she had thought they would be and every glance that turned into a long stare as she passed made her more and more uneasy.

Somewhere in the middle of town was a large, two level building that looked and smelled rather inviting. Scents of meat cooking and baking bread and pastries grew strong as she approached the open doors. The entryway was ornately carved timbers, but she only noticed them absently and she entered without showing any fear, though inside she could not have been more nervous.

Inside, she paused and looked around at the spacious interior. There were many wooden tables distributed about and many patrons sitting at them or walking to or fro paused to look her way. Almost all were men and the few women she saw obviously worked there. Once again Teek refused to show fear and she strode to with her head up. Glancing about, she took stock of what she was entering, and was quick to notice that most of the eyes in there were focused on her, and everyone within was far larger than she was.

She found a small round table near the back of the inn and threw her pack up on it. The table was as high as her chest and she pulled out one of the crudely made chairs and climbed up into it. Sitting down with her back against the rest, the table came up to her shoulders and she crooked her jaw as she glanced about. Pulling her legs under her raised her up a little higher but her chest still barely cleared the table top. No matter. She was trying not to be noticed, anyway.

Folding her hands on the table, she looked about her, seeing that many people were staring at her but most were beginning to lose interest, and that was good.

A few moments passed and she just looked about, and finally a woman in a long white apron, a very low cut white blouse and a long blue skirt strode to her table, eying her suspiciously as she did. This was not a very young woman, but she was very attractive and plump exactly where she needed to be to draw the attention of the men who patronized the inn. Long black hair had a few streaks of silver and was restrained behind her head by a white ribbon and the wrinkles about her face were not deep. When she reached the table, she raised her brow and asked, "What brings ye in here, wee one?"

Teek looked the much larger woman right in the eye and slowly raised a hand to her mouth, touching her lips with three fingers. At the Elf Kingdom everyone pretty much knew that this meant she was hungry, but this woman simply raised her brow a little higher. Teek drew a breath, then opened her mouth and pointed into it.

"Hungry?" the woman asked.

Teek nodded, then made the motion of drinking something.

"And thirsty," the woman concluded.

Teek nodded again.

"What would ye like?"

Blowing a breath out through pursed lips, the elf girl struggled over how to communicate her wishes to this woman.

Raising her chin slightly, the woman added, "And how ye gonna pay?"

This Teek was ready for and her hand slipped into a waiting pouch on her belt, emerging a second later with a silver coin between her index and middle fingers, and this she offered to the woman.

Taking the coin hesitantly, the woman looked down to study if for a second, then her eyes shifted to the elf girl.

Teek raised her brow and offered her another.

The woman's eyes widened slightly and she took the second coin as well, but this one she slipped into a pocked on her apron. A little smile unexpectedly found its way to the woman's lips and she nodded, saying, "I'll just start ye out with some spiced bread and maybe a little wine."

With a little smile of her own, Teek nodded and watched the woman turn and hurry about her way.

She had a few more moments to ponder and did just that, staring blankly at her pack as thoughts danced about her mind in a vain search for resolution. Involving the bigger dragon and his mate had been a stroke of good fortune and she had to concoct some way to exploit it and get the dragons to do battle again. It was not likely that Vultross would stay to fight the bigger dragon to the death, but perhaps he would get the message and go back to wherever it was that he came from.

Three men approaching her did not go unnoticed and her eyes cut that way. They were scruffy looking men with unkempt hair and dirty clothing. They did not have steady steps and had clearly had too much to drink, and the wicked intent on all of their faces and in their bloodshot eyes sent a little pang of panic coursing through the elf girl as they neared.

The largest of them, a red haired fellow with a big belly and long gangly hair smiled slightly as he said, "Well look here, mates. Look what we've found. Lost little girl."

Another, slightly behind him, also smiled wickedly, and he nodded. "Aye, mum should have kept better watch on this one."

Warrior training was not silent within this elf girl and her eyes narrowed slightly as she studied them, and her hand moved slowly toward the old dagger that hung on her belt. These human men were more than twice her size, but she would not back down, would not try to run from them.

The first one reached for her, taking the collar of her shirt and pulling it away from her. "Let's see how grown up ye are in there."

Her hand moved swiftly and before he realized what had happened the point of her dagger erupted through the top of his forearm, then withdrew just as quickly. A little shocked and with wide eyes, he grasped his arm and retreated from her.

Teek stood up in her chair, which brought her nearly to his eye level and pulled the axe from her belt, standing ready with her brow low over her eyes. Her gaze shifted from one to the other and she told them in no uncertain terms that she was going to be very dangerous to approach again.

The first looked back at his comrade's arm, then back to Teek with a scowl, and he pulled his own dagger. "So, ye wants to fight, do ye? I got a fight for ye."

He strode toward her, and when he jabbed his dagger toward her she parried with hers and swiped with her axe, and he lurched away. Holding his weapon at the ready, he approached again, more cautiously this time, and this time he swiped and she dodged backward a step, and nearly lost her footing. Seeing this, he kicked her chair and it overturned, and Teek lost her grip on the dagger as she fell backward. Scrambling up quickly as the chair was pulled away and tossed aside, she tried to resume her battle stance, only to have her wrist seized. She was flung to the back wall and the breath exploded from her as she impacted it. She had little time to regain her wits before a hand clamped down on her throat and pinned her to the wall behind her. Glaring defiantly back at him, she knew she was just no match for him, and she knew this fight was already over.

The others appeared at his sides, and one was tying a cloth around his bleeding arm.

The man holding her throat leaned his head, his lips curling away from half rotted teeth as he sneered, "So what do we do with ye now, puppet?"

"You release her," another man ordered from somewhere in the tavern, "and you go about your way." This was the deep and experienced voice of an educated man, one who spoke clearly and with expert pronunciation of his words.

The men who had attacked Teek slowly turned to face him. The tavern had grown silent but for the heavy and hollow clop of approaching boots on the wooden planks of the floor.

Teek watched nervously as the heathens fanned out, preparing to receive the man who dared to challenge them. When one moved to the side, she finally got a look at the man who came to her rescue.

He was a very tall fellow, very broad shouldered beneath the clean, lace-up shirt he wore. His trousers were black and appeared to double as arming pants. His black boots were well polished and tall, almost all the way to his knees. Many buckles held them tightly to his legs and they reminded her of the boots worn by the Elvan Cavalry. A thick belt was also black and suspended a huge sword on his left, sword breaker and dagger on the right, and an assortment of pouches. He had a pleasant enough face with a graying black beard that was perfectly groomed. Gray also streaked his short black hair at the temples and speckled over the top of his head. He was a thickly made man, more so in the arms than the men who meant to stand against him, and his brow was held low over very sharp eyes that were almost black, eyes that darted from one man to the next with contempt as he sized them up.

With his left hand resting on the hilt of his sword, he motioned to the door with his head and ordered, "Out with you, and leave this wee one alone."

Even the largest of them did not match this fellow's size nor did they seem to be as fit or as strong, but there were three of them, and while Teek found the mismatch a little unnerving, he did not seem to as he shook his head. "I'm afraid you chaps have had a bit too much of the drink. It's best you go and sleep it off before your drunken lack of judgment calls on you to do something very foolish."

The largest of the scruffy looking men sneered back, "Big talk from only one bloke who can't seem to count."

"I count just fine," the big man assured. "There are three of you, and since you clearly mean to fight with me over this matter, I would suggest you go and fetch a few more to even the odds a bit." When the three men laughed at him, he joined them.

The largest grabbed for him, ordering, "Out with ye," but the next thing he realized was that his arm was twisted awkwardly and he was hurled head first into a nearby table.

The second of them attacked immediately, swinging his fist hard at the stranger's face, but he too discovered that this man's skill far outweighed his own. His strike blocked, the stranger grabbed his jerkin and pulled him in to brutally head-butt him and knock him out cold.

With two down, the tall stranger turned predator's eyes to the hesitant third, who slowly raised his palms and backed away.

"A wise decision, friend," the tall stranger commended. "Now would be a good time to attend to that drink that awaits you, perhaps a bar maid with a generous bosom and low standards." As the man returned to his table, the big man set his hands on his hips and looked down to Teek. "Sorry about them, Lass. I'm afraid one has to deal with their kind of rabble almost everywhere these days. Perhaps they'll know their place when they come around."

She nodded.

He strode to her and righted her chair, putting it in its place at her table as he asked, "Mind if an old warrior joins you?"

The way he spoke and carried himself reminded her of her father and a smile touched her lips as she shook her head. Climbing back into her chair, she settled herself on her legs and rested her forearms on the table as she watched him sit down beside her.

He leaned back in his chair and made himself comfortable, then he looked to her and extended his hand. "I am Sir Rayce, knight and soldier of fortune."

She took his hand and nodded to him.

There was a pause between them after they withdrew their hands, and he ended it with the raising of his eyebrows and the question, "You have a name?"

Teek nodded again, then glanced away, unsure how to tell him what it was. Looking back to him, she raised her chin and patted her throat, then she shook her head.

"Hmm," he growled as he nodded. "Mute, eh?"

She nodded.

An unexpected smile curled his mouth. "Well, no worries, wee one. I'm sure I can talk enough for the both of us. Perhaps you'd enjoy an old warrior's company over a hot meal, eh?"

Teek smiled and nodded to him.

Truly, he reminded her much of her father. He had many stories to tell and the way he spoke reminded her of her father. Hushed laughs escaped her a few times as he would say something amusing.

Within the tavern, the mood became more festive. The three ruffians who had tried to assault her earlier had departed more than an hour ago and she felt much safer with them absent, and very safe in this old warrior's company.

He set the bone of a turkey leg down on his plate and shook his head, chewing the last morsel before he said, "I'll not bore you with that, though. I find employment ample in my line of work, though very dangerous. Got to pull out early morning, before sunrise to face down my next challenge." His eyes shifted to her. "Got four dragons to my name and on the morrow I'll make it five or die in the attempt. The fighting of dragons is not a past time or something to be taken lightly, Lass, and the title of Dragonslayer has its own perils." He picked up his mug and took a long drink, slamming it back down before he continued. "I've been told that this beast I face is one of the biggest in the land and but for some enchantments in my possession I'd not even be facing him." He raised his brow. "Locals call him the Desert Lord, and if the bounty on him pays as I hope, I'm likely to retire!" He smiled. "Might just build me a castle and settle in for the rest of my days, live in some degree of luxury for a change. But, we both know the warrior within would call me out at some point."

With a little smile, Teek rested her cheek in her palm and nodded to him, her full and eager attention locked on him.

He looked to the open door, and so did she. The sun was on its way to the western horizon.

Looking back to the elf girl, Sir Rayce raised his chin and informed, "I'd better be turning in, Lass. Got to rest up for tomorrow." A smile touched his lips and he added, "Here's hoping I live through the day and collect that bounty, eh?" He laughed heartily and shook his head. "Don't want to get overconfident now, do we?"

Teek raised her brow as he stood and wiped his mouth on a white napkin before throwing it down onto the table again. It seemed that he had picked up that mug one time too many, though he retained control of his faculties. She had seen her father do this many times over the seasons and he always seemed to know just when to stop, just like this big warrior here.

He patted her shoulder and offered her a little nod as he smiled. "Be well, wee Lass. Perhaps our paths and fortunes will cross again."

She smiled and nodded back to him, and watched as he turned and strode from the tavern.

Now she was alone in this place of humans and she glanced about for a few seconds. Reaching into her pocket, she withdrew a few copper coins and tossed them onto the table before hopping down from the chair and grabbing her pack. Before leaving, she looked back onto the table, taking a few biscuits and shoving them into her pack, then she removed one of the empty tins and scraped some of the meat and potatoes from her plate and the knights before sealing it and shoving it into her pack as well. At least breakfast would be taken care of.

Staying in town would clearly not be wise, so she made for the woods on the west side, then she turned and strode toward the river, instead finding a swiftly flowing creek that flowed into it. The trees all around were almost all sprawling hardwoods and none of them were especially tall, though many had very thick trunks. A flat, grassy area near the creek appeared to be an ideal camping spot, and while it seemed perfect, she did not make camp there, instead favoring the base of a huge oak that had a trunk five times the circumference of her body. There was tall grass growing around it and some of this would be harvested for her bed. Finding a juniper bush nearby, she took some of the clumps of greenery from it and crushed it up in her hands, rubbing this all over her clothing and blanket, her pack and some of it on the oak. This would hopefully mask her scent from night wandering predators that might be lurking about. After a drink from the creek, she pulled the one blanket from her pack, and as darkness fell she cocooned herself inside of it and laid her head on the pack as she curled up to sleep.

Her mind was a whirlwind as she tried to drift off to sleep, and at the center of it was a dragon, and a big human who was a Dragonslayer.

A huge dragon and a Dragonslayer, and her people plagued by a dragon. This was a dilemma she had never thought she would face. Surely she could expect help from one of them. Surely.

CHAPTER 6

Dragonslayer. He would go to kill the Desert Lord…

The big black dragon lived in the desert…

Teek woke with a start and quickly struggled free of her blanket. A couple of hours before sunup, she found herself sitting up and glancing about as the realization began to sink in. The big black dragon *had* to be the Desert Lord! He had to be! If one killed the other, that would be one thing. But what if they both were mortally wounded? It was not unheard of!

In a quick scramble, she rolled her blanket and repacked her pack.

The scarlet dragoness had flown her to the village and walking back would take probably all day, time she did not have. Hopefully there was someone in the village who was already up and moving around, someone she could deal with.

It was time to buy a horse, and she hoped to have enough gold on her to do just that.

A stable was willing to deal, but all he would give her for three Elvan gold pieces was a black pony, one that was only half the size of a regular horse. No matter. Teek was not quite half the size of a human. She could not expect it to be as fast as the knight's war horse, but she was confident that Sir Rayce would not drive his animal too hard and too fast for his battle with the dragon. The horse had no saddle and she had but a thick blanket over its back that was woven of red and white wool.

She left the village right at sunup and headed due west, toward the mountains in the distance. She had packed enough water for both her and the horse—especially the horse—and hoped to overtake the knight well before he got there, or at least arrive ahead of him and warn away the dragon. All kinds of things flashed through her mind as she rode hard on the little pony toward the dragon's lair and she did her best to formulate a plan to stop the coming battle.

A couple of hours into her ride, the sun was climbing high and the heat was indeed building. She stopped her winded horse and quickly swung down. An empty tin was perfect and she took it and one of her water bladders to the pony's mouth, pouring almost all of the water in. The pony drank ravenously and Teek finished the last couple of swallows from the bladder. The air was not very hot, but she could feel it coming as the sun grew brighter and higher. Though feeling pressed for time, she would allow the pony to rest and nibble some coarse leaves from a bush nearby.

She took a moment to look around her, into the desert she had ridden so hard into. Tan sand was speckled with red and black stone and many sparkly bits everywhere. Some pink looking rock had pushed its way up through the sand in places as well. Many bushes dotted the area, many tall cacti and many more that were almost like thorny balls the size of a man's head. Only a few had flowers on them, the tallest of them, and all of the flowers seemed to be freshly opened and were visited by insects and birds. Drawing a deep breath, she could faintly make out the nectars from them, and a little smile curled her lips. This was very flat country, very open. The tallest things out here were cacti, and the odd tree-like bush. The bushes themselves had small leaves that were a dark green, and some of them appeared almost blue.

A short time later, it was time to go, and go she did. She knew that the dragon's lair could not be more than another couple of hours away, and once she was at the mountains it should be easy to find.

Another hour or so later there was very little growing, only a few cacti, some small scrub brushes that were no more than waist high to her, and the occasional tall cactus that reached high over her, though these were very few and very far between. Ahead of her, she could see that even less grew, but the mountains were growing tall and she could feel that she was getting close!

The pony tired and she knew she had to stop and allow it to rest again, which she did. Finding that tin and another water bladder, she offered it another drink, swallowing down the last little bit from the bladder as she held the tin to the pony's mouth.

A horrible shriek sounded from the east and she lowered the bladder and looked that way, squinting under the sun. There, somewhere in the distance was a winged form. The pony grew restless and she grabbed onto the reins as she tried to get a better look at the thing that approached. A long tail swept downward and it stroked its wings. She could make out a long neck and the sun glistened off of black scales. Vultross had found her!

Her eyes widened and she dropped the tin, hurriedly getting back onto the horse and driving it hard toward the mountains, much harder than she had before.

Here in the open, she had no chance of hiding or escape, and ahead of her there were few cacti and even fewer bushes.

She looked over her shoulder, ice sweeping through her as she saw the viper dragon rapidly drawing closer, and stroking his wings to overtake her. He would be upon her in moments.

So close to the black dragon' lair. So close!

Desert blurred by and all she could hear were the hoof beats of the pony and its throaty breathing as it ran ever faster to get away from the horror that bore down on it.

Vultross roared and panic surged through both the elf and the pony.

Teek looked over her shoulder again, terror on her features as she saw it drawing closer, saw those orange, serpentine eyes fixed on her. This was the stuff of nightmares, nightmares that had plagued her since the deaths of her parents. The dragon had made it clear that he would not just kill her, he would kill her horribly! As she looked forward again, visions of being swallowed alive assaulted her and that panic grew even worse!

She frantically swept the desert with her eyes. That Dragonslayer *had* to be nearby! He had to be!

With another horrible roar, the viper dragon angled himself into a descent, his full attention locked on his quarry.

When the dragon's shadow fell over her, Teek pulled the reins hard to the right, turning the pony and thwarting the dragon's aim just barely in time.

Vultross slammed onto the ground feet first, falling to all fours as he swept his wings forward and turned hard, swinging his long tail for balance as he wheeled around to get the little elf back into his sights.

Teek pulled the reins the other way and half turned the pony, and brought it to a stop. Her eyes locked on the dragon's and her breath froze within her.

His scaly lips slid away from his long, pointed teeth and a growl erupted from him. His brow lowered slightly and his eyes narrowed. The thin slits that were his pupils widened. He slowly lowered his head and pushed himself up on his hind legs, holding his body parallel to the ground as he squared himself fully on her. His arms were held ready and his jaws parted ever so slightly.

Her heart thundering within her, Teek could only stare back at him. This chase was already over, and still her mind scrambled to find a way to escape.

A quiet, terrifying moment passed and they just stared at each other.

Vultross' lips slid away from his teeth a little more and he hissed, "Run."

Allowing herself to succumb to the panic within her, Teek kicked the pony forward and sent it galloping as fast as it would go, turning slightly toward the mountains again. She dared to look behind her, drawing a gasp as she saw the viper dragon in pursuit again, this time on foot, and running hard to overtake her. He was less than a hundred paces away and closing rapidly. Clearly, her pony would not be able to outrun him. She *had* to outthink him!

The thumping of his heavy foot falls drew closer, closer… She could not allow him to get within striking distance. She had seen what he could do, seen him spit venom, seen what his teeth could do even against armored soldiers and horses. Looking back, she winced as she saw his jaws less than twenty paces behind her.

His scaly lips drew up and his jaws opened just enough to separate the points of his teeth.

And suddenly he stopped and turned his eyes beyond her.

Before she could look forward again her pony whinnied and locked his hooves, stopping abruptly and she fought to remain on his back, her hands clutching at his neck. He reared up and she was thrown from him, controlling her fall to the ground as best she could, but still landing flat. The breath exploded from her and she somehow forced her wits to return quickly, looking to see her pony bolt into the desert at almost a right angle of their former path.

Vultross roared and she sat up fully and wheeled around.

Something impacted the ground behind her, something huge!

She spun on her haunches, planting her palms on the desert sand as her eyes filled with the huge black dragon!

He had just landed and his wings swept forward, kicking up a hurricane of dust and sand. His eyes glowed red and were fixed on the much smaller viper dragon in a super-predator's glare.

Teek realized that another fight was at hand and she was quick to scramble to her feet and dart away, following the horse for about forty paces before she stopped and turned to watch the outcome.

The black dragon's brow was very low over his red glowing eyes, and slowly his scaly lips drew apart, revealing the white, sword sized teeth they hid. A thunderous growl rolled from him and he stood fully, bringing his head five human's heights from the ground. Holding his arms ready for battle, his tail thrashed violently behind him.

Vultross assumed a similar posture, but this time he backed away a few steps.

His chest swelling as he drew breath, the black dragon's jaws swung open and he roared an ear-splitting challenge to the smaller dragon. The viper responded with something between the black dragon's roar and an air shattering shriek, and this time he half opened his jaws and fire exploded from between them. Quickly closing his wings, the big black dragon shied away as the flames hit him, then his jaws opened and he responded with fire of his own.

Even from so far away, Teek could feel the heat from the black dragon's flames and she punched her fist into her palm as she watched them slam into the smaller dragon and drive him backward.

The fire from the black dragon thinned and he advanced with heavy steps that made the ground tremble. Vultross squared up on him, appearing to be ready to receive him, but he backed away. The big dragon charged, roaring as he did and bringing his open jaws at the smaller dragon head-on. Vultross retreated again, responded with fire, but this time the black dragon ran right through it. The smaller dragon's fangs dropped and he drew his head back, half coiling his neck as he prepared to strike, then quickly dodging aside as his much larger opponent was already upon him.

Turning toward his retreating foe, the black dragon lunged and his jaws slammed shut, barely missing the viper's neck right behind his head. Vultross twisted away and thrust his open jaws at his huge enemy's arm, and the black dragon pulled it quickly out of range and sent his teeth at his smaller foe again. The viper darted around the attacking black dragon, spitting venom as his big opponent turned. Shying away from the cloud of venom, the black dragon finally backed away, and this was what the smaller dragon was waiting for.

With a hard turn toward Teek, he ran as fast as he could, quickly opened his wings and stroked them hard to lift himself into the air, and she found herself ducking as he soared over her. The big black dragon gave chase for a few steps, then stopped less than ten paces away from the elf girl.

Teek watched the viper fly east, then she twisted around, looking back and up to see the black dragon also watching the quick departure of the smaller dragon.

The black dragon huffed a grunt through his nose, then he turned his attention down to the little elf girl and snarled as he raised a brow. He took a step back and folded his arms, growling, "And you're certain you aren't being followed by a white unicorn?"

She nodded.

"Good," the dragon said absently. "That's good. And that's three times, little elf, twice with the same—" Something slammed into his back and exploded in a flash of blue flames and lightning and he stumbled forward a step and roared.

Teek retreated, her wide eyes locked on him as his lips slid away from his teeth and he slowly turned. She looked to the desert and drew a gasp as she saw a knight aboard a huge armored war horse.

The horse could barely be seen beneath the polished plate armor that encased most of its body, but its legs were a dark red-brown that yielded to black near its hooves. It was a huge animal that easily carried the armored knight and the saddlebags and weapons behind the saddle. Even this close to the dragon, the horse did not seem near panic, rather it held its head up almost anxiously.

The knight himself stared fearlessly up at the dragon through the slit in his face shield, hinged on a formed steel helmet that was as polished as the plate that covered his body. The armor looked heavy and awkward but heavy black fabric could be seen through the joints of the arms and legs. Though polished and clearly well oiled, the armor sported a few dents here and there that had been worked by an armor smith and were clearly not as noticeable as they had once been. He squared off against the huge dragon fearlessly and held the long broadsword by an ornately decorated hilt that had a wide tang that was gold in color. The blade glowed brightly even in the sunlight and was engulfed in a blue fire. As he moved the weapon, it spat small shots of lightning with sharp cracks. On his left arm was a big metal shield, one that bore the black image of a dragon impaled on a broadsword.

Lowering his body to bring himself almost parallel with the ground, the dragon's eyes narrowed as he studied this new foe, and a growl rolled from his throat. His claws curled inward and his tail snaked slowly back and forth about a height and a half from the ground.

Dragon and Dragonslayer took a moment to size each other up, and Teek looked on nervously. The knight *had* to be Sir Rayce. He had to be! That meant that she had to do something to stop this fight. She had seen the power of this dragon, seen what he could do, and she did not want to see what he could do to this knight who had been so kind to her. One would not know if it was desperation or bravery, but she ran between the two and stopped, raising a hand to each of them as her attention went from one to the other, and they both turned their attention to her.

"What are you doing, girl?" the knight barked in a harsh tone. "Get out of the way before that thing kills you!"

She gave him her full attention and stubbornly shook her head.

The dragon growled a sigh and snarled as he also ordered, "Teek, stand aside so I can—"

"By God and all Holy!" the knight shouted. "It talks!"

His eyes shifting to the Dragonslayer, the dragon confirmed, "Yes, it talks, fluently in thirteen languages."

"It will avail you but not, beast!" Sir Rayce declared. "I've a bounty to collect on your black hide and I shall collect it or die in the attempt!"

Raising himself up, the Desert Lord glared back at this impudent knight and half opened his wings as he snarled, "You aren't the first to try, human."

"I will be the last," the Dragonslayer announced as he swung his sword.

A blue light and fire lanced from the blade with an accurate aim and slammed into the dragon's chest.

Roaring, the dragon lurched backward as the burst exploded on his chest in a violent, bright blue flash and he took a step back to keep his balance as a shockwave radiated from him. Recovering quickly, he set himself and planted both feet firmly beneath him as the knight swung his weapon again, and this time he raised a hand to meet it.

As the burst from the sword slammed into the dragon's palm, blue and emerald light and fire exploded into a shockwave that radiated out with violent purpose. This clearly did not hurt the dragon at all and he slowly lowered his hand as he bared his teeth, his eyes locked on the Dragonslayer in a challenging glare.

Sir Rayce had not expected this and raised his head slightly as he pondered this new development.

His full attention still on the Dragonslayer, the dragon grumbled, "Teek," and then he motioned with his head for her to move.

Reluctantly, she complied, her eyes darting from one opponent to the other as she cleared the battlefield.

Kicking one of his horse's flanks, the knight directed his horse to the right, bringing his shield against the dragon as he slowly steered his animal toward the dragon's flank. The dragon did not respond but to slowly turn his head to keep the Dragonslayer in his sights.

The knight struck suddenly with that enchanted sword again, and once again the dragon caught the burst on his palm, but this time he struck back, blasting the knight with fire. Sir Rayce raised his shield and took the burst there, then he turned his horse with his heels and retaliated with the sword again. This attack was also blocked and again the dragon responded with fire, but when the knight raised his shield the dragon charged. Before the Dragonslayer could react, the dragon's hand swept in fast and slammed into his shield with enough force to dismount him and knock him about seven paces through the air.

Sir Rayce impacted the ground and rolled to a clumsy stop. He tried to push himself up and struggled to get his wits back about him, and this happened quickly as he heard the dragon's heavy footfalls approaching. Stumbling back to his feet, he held his shield between himself and the dragon as he looked around for his sword. The footfalls stopped and he slowly peered over the top of his shield.

The dragon was only a few paces away, standing fully upright as he stared back, and he appeared to be smiling as he slowly swung the sword back and forth by the tip which he held between his thumb and one finger.

Still holding his shield ready, the knight squared up on the dragon, holding his chest out as he glared back up at his foe. He seemed to know that this fight was already over but he was clearly unwilling to yield and just stood there, awaiting the dragon's next move.

The dragon turned his eyes to the sword and a green glow overtook them as he studied the handsome weapon. A growl rolled from his throat as he raised a brow and nodded, snarling, "As I suspected. One of Zelkton's potions."

The knight stiffened and took a step back.

His attention sliding back to the Dragonslayer, the Desert Lord continued, "His services don't come cheap and you clearly meant to turn this power against dragons. Not a wise occupation, I think."

"I've four dragons to my credit, beast," the knight informed with harsh words.

The dragon growled back, "It doesn't look like you will see five." Turning his head, he looked into the desert, his brow lowering over his eyes, then those eyes slid back to the Dragonslayer. "Then again…"

Sir Rayce raised his face shield, suspicion on his features as he demanded, "What are you saying, dragon?"

"Do you adhere to the code that knights follow?" the Desert Lord asked, turning his head fully to face the knight again.

"Of course I do!" the Dragonslayer barked. "Where there is no honor there can be no knight!"

The dragon flipped the sword over to hold it by the hilt. "Indeed. Very well, then since I've spared your life today, you seem to be in my debt."

"Spared my life?" Sir Rayce laughed. "Our battle has not yet ended, foul beast! I owe you no debt!"

"I see," the Desert Lord said in a low voice. "Very well, then. Shall we continue this foolish battle?"

Teek sprinted to the Dragonslayer and clung to him, craning her neck back to look up at him as she frantically shook her head.

He looked down at her and grasped her little shoulders, pushing her away as he ordered, "You need to stand clear, wee lass. We've a battle to fight and—" His brow curled downward and he turned his attention back up to the dragon. "You called her Teek?"

"That would be her name," the dragon growled dryly.

Rayce looked down to the little elf and asked, "You know this dragon?" When she nodded, he raised his brow and added, "Is that why you don't want us to fight?"

Teek nodded again, then she turned looked up at the dragon with hopeful eyes.

"If we are to continue this," the knight announced, "it should not be in front of her." Raising his eyes to the dragon, he suggested, "We can, perhaps, hold a truce until she is no longer in our company."

"Agreed," the Desert Lord thundered. He glanced at the elf girl and observed, "So you are a Dragonslayer, are you?"

"Yes, I am," Sir Rayce confirmed. "Four beasts have fallen to me and I intend for that to be five."

The dragon raised a brow and nodded. "So you've said. Perhaps your fifth does not have to be a dragon of my power. Perhaps what you seek is a dragon more your—size."

With a wary look, the knight turned his head slightly and raised his chin. "I'm listening."

"I'm assuming you witnessed my altercation with that smaller dragon moments ago," the black dragon guessed.

"I did," the Dragonslayer replied.

"Well," the dragon sighed, "it seems that the dragon I drove off, for the second time now, is causing problems for the Elf Kingdom. Teek here tells me they are anxious to be rid of him. There's no telling what kind of reward would be awaiting one who would kill him."

The knight's eyes slid to the elf girl, who returned his gaze with a nervous expression.

Leering up at the dragon, Sir Rayce asked with a suspicious tone, "And why don't you attend this dragon yourself?"

"I don't care to waste my time with him," the dragon snarled. "If you are truly a Dragonslayer then this is an opportunity that you should not let go. Besides, I'm sure you would be better received by the Elf Kingdom than I would. And, after that, if you still wish for me to kill you then I'll be happy to oblige."

"Hmph," the Dragonslayer scoffed as he folded his arms. "So we'll be at truce while I attend to this other dragon."

The Desert Lord nodded.

"And you'll not try to flee in my absence?" Rayce asked with a slight turn of his head.

Raising a brow, the dragon growled, "From you? Is that supposed to be a joke?"

With a slight nod, the knight assured, "I'll be back here upon my return, then, and we can finish what we've started."

The dragon tossed the sword he held toward the Dragonslayer and watched it land at his feet. "Just try to make the battle worth my time, and see to it that Teek finds her way home." He looked to the elf girl and asked, "You do know the way home, don't you?"

She shook her head.

"Of course not," the dragon snarled, looking away. He huffed a breath and absently said, "I've never been there myself..." His brow shot up. "Unicorns know the way by instinct."

"Unicorns," the knight scoffed.

"I'll attend to it," the dragon assured. "Travel east until you find the Spagnah River. It's a little over half a day from here at a good pace. Follow the river south until it empties into a vast lake and wait there."

Teek thought to him, *If Vultross should catch us in the open...*

"If this Dragonslayer is as good as he says," the Desert Lord interrupted, "then your problems will be over by tomorrow. Just go there. Oh, and by the way, you have something in that backpack you're carrying that is attracting the *vipera*, and he's drawn to it even from a great distance. Someone wanted to see to it you were found easily."

Slowly raising her chin, Teek's eyes widened slightly, then she clenched her teeth and nodded in slight motions. Who would have done that was obvious, but now was not the time to think about it. There were more pressing matters.

"Camp at the lake tonight," the dragon ordered as he opened his wings. "I've something to attend to." He shot a hard look to the Dragonslayer before he turned into the breeze and lifted himself into the air with powerful sweeps of his wings.

CHAPTER 7

The tall grass had turned a dark tan in the late summer heat and was topped with dry clusters of seeds that would await the spring rains. Most of the stalks were made up of thin blades that grew brittle as they dried out to await the next year. With winter coming there was no need for more growth, though some shorter grasses were still stubbornly green closer to the ground. One would expect the field to be dotted with grazers, deer and rabbits and the like, but this day it was not and only one lonely form could be found there.

Snow white in color, the little pony sized unicorn lay on her belly, leaning to the right side with her legs drawn to her and folded almost beneath her. Her neck was curled around and her nose was nearly touching her forelegs as she slumbered peacefully in the sunshine. Ribbons of gold intertwined with the ivory of her spiral horn and glistened in the sunlight. Her whole body sparkled and one might think that she was a source of light independent of the sun that illuminated her so brightly. The only truly unique feature of this unicorn was the gold chain she wore, one which suspended a golden raptor's talon with a perfect emerald sphere in its grip.

From ahead of her, the grass began to slowly crunch under something very heavy. There was a predator of immense size stalking up on her—and she was oblivious to his presence.

A shadow fell over her and much of the surrounding land around her.

She slept on for a moment, then, as if alerted to the sudden absence of sunlight, her eyes slowly opened to thin slits between very long eyelashes. She blinked a few times, opening her big brown eyes wider, then finally she turned her gaze up, and a little smile found her.

Sitting catlike before her with his tail encircling him on the ground, the black dragon stared back down at her.

The unicorn slowly raised her head, admitting, "I was hoping you would visit soon. How have you been, Ralligor?"

The Desert Lord shrugged. "Things have been quiet since others are charged with looking after for you. I suppose you are faring well?"

"I am," she replied.

"And to think," the dragon grumbled, "next spring there will be two of you to watch out for."

She smiled broader and nodded.

He huffed a breath and looked away from her, grumbling, "Not looking forward to that, but from what I understand your foal will be Agarxus' problem, so I'll at least have some peace and quiet when he is on watch."

A giggle escaped her in the form of a whicker.

Ralligor drew another deep breath, one which growled out of him and he finally looked back to her. "Well, you don't seem too terribly busy. Are you feeling okay?"

"Just fine," she confirmed.

With a grunt, he nodded.

"You want to ask me something," she observed.

His eyes shifted away from her. "Well, yes. There's this issue… I seem to have come into possession of a lost elf."

"Oh," the unicorn drawled. "You would like for me to take her home, since they live in the heart of the forest. You sure have become a soft hearted dragon, haven't you?" When he growled, she whickered another laugh. "You know I would do anything for you."

Ralligor nodded again. "That's your nature, Shahly. Think you can do it without getting yourself into some kind of trouble?"

"No promises," she laughed.

His eyes narrow, the dragon turned a disapproving look to her, and she only laughed again.

"I would be happy to help," she assured. "To be honest I've been rather bored the last month or so and I could use some activity. Ammi wants me to walk more but I can only do it in the presence of half the herd these days."

"Well, they watch after you so closely with good reason."

Shahly looked away and nodded. "I suppose they do, and I suppose it's important to stay in your Landmaster's favor."

"More than you realize," he grumbled.

The little unicorn got to her hooves and stretched, then shook and sent her mane flailing wildly in every direction, and when she stopped it settled evenly to the sides of her neck again. "Okay, so where is this lost elf?"

"I've arranged for her to rendezvous with you at the lake, where the Spagnah River enters it."

"I'm sure I can find them," she assured. "It isn't so far and I've met Leedon there a few times and I'm sure I can make it well before dark."

"You aren't going anywhere," a big bay unicorn informed with harsh words as he approached from behind the dragon. This unicorn, about the size of a horse, had a long black mane, tail and a black beard beneath his chin. His horn, which was almost twice the length of Shahly's, had ribbons of copper among the spirals. His eyes were narrow and locked on the big dragon.

Ralligor raised his head and sniffed a couple of times, then his brow lowered and he asked loudly, "What is that foul odor?" Looking over his shoulder, he greeted, "Oh, Plow Mule. Question answered."

The bay snorted to him and paced on to the white unicorn, stopping right in front of her with an irritated, authoritative look. "We talked about this, Shahly. No more crusades!"

With a little smile, Shahly nuzzled him and assured, "This is no crusade, my Love. We must simply return a lost elf to her home."

"She can't find the way on her own?" he grumbled.

The white unicorn looked up at the dragon, and the bay turned to do the same.

Ralligor's eyes narrowed and he snarled, "I'm not this elf's guardian nor am I well suited to traveling in the heart of the forest like that."

The bay's eyes also narrowed and he countered, "We aren't this elf's guardians, either."

"Vinton!" Shahly snapped.

"Hmm," the dragon growled. "I see your impending fatherhood has robbed you of your compassion for others."

Vinton stepped toward the big dragon and whinnied, "Now look, dung-head—"

"Both of you stop it!" Shahly barked as she stepped between them. "Must you two fight every time you are in smelling distance of each other?"

"Yes," they answered at the same time.

The white unicorn turned her eyes up and snorted.

Galloping hoof beats drew their attention and they turned to see another unicorn running toward them. This one was younger than the white one, about the same size and cream white in color with snow white mane and tail. Silver ribbons glittered from the spirals of her horn, which was shorter than the white unicorn's and her green eyes were locked on the big dragon as she quickly approached. "Desert Lord!" she greeted. "You have finally come to visit the herd!"

Vinton snorted at him.

"Not as such," the black dragon corrected. "I've an issue that Shahly and Plow Mule are going to assist me with."

"What!" Vinton barked. "I never said anything about—"

"Vinton!" Shahly whinnied. Drawing his attention, she shook her head and assured, "This is not some crusade that involves facing dangerous predators or humans warring with one another. We must simply return a lost elf to her home." Her eyes narrowed and she stepped toward him, raising her head as she continued, "And I'm bored out of my mind! Ammi wants me to walk more to help my pregnancy, and Ralligor has helped us both many times, and I'm going with or without you!"

The bay unicorn's ears flattened and he grumbled back, "Shahly, we've talked…" He began to back away as she bore down on him, when her nose was nearly touching his.

"Vinton," she growled through bared teeth, "you promised that you would help me in such matters when I needed to help someone and I'm holding you to it!" She finally stopped advancing on him. "Now, are you coming or should Relshee and I go without you?"

Vinton raised his head and snapped back, "Are you forgetting that I'm a herd elder?" When she did not even blink he huffed a hard breath and looked up at the dragon, meeting his eyes. "Your word that there will be no dangers for her to face or anything that could get her hurt or killed?"

Ralligor shrugged. "As far as I know there should be nothing out of the ordinary between here and the Elf Kingdom. I would go myself but narrow roads are not very accommodating to large dragons like myself and I don't know how well I would be received there. It is best that her people see this elf with a creature they hold sacred."

"And that's all?" Vinton snarled.

Ralligor looked away. "No, not entirely. There is the matter of the other dragon, a half-witted *vipera* that seems to be at the heart of this whole matter, the elf being banished and all that."

"So naturally you want to send Shahly," the bay unicorn growled.

"I expect you two to be gone before he returns to the Elf Kingdom," the black dragon informed, his eyes sliding to the stallion. "You only have to get her home and leave, then the Dragonslayer can do the rest."

Vinton raised his head. "Dragonslayer?"

"The human she has with her," Ralligor explained. "I didn't mention the Dragonslayer?"

"You did not," Vinton confirmed.

"Oh," the black dragon conceded with a nod. "Well, she seems to have… Actually, I don't know why he's with her. He and I tangled about an hour ago and I spared his life for the moment to—"

The bay unicorn interrupted, "So now it's an elf, a human, *and* we have this dragon to avoid. Was there anything else that might have slipped your mind?"

Ralligor turned his eyes up. "Well, let me think…"

"I'm already not liking this," the stallion grumbled.

"It's a simple task!" the dragon argued. "Get the elf home and leave. Not even you could botch it up! Just be gone before the dragon finds her again."

Looking across the field, Vinton heaved a breath before asking, "And he finds her, how?"

The dragon growled, "she has something on her that the *vipera* seems to be able to sense. Apparently someone from the Elf Kingdom was determined that she be found by this *vipera* and killed."

"And how easily can he find her?" the stallion asked, still looking across the field.

"Pretty much at will," Ralligor answered. "I could sense it on her as well, so it's some kind of charm that has specific spells that call to dragons. Whoever banished her appears to want to make certain that she never returns."

Vinton nodded, his gaze still fixed across the field. "So, she's being hunted by a dragon, keeps the company of a Dragonslayer who tragically failed to kill you, is a fugitive from the Elf Kingdom that clearly does not want her back and she has a charm with her that attracts not only the dragon that hunts her but all dragons." He turned his eyes up to the Desert Lord. "Are you sure those are the *only* complications we will face?"

Ralligor's eyes slid to the side, then he hesitantly nodded. "I believe so." He looked down to the stallion again and pointed out, "Of course, you'll have Shahly with you so things will be complicated from the beginning."

Narrow eyed, the white unicorn snorted at him.

Loosing another hard breath, Vinton nodded and turned toward the forest, ordering, "Stay here, Shahly. We'll leave shortly. I need to go to the creek and get a drink, maybe bang my head against a rock for a while."

They all watched him pace toward the forest.

The cream colored unicorn danced restlessly and whinnied, "An adventure! This is so exciting!"

Watching the stallion pace away with a low head, Ralligor grunted, then he lowered his body and set off in pursuit with long, bipedal strides.

Vinton looked over his shoulder as he heard the big dragon approaching, then he turned his attention forward again, snorting as he laid his ears flat.

As he caught up to the bay unicorn, the black dragon growled and admitted, "You have to know that I don't relish the idea of putting her in harm's way, but I need someone I can trust to get this elf home."

Heaving a heavy breath, the unicorn grumbled back, "I understand, Ralligor, but…"

"We both know why Shahly is best suited for this," the Desert Lord informed. "She communicates with other species in ways none of the rest of us can. Elves hold you unicorns in high regard anyway and the presence of a white one always has the effect of swaying humans and their kin."

Vinton stopped, looking up at the dragon who stopped beside him. "There's more, isn't there?"

Staring off into the forest, the black dragon nodded in slight motions.

"The Heart of Abtont," the unicorn answered for him.

Ralligor growled. "If that *vipera* gets his talons on it he would have almost unlimited power at his disposal, and no wisdom to guide his use of it."

"It would also make him immune to unicorns," the stallion informed.

The black dragon looked down at him with eyes that showed concern for this threat. "According to the elf, this dragon has declared himself the Lord of Abtont, and if he gets his talons on the Heart of Abtont, he will be."

"Do you think you could defeat him if he did?" Vinton asked.

After a pause, the dragon grimly admitted, "I don't know." His eyes shifted aside. "You'll only have to get the elf home. The Dragonslayer should attend to the *vipera*, but if that doesn't happen the *vipera* will have to be killed one way or another."

"I've killed dragons before," Vinton disclosed. "It's not something I'm proud of, but if I must do it again I will."

Ralligor heaved a breath and looked back down to the big unicorn. "I don't think it will come to that. I hope it doesn't."

"We'll have to cross a vast sea of grass," the unicorn informed, "one grazed by every kind of creature that eats grass, including grawrdoxen. There is almost no cover there and it is hunted by terra-dragons and terror birds among other big predators. That could be a problem."

"I'll make sure it isn't," Ralligor assured. He turned his head and looked into the forest, over the forest, and a low growl rumbled from him. "I have somewhere to go, somewhere that I might not be very welcome, but information will be our best weapon."

"Information?" Vinton questioned.

"I must know more about the Heart of Abtont," the dragon confirmed. "If this other dragon is after the Heart then I'll have to know exactly why."

"That's foolishness," Vinton scoffed. "One cannot possess the heart."

"Someone wants to, and I'll need to find out why." Ralligor looked down to the unicorn and asked, "Do you think you can get the elf home in short order?"

"I don't foresee any problems beyond what you've already told me."

"Just stay on your guard, Plow Mule. I'll catch up to you as soon as I can."

The stallion's ears flicked up. "Do you realize we're voluntarily working together?"

The black dragon grunted and turned, striding back to the waiting white unicorn as he grimly admitted, "I know. I don't like it, either."

Vinton smiled and whickered a laugh.

CHAPTER 8

Some days I remember more fondly than others, and this would be one. I had never met the Desert Lord face to face nor him me, but destiny would see to it sooner or later, and now was as good a time as any.

Ralligor approached my cave apprehensively. Not wanting to seem like he posed a challenge, he was sure to keep his dorsal scales down, his wings tightly to him and his teeth concealed for the most part. Any large dragon could walk easily through the entrance to my cavern, my lair, but still he felt compelled to duck down and give a good eyeing to the crystal embedded tan and red stone that make up the mountain where I live. This whole area, this valley where I live, could best be described as desert, though right on the other side of the pass one can find lush forests and river valleys, fertile fields and pastures dotted with trees and scrub that attract many creatures. It looks much like the Abtont forest but the Territhan Range has its uniqueness, one that leads many to wish to possess and rule it. That is a story for another time.

The inside of my cave is much what one would expect. White and tan stone make up most of it and it is oval, about seventy human's paces deep and eighty or so wide. The floor is relatively flat but gives way to a few pools here and there where water collects, water that is so pure and still that one could hardly know it was even there. Many paces inside the huge room and to the right of the entry is a huge mound of gold and treasures and weapons and artifacts I have collected over the many centuries of my life and here is where the black dragon's attention went first. Directly in front of the entrance and to the very back is the podium where I do most of my work. It is sized appropriately so that I can sit behind it and write in the Books of Knowledge and I crafted it out of the stone of the cave with the *sortiri*, which I spent many a season learning to master. One might think it a stalagmite on a glance but for the angled stone shelf atop it that holds the Book of Knowledge that I write in. All along the ceiling are stalactites that grow from between the tens of thousands of jewels and gems of different kinds that are a part of the cave, jewels that glow when one of power is present and alert, and this glow would grow stronger as the Desert Lord entered, and would not go unnoticed.

Ralligor's eyes and attention found me quickly as I worked behind the podium, the old silver gray dragon he had sought. My dorsal scales are as black as his, as are my horns and claws and the scales of my belly. There was once a cobalt blue tint to the black, but that has since faded with time to obsidian black. I wear spectacles before my blue eyes, the same cobalt blue that I mentioned before, in part because they have grown somewhat weak over the last two and a half eons and I find focusing up close very tiring without them.

This is where he found me, how he saw me that first time, laboring away in the Book of Knowledge, the very chronicle I've kept since the Great War between my kind and the mages of mankind and elfkind that is described in an earlier volume. He stood quietly, respectfully watching me as I scribbled away with my claw, burning the words into the pages of the great book which is over a man's height square when open and rather thick with the many pages that make it up. Yes, this young dragon and wizard's apprentice was very silent those first few moments. I could not tell if he just wished to study me and what I was doing or if he did not want to disturb my train of thought, but I finished those thoughts before looking up from my labors to meet his gaze.

Raising my nose somewhat—I was sitting and he was standing—I looked him eye to eye over my spectacles and greeted, "Ralligor. At long last you have come to visit." I could see and feel that my knowing of him and knowing his name made him uneasy, but he merely leaned his head slightly, his brow tensing as he stared back at me. I removed my spectacles and laid them on the open book, and closing my eyes I gently massaged them with my thumb and finger as I stood. Though very old, I found myself only slightly larger than this young, powerful drake, though any conflict with him was furthest from my mind.

As I looked back at him, he finally said, "Since you know me and you knew I was coming, I suppose I can also assume that you know why I'm here."

"I do, indeed," I assured. "The great Desert Lord, the first subordinare to Agarxus the Tyrant, wizard's apprentice…" A smile curled my mouth, one that I could not avoid. "And friend to unicorns."

Ralligor growled and turned his eyes away from me. One does not need to be empathetic nor clairvoyant to see that this annoyed him.

I turned to the other side of the cavern and approached the stone recesses that hold other books, those I've completed. About twelve in number, I knew which one he would want. "It's nothing to be embarrassed about, my friend. I am friend to many unicorns, many creatures who should know fear of me." I pulled down the appropriate book and turned back to him. "To be feared by all around you is all fine and well, but to be respected… There is real power. You can influence more by your demeanor and your oratory than your ability to instill fright and terror." His eyes slid back to me and I could see in them he did not want to talk about this. "You have concerns, young drake, concerns over the *vipera* that means to declare himself the Lord of Abtont." I patted the book. "In here you will discover how well founded those concerns, and how much."

He watched as I approached the podium and removed my spectacles from atop the book there, watched longer as I hooked them behind my horns and settled them back on my nose again. As I closed the book there, he finally approached and I picked up the book by the spine and offered it to him, waiting for him to take it before I set down the one he would want to read from, I then took that one from him and leaned it on its bottom against the podium.

"How go your teachings in the *wizaridi*?" I asked.

He raised his head, not expecting such a question, then he cocked his head over and replied, "Very well, I suppose. I think I've learned most of what I need to."

With a nod, I opened the book and commended, "Good. That's good." Having opened the book to the appropriate page, much by instinct by now, I looked to the young drake and raised my head. "In here is the knowledge you seek, Ralligor, but some learning cannot be unlearned nor can it be learned in its completion by the written word."

"You seem to be speaking in riddles," he grumbled.

I smiled and shook my head. "No, Ralligor, I must simply warn you about that which you seek. Often, what you most need to know is what is most likely to change your life in unexpected ways."

He growled and looked past me. "While I would love to stand by and debate philosophy with you, I find that time is not exactly working in my favor." He looked to me and was clearly struggling to hold onto his patience. "I only need to learn about the Heart of Abtont, what it is and what a simple minded *vipera* might want with it, and I need to figure this out as quickly as possible."

"You know of the Heart," I said to him, "but you do not know *about* the Heart, the essence of the Heart or what it is." With another nod, I beckoned him closer and motioned to the book with my nose. "There are your answers, Desert Lord. Do not expect the Heart to be what you would assume it is. Sometimes what you seek can be too small to be seen, or too vast."

He kept his eyes on me as I backed away, and still longer as he took hesitant steps to the book. Sitting behind the podium in traditional dragon fashion, he finally looked to the Latirus words I had put there. His eyes panned back and forth as he read, then faster and faster as he absorbed what the words said.

I also sat. There was much for him to learn this day and it would take some time. I also knew that when he had finished with the text he read, there would be many questions.

That time passed. I occupied myself with meditation, closing my eyes and directing my head downward, and when I felt his attention stray from the book to me, I looked to him and showed that I was ready to answer the questions that were a whirlwind in his mind.

"First of all," I started, "what you read makes perfect sense, but only if your mind is open to possibilities you've not yet accepted. Truly, to possess the Heart of Abtont, one must make one's self one with it."

"More riddles?" he growled.

I couldn't help but smile. "No, no riddles today. Many of the answers you seek will lie with unicorns. Perhaps that is why destiny led a small white unicorn to you this spring, and why destiny called upon you to aid what you have always perceived as an enemy."

Seeking pure truth, Ralligor snapped back, "I used her for a specific purpose that day, the purpose of destroying Red Stone Castle's talisman and getting Falloah away from there." He looked away and grumbled, "And she would not leave me alone after."

I raised my brow as he looked back at me, letting him know that there was much more to that story than he was willing to admit.

He looked away from me and growled, a snarl on his lip as he grudgingly admitted, "She does have her way of boring into one's heart, I suppose." When I huffed a laugh, he turned those annoyed eyes to me and growled again.

"You discovered this," I told him, "just as your Landmaster has. He is no more immune than you or any other to the magical and emotional influences of unicorns. But, that is not why you are truly here. Rest assured that the secrets you seek of the Heart of Abtont lie with her kind, and that is an advantage you hold over all others. Know the unicorns, Ralligor, and seek the council of the wisest and most experienced of them when the time comes."

His eyes narrowed and he demanded, "When what time comes?"

"On this journey," I explained, "you will seek the Heart of Abtont, but to find it, you must become one with it, and to do so, you will first have to face it."

"You're still not making sense," he complained.

"It will all make sense," I assured. "All you've read and heard today, all of what you know but do not yet realize or understand will find its way to your consciousness when the time comes."

"How will I know when the time comes?" he asked.

Another smile found me as I replied, "You will not, but the knowledge will."

CHAPTER 9

Sir Rayce stopped his horse on the grassy flood plain of the Spagnah River, and Teek stopped her pony beside him.

Ahead of them was the lake the dragon had described, one that was so vast it stretched to the far horizon. Wind born waves lapped at the sand and stone shore and grasses grew to about five paces of the water, clearly kept at bay by the lake's temperament. A few bushes also dotted the flood plain, many burdened with dark colored berries. The wind coming off of the lake was very cool and hissed through the trees behind the two travelers. The river that fed into the lake met another and both flowed very slowly and widened as they met the big body of water. Many birds were crowded by the edge of the water for a good length, but avoided another stretch.

Looking around him, Sir Rayce nodded and observed, "Good place to camp, I think." He looked up and squinted against the sunlight, looking to the few clouds that drifted overhead. "My bones don't tell me about rain tonight, so that will be one less concern." Turning his gaze down to the elf girl, he smiled and asked, "So where would you like to pitch camp, Lass?"

Teek looked over her shoulder to the forest, then up to the knight and pointed back to it.

"The safety of the trees," he surmised.

She nodded.

"I can see where a wee one like yourself would not want to be found out in the open," he said with a nod, "especially with a dragon coming for you." He looked out over the lake, scanning the surface and watching the birds for a moment. "Crocodiles out there, too. We won't want to be too close to deeper water with them lurking about. We'll refill our canteens and find a place in the trees to sleep tonight. Of course, that dragon thinks we'll be found by a unicorn here so I suppose we should not hide." He pulled the reins and turned his horse. "Come along, Lass. Your people come from the forest so you'll know the best place to bed down.

Setting up their camp took time, but that time seemed to go by quickly. To Rayce's surprise, Teek was amazingly swift and efficient at this task. He had gathered wood while she flattened out a place in the tall grass near the trees to make their beds, and once he had dropped a considerable pile of wood near a ring of stones she had put around a shallow depression she had dug, she had a fire built before he returned with the next armload. He just stood there and watched for a moment as she labored away to stoke the fire and level a flat stone she had drug from the nearby creek to have nearby, and she paused to flash a little smile at him.

Rayce went for still more wood and found a good stockpile left over from when the creek had flooded some time ago. With a small axe that had hung on the back of his saddle, he hacked up a few of the logs and took another armload to their campsite, stopping in his tracks as he saw the wooden tripod erected over the fire and tied off with course vines at the top. Thick sticks had been driven into the ground on two sides of the ring of stones, sticks that had "Y"s at the tops that supported another stick held at about Teek's waist level, and hanging on these were strips of meat that he was certain they had not brought with them and two fish almost as long as his forearms. Hanging from the tripod was a little black iron pot she found in his saddle bag that had steaming water within and was filled with greens and roots she had collected. Dropping the wood near the fire with the rest, he set his hands on his hips and looked around him for the elf girl, seeing her finishing a little structure over their beds that was made of a long limb that was settled into a V that was made by two shorter limbs tethered together to form A-frames. She was just completing the last of which consisted of a framework of long, thick sticks with shorter ones woven between them.

Teek looked up at him as she dusted her trousers off and offered a little smile.

He scanned the campsite once more and finally grumbled, "Did you leave anything for me to do?"

She looked around at everything, then back up to him and shook her head.

With a hearty laugh, he shook his head and said, "Let's see what you've made for dinner!"

Sir Rayce rather enjoyed the meal that the elf girl had scraped from the land and creek. They both ate well and after their dinner they sat on a big log by the fire and enjoyed the sunset. Teek listened with her full attention as the knight shared yet another story with her, and a little smile would curl her lips as he spoke.

"I don't know what dark reaches the beast lurched out from," he went on, "but it was none too happy to see me there to defend the village and the people it had been eating. That kind of dragon is awfully straight forward and will charge right at you, and when he did I knew fire was coming." His face went blank and his eyes flitted away from her, just for a second, then he continued, "It came for what it thought an easy meal, but it found me instead." His sword was leaning on the log beside him, still in its sheath, and his hand slowly and subtly found it and stood it on its point, moving it between his legs. "When I saw those jaws gape I knew it was going to be teeth or flame and either way I meant to respond with steel. It loosed a burst of fire and I took it on my shield." He pulled his sword. "And I replied with steel born fire of my own! Sent my burst right between his jaws and down his gullet! Felled him with a single blow and when he went down I took my lance and awoke the power of the enchanted steel point and finished him off." He drew a breath and tightly grasped the hilt of his sword. "Slaying a beast like that is normally a complicated matter, but not so complicated as…" He suddenly swung around and swung the sword, directing the tip at the chest of the stranger who stood two paces behind them, and he snarled, "running through some foolhardy bandit who would try to strike from behind."

Teek gasped deeply and sprang up, spinning around to face the intruder as she reached for her own dagger.

The man who stood behind them leaned heavily on his walking staff and wore a smile and a certain gleam in his eyes. His long beard was white, as were his bushy eyebrows. He wore the dark green robes of a wizard with the hood that would cover his head hanging behind him. With a simple raising of his eyebrows, he looked to the knights sword and commended in a gentle, experienced voice, "That is a fine blade you have there, and you hold it with a steady hand."

Slowly, Rayce got to his feet and turned to face the wizard, steadily directing the blade toward the old man's chest as he demanded, "What business do you have creeping up on us so?"

The wizard chuckled. "Well, I can't say I've been accused of creeping up on anyone for a while. At my age it's not something that comes easily, especially with such creaky joints as mine."

Slowly lowering his sword, the knight suggested, "Then perhaps you'll state your business."

"Merely reassurance," the wizard replied. Turning his eyes, he looked over his shoulder.

Movement caught Teek's eyes and she looked that way. A chill washed through her and her eyes widened as far as they could, her mouth also falling open as the unicorns emerged from the forest. Even in the dimming light of dusk they sparkled as they paced from the cover of the trees and underbrush, coming seemingly from everywhere. The one that captured her attention was a snow white one that looked no larger than a pony.

Shahly wore a rare expression of annoyance as she glanced to the big bay unicorn who veered to her side. Her head was held low, her ears flat against her head and her eyes seemed a little narrow as she whickered, "I told you it was okay to approach them."

"He has a weapon in his hand," Vinton defended.

"You can't feel how nervous he is?" she snapped. "Night is coming and humans don't like to be out of their houses after dark. You know that. You're just being too cautious again."

The bay huffed a throaty breath and looked to the humans and elf they approached. "And you're being too reckless. And there is no such thing as too cautious as long as you are carrying our baby."

Shahly snorted.

The wizard turned fully and reached to the little white unicorn to stroke her mane, offering a smile as he greeted, "And how is the expectant mother today."

She looked back at him and replied, "I'm tired and my hocks are swollen."

He reached into a pocket in his robes and produced a bright red apple, holding it to her as he assured, "I know just how to make you feel better."

Shahly ate the apple from his hand and looked him in the eyes once more, nodding as she agreed, "You sure do." She nuzzled him before turning to walk around him, right toward the awestruck elf girl.

Teek did not know what to do. Elvan law was clear that it was expressly forbidden to approach a unicorn, to try and touch a unicorn brought the penalty of death. She had always respected the law, but always dreamed of seeing a unicorn up close. Now it was happening. She was finally within touching distance of a sacred unicorn and exhilaration and fear whirled within her.

"Ralligor told me about you," the white unicorn informed in a whicker. "He said your name is Teek and that you cannot speak out loud. It's okay. I can hear you if you speak to me with your thoughts and heart."

Teek understood and responded with a quick nod.

"We will take you home," Shahly assured, "and get you back to your people." Her eyes narrowed. "And we'll deal with this dragon that has been bothering you."

Vinton took the white unicorn's side and countered, "No *we* will not! He'll be left to Ralligor and this Dragonslayer." He turned his eyes to Sir Rayce, who stared back at him with the same bewildered expression Teek wore. Raising his head, he demanded, "Can you understand me?"

The knight did understand and struggled to stammer, "Uh… Um…"

"Good enough," the bay accepted. He looked over his shoulder to the wizard and asked, "I guess we'll bed down here tonight. Will you be staying with us?"

"Of course!" the wizard replied in a scoffing tone. "I'll not miss the opportunity to share a journey to the Elf Kingdom, especially in the company of you beloved unicorns. It has been many seasons since I last visited there." He turned his eyes to the elf girl and approached her with quiet steps. "I am sorry to hear of the passing of your father. Leumas was a brave elf and I considered it an honor to call him my friend."

Teek stared back up at him for long seconds, her mouth tightening as she offered a little nod.

Looking to the knight, the wizard suggested, "And you need to find a new line of work, my friend. Dragonslayer will not see you enjoy your later years and you have many ahead of you."

Sir Rayce picked his sheath up and carefully slid his sword back into it, pointing out, "I'd say a Dragonslayer is exactly what you need right now, especially should that dragon that hunts our little elf lass decide to descend upon us in the night."

"Among all of these unicorns?" The Wizard smiled and shook his head. "I think only a very foolish dragon would risk that." He looked to the elf girl and took her shoulder. "We've a long journey ahead of us, Teek, and many unicorns who are anxious to get acquainted with you."

CHAPTER 10

Teek had never been fond of long journeys but this one seemed worth it! In days past, her attention would be occupied with her father's stories and his teachings about the wilderness and how to be a part of it. This journey, in the company of unicorns, the big human who reminded her so of her father and the old wizard who rode with them, she felt more safe than she had for many days. Inside the dense forest she had little fear that the viper dragon would find her and in her mind she secretly hoped that he would, but this time he would be facing the Dragonslayer, the wizard and unicorns. The odds seemed to have finally tipped in her favor.

Astride her pony, the young elf girl rode to the left of the big Dragonslayer, her attention on him fully as he told yet another tale of his adventures. Shahly paced along his right, also listening intently while Relshee followed close behind. The big bay unicorn and slightly smaller silver stallion listened as they led the procession.

"Well," the knight went on, "one couldn't really say why they chose to go that route or what might have put the idea in their heads, but it is a recurring problem. It seems to make sense that if one does not feed a dragon he will simply go about his way looking for food, but there are those who choose to placate him by giving him virgin girls."

Relshee drew her head back and whinnied, "To eat?"

Sir Rayce glanced back at her and nodded. "I'm afraid so. It always happens that those giving their daughters to this futile cause are the ones most determined to put a stop to it, and that's when I usually find myself in the middle of it. Even when the local lords and landowners object, a village will pay handsomely to rid themselves of such beasts. Seems like taking blood money sometimes, but one has to make a living."

"What kind of dragon was it?" Shahly pressed.

"Most call them terra-dragons," Rayce replied. "They don't fly and they have quite a taste for women and girls."

Vinton looked over his shoulder and added, "They'll eat anything that doesn't eat them first."

"And that makes them all the more dangerous," the Dragonslayer informed. "This was no timid beast, either. When I rode to his lair he came right out to meet me and a fierce battle was to follow."

He paused as if collecting his thoughts.

"Well?" the white unicorn beside Teek demanded. "What happened next?"

Teek's head whipped around and she looked to the little, blue eyed white unicorn who had suddenly appeared beside her.

Rayce also looked, then he looked to his right to see Shahly still at his side. His attention went back and forth many times and he announced, "I didn't know there were two of you!"

Shahly looked up to him and smiled. "This is my mother. She joined us a few moments ago." Quickening her pace, she came ahead of the Dragonslayer's big horse and asked, "Where is Ahpa?"

The other white unicorn also quickened her pace to look around the horse and replied, "He is up ahead still and seeing that there is nothing in our path that might pose a danger." Looking back up to the knight, the blue eyed white unicorn urged, "Well go on. What happened next?"

Their trek continued for a few more hours and all listened to the stories of the Dragonslayer, and he seemed never to run out of them.

A league or so later they were joined by a sixth unicorn, a big, tan colored stallion with a black mane, white beard and very experienced brown eyes. Silver sparkled from the spirals of his horn and he was quick to take the blue eyed white unicorn's side after saying his hellos to everyone.

Teek traveled behind the others for the most part. Even in this motley group of unicorns, a wizard and a Dragonslayer she felt different, as an outsider would. She had been largely accepted by the elves of her home, but even there she had always felt different, a mute who had to gesture just to communicate, and this had only grown worse since the passing of her parents. She distracted herself in the knight's stories and enjoyed being in the company of the unicorns. They were magical beasts and having spoken to them and spending the day with them the way she had, they seemed even more magical. As varied in their personalities as anyone else she knew, they soon became more than creatures of myth and legend, and she felt the stirrings of forbidden friendships begin with them. Observing them was another fine distraction, but still she felt excluded, knowing that they were not doing this, she just felt so.

So, she lagged a few paces behind and just watched, and listened.

For two days.

Even at a fairly quick pace and many, many leagues behind, Teek felt as if they would never get there! With the unicorns in their presence, they avoided human villages and settlements and simply stuck to the main roads that did not go to close to them. Teek would often find herself looking skyward where the forest opened and she could see the sky. Any time there appeared to be enough room through the trees for broad wings, her eyes darted about above, scanning the sky for that viper dragon. She felt safe in the company of the Dragonslayer, the wizard and the six unicorns, yet she was still afraid of him finding her again. This was easy to push to the back of her mind, yet it still crept up on her from time to time.

Evening fell that third day and they found a wonderful campsite near a fast running creek. As usual, Teek occupied herself with the setting up of the camp, something she did with speed and efficiency that the men with her could not match. Sir Rayce gathered firewood and the wizard and unicorns looked around for fruits and nuts and roots that they could eat. Teek discovered fish in a wider part of the creek and put her bow to use, ending up with three large ones the length of her forearm and two smaller ones. Quickly scaled and gutted, she had them over the fire and cooking in short order and the wizard and knight marveled over her skill.

She spent their mealtime listening to the wizard and Dragonslayer exchange stories as the unicorns browsed on berries and nibbled grasses by the creek. After their meal, Teek excused herself to go to a remote part of the creek where she could not be seen by others to wash herself. In her mind, she would not be missed, anyway.

Kneeling down by the water, she stripped her shirt off and hung it on a low hanging tree limb. With both hands, she scooped out as much water as she could hold and splashed it on her face first, running her hands down her face and neck on each side, and she repeated this two more times. Wetting her hands well, she rubbed water all over her, just getting a good rinse in to wash off two days of travel on horseback and feel clean again. It was not quite working. Covering her chest as best she could with both arms, she looked around her to be sure there were no prying eyes, then she stood and unbuckled her belt.

Only a few steps upstream the water was deep enough to immerse herself in and she laid down in it and submerged herself completely. The current was relatively slow but still swift enough to make her feel as if she was being cleansed. Slowly lifting her face from the water, she raised up just high enough to breathe and allowed herself to relax for a moment. There was still a long journey ahead and she wanted to just clear her mind, to be at peace if only briefly.

That moment passed as she had hoped, and as she opened her eyes it ended with a start and she found herself splashing awkwardly to cover herself as she sat up and stared back into the cream colored unicorn's eyes.

Relshee was standing right at the water's edge and her nose was within touching distance of the little elf. She leaned her head, then drew back and said, "I was wondering where you were and picked up your scent and followed it here."

Teek drew and released a calming breath, still covering her chest with both arms as she nodded.

"That doesn't look deep enough to swim in," the young unicorn observed.

Knowing the unicorn could hear her mind, Teek shrugged and thought, *I'm just bathing.*

"Oh," Relshee responded. She turned her eyes to the water, then stepped in, and as the elf moved aside she rolled from her hooves and splashed into the water herself, coming to rest on her back.

The elf girl smiled as she watched the young unicorn settle into the water.

Relshee held her head up just enough to keep her eyes out of the water and looked to the elf, informing, "I don't see the point." Rolling toward the elf girl, she ended up on her side and drew her legs in. The water running around her was much swifter and little waves and eddies were formed all around her. "Is this what elves do for fun?"

Teek shook her head again and replied, *This is what we do to get clean.*

The unicorn stared back at her for a moment, then her ears swiveled and she jerked her head, looking abruptly upstream. "Uh, oh," she mumbled as she slowly got her hooves under her to stand. "We need to go."

Looking that way, Teek could see nothing but the creek that disappeared into the rocks and ferns and undergrowth of the forest, but she knew if the unicorn was becoming uneasy, she had cause to be as well.

Relshee pushed herself up from the water, her eyes dancing about as she seemed to look for whatever she sensed out there. "Move slowly," she said in a low voice. "There are many of them."

Teek felt panic begin to well up within her but she fought it back and slowly stood, maneuvering herself behind the unicorn as she made her way to the bank and reached for her shirt. Unseen splashing beyond the undergrowth drew her attention and she jerked her shirt from the tree limb and hastily pulled it over her head, allowing it to dangle just below her hips.

"Make your way back to the others," the young unicorn ordered in a low whicker. "I will try to distract them." Her eyes were locked wide on some point up stream and her head was held low as she commanded, "Go on, and bring help."

As quietly as she could, the elf girl darted away and hurried back toward the camp, suddenly finding herself aware of every sound, every shadow. Something horrifying had to be out there, something terrible, and she had left a sacred unicorn alone with it. Them. She had said there were many.

Something darted into her path and she came to an abrupt stop, instinctively taking her battle stance as it turned on her.

Standing on two legs, it was just a little taller than she was and built much thicker. It seemed to be wearing part of the forest and was covered with leaves and both green and dead grasses, twigs and vines. All of this made up its clothing, or was woven over or in its clothing. Its skin appeared to be gray, what little she could see, and it hands were dirty—and human or elf hands! Its eyes were much like any elf she had ever seen, were deep blue, and held her gaze in a mesmerizing stare.

Unarmed and wearing only her long shirt, Teek braced to meet it hand to hand, hoping that she was quicker and more maneuverable.

It just stood there, staring back at her.

Something stung the side of the elf girl's neck and she flinched and quickly reached for that spot, feeling something sticking in there. Quick to pull it out, she looked down at it, seeing that it was some kind of dart that ended in black and white feathers, one about as long as her hand with a long needle at the front that was half the length of her index finger, very thin and stained with her blood. It looked like a thorn, one cut off of some kind of tree and was black at the end with red leading to the wooden shaft of the dart.

She wheeled in the direction it had to have come from just as another flew at her, this one sinking into her chest just below and to the left of her throat. Her hand darted up and pulled this one out as well and she backed away, her eyes sweeping about to find the source, to find who was shooting them at her. She felt another sting the back of her right shoulder and she turned that way, her eyes darting about, but very quickly she could not focus and balance began to elude her.

Still ready for battle, she staggered sideways, blinking to bring the world around back into focus, but to no avail. Consciousness began to slip away and her knees buckled, and she barely remained upright. Her vision began to close in as everything around her began to darken as if the sun was setting very quickly.

Someone grabbed onto her arm, apparently to steady her. Someone else grabbed the other.

Teek could not keep her eyes open, but stubbornly forced them open each time they would close. Soon, she was barely aware of what happened around her. Strong arms wrapped around her legs as she was picked up and cradled by at least two people, and she could feel the foliage they wore against her skin. Whispering caught her ears but she was unable to make out what was said. Soon, that whispering was very faint, very distant, and as she was carried into the forest, her eyes could not be forced open again and consciousness finally slipped away completely.

**

The air was very still, cool, heavy and damp. Quietness was all around her.

Teek opened her eyes only to have them met by darkness. She lay on something hard, something relatively flat and cold. Her hands groped about at her sides, finding a smooth stone beneath them that she lay on, and as she felt around her, she realized that the stone dropped off sharply as if it had been carved out that way. Fear gripped her. She had never been in absolute darkness and silence before. The heavy air was not moving at all and there was the smell of stone and earth about it. Her imagination was harassed by all of the possibilities of what might be around her. What surrounded the stone she was on? How high up was she? If she hopped off of the stone, would she plummet to her death? What might be lurking down here, waiting for her?

Slowly she sat up, her hands braced on the stone she lay on as she looked about for any sign of light, any sound. There was nothing. Carefully turning, she felt along the edges of the stone to find out what she lay on. It felt to be almost a pace across, perhaps two long, just large enough to accommodate someone the size of an elf laying on it. New and horrible thoughts assaulted her. There were few reasons anyone would find themselves lying on something that seemed like a stone alter and sacrifice was the first thing that came to her mind.

A noise to her left drew her attention and she pulled her legs under her as she spun that way. Settling her behind on her heels, she faced the source of the faint sound, her heart thundering as she heard it again. It was like someone had shifted ever so slightly on the stone some distance away. Then the rustling of some kind of fabric reached her and she felt herself near panic.

A blinding light preceded a loud pop and she shielded her eyes from it, turning her face away as she blinked to slowly allow her eyes to become accustomed to the light again. Still squinting, she looked toward the light, seeing two small, thin flames burning about a pace and a half apart. An old man sat cross-legged between them, an ancient looking elf with long white hair, a long white beard and bushy white eyebrows. His dark eyes were fixed on her, his brow low over them. He looked dirty and wore tattered robes that may have once been white. He appeared to be a rather large fellow for an elf, but age had clearly robbed him of a warrior's physique.

Teek's attention remained on him, on his eyes. Breaths entered her reluctantly as she planted her palms slowly on the stone at her sides. She could now tell that she was in a cavern, but barely noticed the white stalactites that hung randomly from the ceiling all around, the stalagmites that reached up to join them, and the reflection of the still and shallow water that covered the stone all around her. Finally daring to look away from him, she noticed that she was in the center of a room that appeared to be fifteen paces in any direction. The ceiling was rather high in the middle but domed downward to meet the floor which rose at the sides to meet it. Swallowing back hard against a dry throat, she looked back to the old elf who sat ten paces away, directly between her and what appeared to be the only way out.

In an voice that was rough and gravely from age, the old elf demanded, "Speak your name."

She tensed, then raised her chin slightly and patted her throat, then shook her head.

"You are the mute," he guessed, and when she nodded he informed, "The voiceless one the prophets spoke of, the one who would bring the wrath of the black dragon to the Elf Kingdom."

Her lips parted slightly in fear and surprise, and she could only stare back at him through wide eyes.

"You have broken elvan law," he went on. "Contact with unicorns is forbidden and you have sought them out to do battle with the black dragon."

She frantically shook her head.

"And," he continued, "you have sought the aid of humankind and you keep their company. This was all foreseen. The black dragon will unleash a terrible vengeance and when he is one with the Heart of Abtont his power in the forest will be limitless, bound only by the forest itself." He looked away and his eyes became blank. In what sounded like a different voice, he absently said, "His shadow grows long with the sun at his back, a shadow that is the black dragon. That dragon shall be one with the Heart of Abtont and shall hold judgment over the elves." He blinked and looked back to her. "The great sea of grass is where he will find you. You will be taken there and kept until he sees you from far above. He will find you and he will come for you. You will be held to the ground and kept for him, and revenge is to be denied you, as dragons do what dragons do." Raising his chin, his eyes narrowed and he said, "Revenge for your lost line is an insult to the unicorns and you are not worthy of their company. Stand tall and let the black dragon take you, and be worthy of the unicorns." He looked over his shoulder.

Two figures carrying torches before them entered the room, two figures that had attacked her before, and she cringed as they approached through the ankle deep water and reached for her.

**

Teek was bound and taken in some kind of small wagon that was a covered wooden cage of some kind. For hours she struggled to free herself, fought the course ropes that bound her hands behind her until her wrists were sore and raw. She bent her body to at least reach her ankles, but to no avail. There would be no escape for her. So, here she stayed for more than a day, sleeping when she could. When night fell she was aware that the wagon did not stop.

Sometime before sunup the journey ended and the wagon came to an abrupt halt. Now, fear began to creep along every part of her and her stomach was a squirming mess. The door at the back of the wagon opened with loud creaks from its protesting iron hinges and those two figures who had taken her more than a day ago reached in to drag her from the wagon's wooden floor. By the time the sun rose, she found herself standing in the tall grass that came up to her hips. Course ropes still bound her hands behind her, but now she was tethered to the ground by them. She watched with blank eyes as the old wooden wagon, pulled by some kind of small oxen, slowly retreated toward the edge of the forest more than half a league away. Safety was there in the forest, safety she could not reach. As the wagon disappeared, she looked around her, seeing that behind her was nothing but open field dotted with the occasional bush or tree, and this extended to the horizon. Gently rolling hills were in the distance, but not much else in the way of terrain features. Ahead of her was the forest, tall trees that seemed to abruptly stop growing where the grass took over. Against the tan and green and amber grasses and seed stalks, her white shirt stood out like a beacon to any predator that might venture by, or fly overhead.

Her thoughts drifted to her companions. She had always loved unicorns, always wanted to be near one, to touch one. With six unicorns in her company, she found that elvan law was engrained deep within her and she could not allow herself to become close to any of them, even at their beckon. Perhaps the old man in the cave was right. Perhaps her want for revenge against Vultross made her unworthy of their attentions. The Dragonslayer was very nice, very fatherly, and did in fact remind her so of her lost father. She would miss him the most. She knew she was here to die, and she knew it would be as painful as she could imagine. Vultross wanted her to suffer, and suffer she would.

Teek found herself hurting, hungry and dehydrated, but she would not allow discomfort to distract her for long. In a short time the black dragon would find her and it would be over. She lowered her eyes, bowing her head as she did so. At least this way she would be with her parents again.

Horns blowing loudly in the distance from the forest drew her attention and she looked that way. This was a call, a call to the dragon that meant to find her. Whoever the elves were who had captured her clearly meant that the dragon should find her, and clearly meant to make that as easy as they could.

"This really isn't very fair," Relshee grumbled from behind her.

Teek swung around, startled and surprised to see the young unicorn right behind her.

Relshee looked back to her and offered, "I'm sorry, but I could not risk them discovering me, so I concealed myself from them and you as I followed. I saw them take you and didn't know what else to do."

Turning fully, Teek faced the young unicorn, her mouth hanging open as she could barely believe that she had followed all this time to look after her.

The trumpet of the viper dragon sounded overhead, over the forest, and unicorn and elf looked that way as he soared over the treetops.

All of the horns suddenly stopped blowing.

Laying her ears flat, the young unicorn observed, "That must be the dragon that is coming for you." As the elf girl turned to face the approaching dragon, Relshee lowered her head to the girl's bound wrists and touched the tip of her horn to the ropes, her essence easily cutting and dissolving the course ropes with a yellow flash.

With her hands now free, Teek allowed her arms to drop to her sides, her eyes on the winged black form that soared over the treetops.

Vultross trumpeted with horrible intent as he saw his intended victim, but he failed to see the unicorn who had folded her essence around herself and backed away.

As the dragon descended to touch down, Relshee suddenly made her presence known, rearing up and whinnying as loudly as she could.

The viper dragon swept his wings forward in air grabbing strokes and quickly slowed himself, settling feet first to the ground about fifty paces away. With his wings still fully extended, he just stared down at the unicorn as he seemed to ponder this new development, and how to respond to it. He seemed confused, and yet he also seemed to know that this was an enemy of his kind, one that could be rather dangerous. He slowly leaned forward, lowering his body and bringing body and neck parallel to the ground as he stared back at the unicorn almost curiously.

Seeing his hesitation, Relshee found her courage and snorted, directing her horn at the viper dragon as she paced in front of the elf girl, holding her ground about forty-five yards away from the dragon. A yellow glow overtook her horn and she bayed a warning to him, a clear invitation to withdraw.

His eyes narrowed, his brow slowly lowering between them. His lips slid away from his teeth and a growl erupted from him.

This time, Relshee raised her head and whinnied at him.

He responded with a loud roar through his bared teeth.

The unicorn cringed and backed away, lowering her head and her ears as she watched him stomp toward her a few steps. Abreast of the elf girl again, she mumbled. "I don't think he is scared of me."

Teek glanced at her, then she turned her wide, fearful eyes back to the dragon. Drawing a breath, she thought to the unicorn, *I will run. He will be distracted by me and allow you to get back to the forest, back to safety.*

"He'll catch you and kill you," the young unicorn pointed out.

But you will be safe, the elf girl assured.

"I'm here to keep him from getting you," Relshee informed through clenched teeth, "and that is what is going to happen.

You are more important than me, Teek insisted, *and I'll not have you sacrifice yourself for me.*

The unicorn turned her head slightly, sliding her eyes to the elf girl as she countered, "You'll have to be faster than me, then." Without warning, she bolted toward the forest, toward the dragon, then veered hard to the left on nimble hooves.

Taken off guard, Vultross watched the unicorn as she sped away from him, then he growled and rose up slightly as he set off in pursuit.

Teek drew a gasp as she watched the viper dragon chase the young unicorn, and it was quickly obvious that he was faster.

Relshee seemed to know this and when he was almost upon her she turned hard toward the forest and bolted that way.

He overran her, turning his head as he stopped awkwardly to turn and continue the chase, and as he got back into his stride the unicorn changed direction again. She was clearly much nimbler than he was on the ground and knew how to exploit this, but the elf girl knew she would not be able to keep this up for long.

Trotting after them through grass that was up to her waist, she did not have a plan in mind but felt that she could be of some help should things begin to go badly.

Relshee was zig-zagging toward the safety of the trees and seemed to have purpose in doing so beyond running to safety. Vultross looked like a cat trying to catch an elusive mouse and he growled and bellowed as his frustration grew. When he was close enough, he would swipe at the unicorn, finding himself just out of range and finding her able to anticipate what he was doing. Each time his claws came for her she dodged away and he was simply unable to get close enough to get her. After a moment he was running on all fours but was still unable to catch her.

Halfway to the forest the unicorn stumbled, succumbing to fatigue, but she was quick to change direction again and elude him at the last second. This was, however, what he seemed to be waiting for. He was closer now, and as she darted toward the trees again he drew closer yet and his claws slammed onto the ground right off of the back of her haunch. She was whinnying loudly, fearfully, and Teek could only pray that help was close enough to hear it.

It was inevitable. Relshee turned hard and stumbled again when a hoof found loose soil beneath the tall grass, and his hand found her this time and the unicorn slammed onto the ground on her side, the breath exploding from her as she hit.

Teek watched in horror as the unicorn tumbled to the ground and her trot to catch up became a sprint through the tall grass. She was about sixty paces behind them and knew she could never overtake them in time. Pausing, she looked down for something to throw, finally finding a stone about the size of her palm. It was flat and fit her hand perfectly, an ideal stone for throwing accurately over a great distance.

Relshee struggled to right herself as his shadow covered her, and as his hand slammed down on her side she bayed in pain

The stone flew true and glanced off of the dragon's head, right below his eye, and he shied away. Growling, he snaked his neck around, turning his head to the source of this attack on him, and his serpentine eyes fixed on the little elf who stood only forty paces away.

Teek had another stone in her hand, this one much like the first, and her gaze was locked on the dragon's. She dared to hold her ground, dared to defy him to turn on her. With only a stone to throw, it was clear that she stood no chance against him, but she defiantly challenged him with her eyes anyway.

His scaly lips slid away from his pointed teeth as another growl erupted from him. Abandoning the unicorn, he turned fully on all fours, raising his head to intimidate the elf girl as much as he could before he charged.

Teek's eyes narrowed and she twisted slightly at the waist as she poised the second stone to throw.

With his attention fixed on her fully, Vultross crept forward a couple of steps, suspicion in his eyes as he studied her and pondered why she would not run.

The standoff lasted only a few seconds.

Teek hurled the second stone hard at his eye and he shied away when she did and it glanced off of the side of his snout. She backed away a few steps, looking to the ground around her for another, and found one. The dragon roared furiously and charged as she stood with her next weapon and she backpedaled away from him, hurling the stone with a clumsier throw this time.

This third attack glanced off of his nose and he did not react to it this time.

She retreated backward as fast as she could as the terror of her situation finally struck home. A vine or root snared her ankle and she fell, landing hard on her backside but quickly scrambling away from the dragon again. Vultross was upon her quickly and she rolled aside as his hand slammed onto the ground where she had been a second ago and in doing so she realized that whatever had tripped her had wrapped around both ankles. There was the desperate urge to free them, but her eyes were locked on the long, pointed teeth that were only two paces away from her.

Another growl rolled from the viper's throat as his jaws slowly opened.

Looking inside the dragon's mouth, she could see where her parents had disappeared more than a season ago, and this made horror and rage vie for control of her.

The viper dragon's fangs slowly swung forward. He lowered his nose to see her better, the black slits of his eyes growing wider.

Teek could see herself in his vertical pupils and slowly she lay back to the ground.

His eyes shifted quickly behind her and he abruptly raised his head.

The elf girl rolled to her side and looked that way, brushing the tall grass aside to see the big bay unicorn standing only a few paces away.

With his horn glowing inside a crimson fire, Vinton narrowed his eyes and snorted.

Vultross hesitantly drew back, raising himself up on his hind legs as he stared this new threat down. His long, slender tail began to thrash behind him and he took a step back. He clearly sensed that this unicorn was much more powerful than the first, much more dangerous, and he would not be so quick to attack.

Vinton was still as he watched the dragon slowly retreat, but he kept his gaze fixed on the viper's.

Snarling, Vultross held his ground ten paces away, half opening his wings. When the unicorn bayed at him, he swung his jaws open and roared loudly in response.

The roar of another dragon answered.

The unicorn swung around and looked up as the viper dragon backed away.

Slamming onto the ground with horrible purpose, the newly arrived dragon swung his jaws open and roared in nightmarish fashion through bared teeth that were like curved swords. The metallic green scales of his back and sides faded into dark green. The scales on his belly were glossy black as were the dorsal scales that stood erect as he found his footing and stood to face the dragon that was only two thirds his size. His dark blue horns curled downward and then back up, their points angling upward from his head.

With his wings half spread, the larger dragon bared his teeth and strode forward with heavy steps, his eyes boring into the smaller, retreating dragon.

Vinton leapt to the elf girl and stood over her as the big dragon strode right over them, and they both watched as he prepared for battle.

Vultross circled away, roaring back as he lowered his fangs, then pulled them halfway back and sprayed his venom toward his enemy's eyes.

The metallic green dragon shied away and sidestepped to avoid the venom, then he responded with fire, keeping his left eye tightly closed as he did.

Darting away, the viper tightly closed his wings and was scorched only slightly, looking back to find the big dragon bearing down on him again with gaping jaws and bared teeth. Turning slightly, Vultross opened his stride and his wings and ran has hard as he could into the wind, stroking his wings for speed and height.

Running after him, the green dragon also extended his wings, soaring just over the ground as he sent another burst of fire toward the departing viper, then he settled back to the ground and trotted to a stop.

Teek had watched this brief exchange from beneath the bay unicorn and slowly reached out to grasp his leg, and when she did so, he whickered in response and turned his head to look under him.

The metallic green dragon turned and strode toward the unicorn, his gaze locked on the big bay as he approached. His left eye was red around the green that surrounded his pupil, half closed and weeping.

Vinton looked fearlessly up at him, greeting, "Drarrexok. Good to see you again."

"What was *that* about?" the dragon roared. "And why are you leading a *vipera* into my territory?"

"Long story," the bay replied. "Ralligor should be on his way and I'm sure he'll explain everything."

Drarrexok looked away and growled. "I don't really care for him coming into my hunting range, either."

"You share the Grass Sea with him," Vinton reminded. "We are on a quest to get this elf girl home."

Huffing a throaty breath, the green dragon looked back down to the unicorn and snarled, "The Elf Kingdom is near the very center of my territory, and I surely don't want him there."

"There are other issues," the stallion explained, "and I am certain that you don't wish to be caught up in them. Believe me, Ralligor has no interest in your territory or anything in it."

"Except the Elf Kingdom," Drarrexok grumbled. Something caught his attention and he looked away from them, where the grass was trampled down.

Vinton and Teek both heard the distant bay of the blond unicorn, and Teek scrambled from under the stallion to run that way.

It seemed to take forever to arrive, but finally she dropped to her knees beside the young unicorn, who seemed to labor to breathe. Gently laying her hand on Relshee's neck, she stroked her nose and tried to soothe her, not knowing just what was wrong.

In a moment a shadow fell over them and Teek turned and looked up, her wide eyes finding the big green dragon as he looked down at them. Vinton appeared on her other side, his horn enveloped in a ruby glow as he lowered his head to the injured young unicorn.

The stallion whickered, the glow about his horn intensifying as he reported, "She has broken ribs and is badly hurt inside. This will take a while."

Teek nodded, then she stood and turned to the big dragon who looked down on the unicorns. Waving to him, she snared his attention, then touched her mouth and extended her hand to him.

He understood and nodded once to her. His eyes shifted behind her and narrowed, summoning her attention that way.

She spun around as she saw the other unicorns approaching with the wizard and knight, dressed fully in his armor with his shield on his arm and the faceplate of his helmet raised, riding behind them. When another growl erupted from the dragon, she turned and looked back up at him, waving her arms to get his attention, and when she got it, she pointed to the approaching men and unicorns, placed a hand over her heart, then clasped her hands together.

"I recognize most of them," he snarled, looking back to the riders and unicorns, "but there is one among them I do not, one who seems to fancy himself a Dragonslayer. I can tell by the crest on the shield he carries."

The unicorns gathered around the injured Relshee as the men stopped short of them and looked up to the dragon.

Leedon raised a palm to the big green dragon as he greeted, "Drarrexok. So good to see you again."

Motioning to the Dragonslayer with his nose, Drarrexok countered, "So good as to bring one of his kind with you?"

"Don't worry over him," the wizard assured. "He has an accord with Ralligor, and if I have my way he'll be seeking a new profession when this is all over."

"That would be a wise decision," the dragon snarled, "and I don't worry over him. I've killed many of his kind and have no qualms about killing more."

Sir Rayce raised his chin and spat back, "Rather sure of yourself, aren't you?"

As Drarrexok's lips slid away from his teeth, Leedon intervened with, "It seems your foe got you with a spray of his venom. Perhaps you would do me the honor of allowing me to clear that up for you."

The green dragon looked away and growled.

Shahly was standing behind the silver stallion and her father as they worked to heal Relshee and had been listening to the exchange. She looked up at the big dragon and observed, "That looks like it hurts. Leedon can make if feel better if you'll allow him to."

"Advice from Ralligor's pet," the dragon snarled.

Laying her ears back, the white unicorn snorted and looked to her fallen friend, grumbling, "Fine. Go ahead and suffer then."

"I would consider it an honor," the wizard informed. "You must know that I hold your kind in very high esteem."

With a soft growl, Drarrexok considered a few seconds more, then he rubbed his burning eye with the side of his hand and finally crouched, then laid to his belly to allow the wizard to heal him.

Teek found herself consumed with what the unicorns were doing. Four of them held their spirals to the injured Relshee, and each horn glowed with a different color. Vinton's was red, the silver unicorn's almost a white glow, Shawri's was blue and Dosslar's glowed a golden yellow. The stricken unicorn's strength seemed to return quickly and she no longer breathed like she was in such pain, though she kept her eyes closed while the other unicorns healed her. Elvan law was still at the forefront of the girl's mind, a law that threatened imprisonment or even death for any elf who would dare disturb a unicorn, much less try to speak to one. She felt for the young mare and wanted to comfort her, yet she was hesitant to even approach further, even after comforting her before.

Relshee finally lifted her head and the other unicorns backed away to allow her to stand. When the young unicorn was on her hooves, she shook her head, her mane flailing in every direction until she was still again, and it fell evenly to both sides of her neck. She whickered her thanks to the other unicorns, then looked to the elf girl who stood nearby, closing the short distance between them with two steps, and she shook her head, admitting, "I slipped."

Teek smiled and nodded.

"Next time," the young mare assured, "I'll be sure to—"

"There will be no next time!" Vinton whinnied.

The young unicorn lowered her head and flattened her ears as the stallion approached.

A whicker escaped him, one that sounded like he was rather annoyed, and this showed in his eyes as he announced, "You are to remain at Shahly's side until we get to the Elf Kingdom." His eyes shifted to Teek and he added, "Both of you. You will remain under someone's watch at all times."

Relshee grumbled, "I'm not a foal anymore." She cringed when the bay snorted and, with her head held low, turned away from him and paced to Shahly's side.

Vinton then turned his eyes on Teek, who also cringed, drawing her shoulders up as she slowly made her way around him and toward the other young unicorns.

Shahly had her eyes locked on Vinton, and when he looked to her with his usual authoritative expression she turned away, shaking her head as she paced toward the forest and ordered, "Come on, mares. Let's get to the safety of the forest before the sky falls on us."

They had barely made it a few paces when all of them stopped and looked up to see the black dragon swoop in low over the treetops, and everyone present watched as he turned hard, banking at such a steep angle that his wingtip drug the ground as he turned.

Ralligor landed hard and one foot at a time with loud thumps, kicking up a cloud of dust as he lurched forward and caught himself on one hand. His tail swung hard behind him, brushing over the tops of the tall grass and sending a wave of air that bent them over as his tail passed. His eyes darted about after he settled, and in a couple of seconds he stood fully and folded his wings, striding first to the green dragon who turned to meet him.

"The vipera," the black dragon demanded. "Did you see him?"

Drarrexok growled, showing his annoyance in his eyes as he confirmed, "I saw him. He's been driven away and—"

"Which way?" the Desert Lord snapped.

The green dragon motioned with his head and replied, "That way."

Ralligor looked that way, south, and his eyes narrowed.

Striding toward the black dragon, the wizard called up to him, "What did you learn from the Keeper?"

With a deep growl, the black dragon continued to stare to the south as he answered, "He speaks in riddles and says he does not. He also tends to repeat himself." He finally looked down to his wizardry teacher and added, "We need to stop that vipera and stop him soon. He gets his talons on the Heart of Abtont and we'll have real problems." His eyes shifted to the green dragon and he added, "Big problems." As he saw Shahly, Teek and the other mares with them approaching, he asked, "How quickly can you get to the Elf Kingdom?"

Shahly looked to Vinton.

Vinton wickered, then replied, "At least four more days, more likely longer."

Ralligor growled again. "That's going to be far too slow."

Raising his chin, Leedon observed, "Something has you awfully anxious, Mighty Friend."

The black dragon nodded. "The vipera cannot be allowed to possess the Heart of Abtont, and I think there is someone at the Elf Kingdom who may be aiding him."

Relshee whinnied, "Teek was kidnapped yesterday and brought here, then they made sounds with horns that called to the littler dragon."

His eyes fixing on the elf girl, Ralligor confirmed, "I heard the horns. Who took you? Were they elves?"

Teek nodded.

The black dragon looked to the wizard and insisted, "You have to get there quickly, now if possible."

"That's four or five day's travel," Vinton spat. "Getting there right now probably won't happen, especially since we've still got to cross the Sea of Grass and dodge all of the snakes and predators that lurk there."

"The mist!" Shahly declared. She danced anxiously and looked to the wizard. "Do you remember when we walked through the mist to cover long distances before?"

He nodded. "I do, my dear Shahly, but this is a much larger group, and holding the portal open for so many to pass is rather tiring at my age." He raised his brow and looked up at the black dragon.

Ralligor growled and looked aside. "I would need to be able to see where to open the other end, and even then it would be important not to have everyone materialize out of thin air right in view of everyone." He looked down to the elf girl as she waved at him.

When Teek had his attention, she patted her chest, then pointed to her eyes with the fingers of one hand.

A soft growl rolled from the dragon's throat as he stared down at her. He leaned his head, cocking an eyebrow up as he asked, "You're telling me you know where to open the other gate of this portal." When she nodded, he responded with one of his own and held a hand to her, commanding, "Show me." A green glow overtook his claws and the elf girl drew a deep, hard breath, her eyes widening as the same glow emanated from them.

Teek found she could no longer see the huge dragon that was right in front of her, could no longer see the grassland she was standing on. An emerald mist seemed to form in front of her vision and in a second her eyes filled with the forest where she had camped with her parents for the last time, that last spot where she had spent time with them. It looked much the same and as she looked about she could still see the ring of stones where their campfire had been. Memories and feelings were a whirlwind inside of her as her eyes slowly panned back and forth, finally finding the road.

"Quit moving your eyes," the dragon snarled.

Nodding, she fixed her gaze on a point in the road ahead of her. Amazement found her as a small vortex of mist began to swirl on that spot, growing larger and larger until it was a human's height and a half tall and about six paces across. She just watched as bright emerald light shimmered around the irregular rectangle of mist that did not seem to dissipate, and as the green glow around it grew in intensity, she felt someone gently take her shoulder and push her toward it. Not wanting to move her eyes for fear of drawing the dragon's ire again, she just watched the portal gate as she was pushed to it, watched as the white and bay unicorns paced around her, ahead of her and disappeared into it. A few steps later found her stepping into the mist herself. It was cold within, and still, and absolutely silent. Time seemed to slow and she strode forward though air that seemed very thick, like walking through water. She found herself becoming afraid, drawing some comfort from that hand that still grasped her shoulder.

She did not know how much time passed in the mist. It seemed like a long time. As she strode hesitantly forward with that hand gently grasping her shoulder, she could see light ahead of her, then she could make out shapes. Wind began to blow the mist about, thin the mist, and she could see trees, hear the wind blowing through them, hear birds. Warm air filtered in and touched her randomly.

Like stepping through a door, she found herself emerging just down the road from where she had been, from what the dragon had seen through her eyes, and she stopped. Turning, she looked up to see the knight right behind her and looking a little puzzled, but a smile found him as he met her eyes.

"That was quite strange," he admitted.

Leedon patted his shoulder as he strode by and shook his head. "This day plans to get stranger yet, my friend."

In a moment they were all assembled on the road that would take them to the Elf Kingdom, a road Teek was very familiar with, though she had not traveled on it for more than a season.

Sir Rayce took her shoulder and drew her attention, and when she turned he asked, "How far to the Elf Kingdom, Lass? How long?"

She stepped back to gesture, swept a hand from one side to the other, then held up two fingers and motioned as if cutting through one with her other hand.

"Two days?" he prodded.

Shaking her head, she held those two fingers up and gestured with a sweep of her hand halfway down it again, this time curling it over."

"A day and a half," the knight corrected.

Teek nodded, then turned and pointed down the road.

"That way to the castle," Rayce observed as he looked that way, "and none too much time to get there."

**

The decision was made quickly to travel at a rapid pace until after sundown. Even when darkness fell they had unicorns who had excellent night vision to take them another league.

Though exhausted from her ordeal, Teek forced herself to remain alert and vigilant, as much as she could, and only after she had nearly fallen from her pony for the second time did Sir Rayce and the wizard Leedon insist that everyone stop for the night. There were no protests.

A cold camp was quickly pitched in the tall grass about twenty paces off of the main road and Rayce unrolled his bedroll, kicked his boots off and fell to his back on it. Heaving a hard breath, he laid his arm across his eyes and announced, "I'll be off to sleep. Someone wake me when the sun's up." When he felt someone cuddle up beside him, he raised his arm and looked to his side, smiling as he saw the small elf girl had curled up beside him and was quickly drifting off to sleep.

Relshee laid down in the grass beside the elf, and Shahly beside her.

Sir Rayce smiled as he saw this and just stared at the unicorns as they put their heads down and closed their eyes. Hearing a rustle on the other side, he turned his head just in time to see Shawri lay down to her belly beside him and meet his gaze.

"I hope you don't mind," she said with teasing words.

He huffed a laugh and replied, "My Lady Unicorn, I would consider it an honor to share my bedroll with you."

CHAPTER 11

Awakening meant haste and weary travelers were on their way quickly. For the men and elf, breakfast was a mean eaten on horseback and consisted mainly of fruit and berries that had been gathered from just inside the forest before departing.

Despite pregnancy woes from a young white unicorn, they traveled at a rather quick pace down the forest road that led directly to the Elf Kingdom. They were met by an Elvan patrol that was ten in number and slowed to give them a long, silent stare as they passed. The unicorns held their interest, of course, but three of them knew Teek, and this day knew her on sight. She knew them as well and could only briefly meet their eyes, knowing the disapproving looks she got from them.

There came a spot that was only a league away from the castle, one that was marked with two height tall stone pillars that were constructed of the local limestone and topped with emerald colored glass orbs about the size of a human's head. It was here that Teek finally felt herself becoming anxious about her return home. She had been banished and only now did it occur to her that she may not be exactly welcome back at the Elf Kingdom.

Such thoughts were shattered by a dragon's roar in the distance, ahead of them—from the castle!

Teek's heart jumped and she drew a wistful gasp, her wide eyes locked on the source of the horrible noise. A second roar drove her to panic and all that was in her mind was her kingdom in peril. Without a second thought, she kicked her pony faster, urging him into a full gallop toward the imperiled castle. What she could possibly do was not on her mind. She only knew that she had to get there. Protests from those behind her were heard but not heeded as she raced toward the sound of the attacking dragon.

Emerging from the forest, the elf girl reached behind her and took her axe from the strap that held her pack behind her saddle, positioning it in her hand as her eyes scanned for the dragon. The grain field was afire and a line of flames swept toward her, toward the castle, toward the forest. Looking up, she saw two turrets of the castle blackened and flames erupted from many of the windows of the two. Smoke billowed from several places behind the castle wall and much of the vine coverage had been burned away. Atop the wall was still more smoke and fire.

Blinded by the smoke from the burning field, she stopped her restless pony and rubbed her burning eyes, then she turned them upward and scanned the sky all around. Her chest heaved with each hard breath she took and she expected to see the viper dragon soar in from anywhere at any second. Hoof beats behind her drew her attention and she looked over her shoulder to see her companions finally catching up.

Leedon stopped a few paces past her, his full attention on the burning grain field. He raised his hand, directing his palm toward one end of the fire line. With a cool blue glow enveloping his hand, he slowly swept it from one side to the other, and as he did eruptions of steam seemed to bellow from the ground to extinguish the flames from one end of the burning line to the other. In seconds the fire was gone, replaced by white billows of vapor that boiled up from the ground for long seconds after he lowered his arm.

Sword in hand, Sir Rayce stopped beside the elf girl and glared down at her, scolding, "What did you think you were doing, Lass?"

She looked up at him with defiant eyes and clutched her axe with a tight grip.

The unicorns surrounded them, also scanning the sky all around, and it was Dosslar who observed, "He's moved on. I don't know if he sensed us coming or if he made the statement he wanted to and just left." He looked to Vinton and added, "I don't think we've seen the last of him today. He belched quite a bit of fire and may be off looking for brimstone to replenish his crop."

The Dragonslayer growled, also scanning the skies. "So he'll be back in short order. We'd best be prepared for him."

"There are things to be attended before that happens," the wizard informed, his full attention on the burning castle. Raising his hand again, he directed his palm to the first burning tower, extinguishing the flames as he had before, then he moved his attention on to the next. His companions watched in amazement as he worked.

In short order the only fires that were left burned behind the perimeter wall and out of eyeshot and the old wizard looked down to the elf girl and offered a little smile. "Time to get you home, little Teek, and time for my long overdue reunion with King Arlo."

That nervous crawl would not leave Teek's stomach no matter how hard she tried to banish it. In fact, as they drew closer to the open gate, it only got worse. At some point she simply lost count of all of the Elf Laws she was breaking, the most serious of which were daring to approach unicorns, bringing tall humans to the castle and returning home once banished, any of which warranted execution in any of a number of horrible ways. It was that penalty that stayed at the forefront of her mind as she glanced about at the elves who stared at her as she and her party entered the gates of the castle.

Chaos had been rampant moments ago, but with the departure of the dragon, the mood within was about cleaning up the mess, attending the dead and injured, and putting out the many fires that still burned. Everyone entered the Elf Kingdom confidently but one, the only one who actually had a place there.

They all stopped just outside of the palace and Teek and Leedon dismounted, and it was the elf girl who expected the worst when many guards filed out of the largest door inside and strode right toward them, each of them brandishing bow or halberd. Sir Rayce stayed atop his horse, making no secret that the soldiers who approached did not intimidate him, but he kept a grip on his sheathed sword, anyway.

Leedon raised a hand to the soldiers and bade, "Good day to you. We return one of yours that was lost."

Councilwoman Gisan strode out behind the last guard and quickened her pace around them. Dressed in long, loosely fitting red trousers, a white blouse and a red jacket over it, she walked with heavy, imposing steps on knee high black boots that were polished to a high shine. Her hair was worn up and a white and red silk headpiece helped keep it so. As the eight guards assumed a shoulder to shoulder line between the visitors and the palace, Gisan walked around the line, her eyes fixed on the elf girl as she approached. She seemed not to notice the unicorns, and it was soon clear that this was by the will of the unicorns not to be noticed.

Yet.

Stopping only a pace away, Gisan loomed over the elf girl and set her hands on her hips, glaring down at her as she barked, "Such an unbridled display of cowardice I have never before seen. This explains why we received the brunt of Vultross' wrath today! You had to bring his anger back to the Elf Kingdom with you, didn't you? Guards, take—"

Sir Rayce interrupted, "She has not brought you that lizard's wrath, she's brought his death." When the councilwoman looked up at him, he raised his chin and announced, "She's brought a Dragonslayer to meet him, and meet him in battle I will."

Glaring up at him, Gisan snarled, "Your kind is not welcome here."

Leaning forward in his saddle, Rayce smiled as he rested his forearms on the saddle horn and asked, "Less welcome than that dragon that plagues you?"

Still glaring at the knight, Gisan ordered, "Guards, take the girl to the dungeon and escort these men out and away from our lands."

Even as they made their first steps, the unicorns finally made themselves known, and all six of them formed a shoulder to shoulder line between the guards and the elf girl. Shahly even butted the bewildered councilwoman back two steps with her nose as she took her position.

Gisan retreated a few more steps, running back-first into one of the guards.

Leedon raised his brow and informed, "I think the unicorns would have their say in this matter, Gisan."

Staring wide eyed at the brown eyed white unicorn, Gisan stammered, "Bring… Bringing unicorns within the castle wall is… It's forbidden!"

Shahly corrected her with a harsh snort and, "Nobody brought us. We came because we wanted to."

The silver unicorn added, "You would deny unicorns entry into the Elf Kingdom?"

Shaking her head, Gisan assured, "No! No, I… We would not. You are welcome here, but…" She tried to retreat another step as the white unicorn closed the distance between them, but she backed into one of the guards she had summoned.

Bringing herself nose to nose with the councilwoman, the white unicorn growled, "Teek is with us, and if you mean to take her to your dungeon then believe me you and I are going to have words." Her eyes narrowed and she snorted again.

Leedon smiled again and advised, "You'd best listen to this one, Councilwoman. She's been a might grouchy the last few days."

Shahly snorted again, this time right in Gisan's face.

The palace door burst open and King Arlo stormed outside, shouting with slurred words, "What is the meaning of this commotion? There's a dragon about, you know!" His clothing, comfortable looking leather shoes, loosely fitting light green trousers and a white shirt that was wrinkled and unkempt, looked as if he had slept in them. His hair was a frightful mess and he did not walk with deliberate steps, rather he seemed to struggle to walk upright at all. In his hand he held a half empty wine bottle by the neck. When he pushed through the guards and his bloodshot eyes saw the line of unicorns, he froze where he was, just staring at them for long seconds before he looked to the bottle, and raised it to his mouth once more.

Teek darted around the line of unicorns and rushed to her king, taking his arm and looking up at him with concern in her eyes.

"Teek," he greeted with a very slight voice. "What are you doing here? Why…" He looked back to the unicorns, then behind them to the Dragonslayer, to the wizard. "Leedon."

The old wizard smiled and bowed his head to the Elf King, greeting, "King Arlo. It has been far too long since we enjoyed each other's company."

"That is has, old friend," the King confirmed. His unsteady eyes darted about again, to the Dragonslayer, to the unicorns, to the elf girl, then back to the wizard. "Guards," he barked. "See to their horses and escort my guests to my personal sitting room. And have a couple of those larger chairs brought in. See to their comforts." He looked to the unicorns. "And to theirs. Bring them anything they desire." He took Teek's hand and turned back into the castle, pulling her along as he entered.

The King did not speak the entire way as they strode side by side and hand in hand through the palace, up a wide stone staircase to the second level and on toward the end of a long hallway. He reached toward a heavy wooden door, one that was as ornately carved as most of them on this level, and pushed it open, pulling the elf girl inside with him, and when he turned and closed the door, he enveloped the girl in his arms and held her tightly to him. Teek hugged him back, burying her face in his shirt and nuzzling into his chest and feeling wrapped in his love for her, and her for him.

"I should scold you," he informed as he laid his cheek on top of her head. "I should give you a tongue lashing that would send shivers through you. I should." He tightened his grip on her. "Perhaps later. It's so good to see you, my dear. I've missed you."

She nodded.

"Most won't understand why you've defied your banishment and returned," he informed, "but I know full well. You've brought someone to face down that bastard dragon and rid us of him. And you've brought unicorns. At times like this I wish you could talk. I wish you could tell me everything you've seen and experienced." He vented a deep breath and was almost sobbing as he finished, "And I wish I didn't have to tell you... Oh, Teek. He's gone."

The elf girl pulled away and looked up at him, but he would not meet her gaze.

Arlo stared across the room, his eyes glossy and filled with tears as he shook his head. "I told him not to go. I ordered him, commanded him not to... He took his garrison and rode against the beast two days after you left. He was determined to spill the dragon's blood, to avenge..." The King closed his eyes, bowing his head slightly as he struggled to continue, "Only a few of his garrison survived, but... but he did not." His body quaked as he began to weep. "Teek, I've lost my son. That thing has killed my only son!"

She allowed him to pull her to him again, her wide eyes fixed on some unnoticed point across the room. Her heart broken anew, she just held onto her king, the last person in the world she considered family.

**

The King was called away and composed himself as best his drunken state would allow.

Teek needed solitude and slipped away from everyone she knew, prying eyes, and away from the palace.

There was this place in the forest at the back of the palace that she liked to go, an enchanting place where the river continued on into the forest and the trees grew right to the water's edge. Here, there was a large, flat stone that looked a little out of place and was buried in the ground on one side and out in the open water on the other. This time of day the sun shined on it, the sound of the waterfall two hundred paces away was not too loud and just a little mist from the falling water would occasionally have just enough wind to reach so far.

Huddled in the center of this large stone with her legs drawn to her and her arms wrapped around them was a heart broken little elf girl.

Teek stared with blank eyes into the forest across the river. Memories of coming to this place with her beloved Prince Wazend swept through her mind over and over and the pain in her heart had simply become unbearable.

Even over the distant roar of the waterfall she could hear someone coming up on her, a distinctive clop of hoof on stone, and she raised her head and looked over her shoulder.

Shahly stopped only two paces away, staring back at the little elf girl for a moment before she finally, gently greeted, "Hi."

Teek's mouth tightened and she lowered her eyes, then turned her attention forward again.

Quietly approaching, the white unicorn stopped right beside the elf girl and also stared across the river, into the forest.

For a moment, silence gripped them, one that was broken when the unicorn dreamily observed, "It is beautiful here."

Her chin resting on her knees, Teek nodded.

Shahly gingerly lay down to her belly beside her and scanned the far bank, the forest on the other side. "I'm guessing you come here a lot. I know I would. I cannot really understand why I've never visited here before. Your people brought us some really good grain and apples and strawberries… Oh, I love strawberries! I'm sure the little unicorn in my belly enjoyed them, too."

Teek finally looked to the unicorn, and found her looking back at her.

"I can feel your sadness," Shahly informed. "I spoke to some of the elves to learn more about you. They said you lost your parents to Vultross." A sadness took the unicorn's eyes and she added, "Now you've lost your dearest love to him."

Her features tensing, Teek clenched her jaw, but could not look away from the unicorn.

Leaning her head slightly, Shahly asked, "You've never wept for them, have you?"

Slowly, the little elf girl shook her head.

"I know it is important to be brave," the unicorn said, "but it is just as important to feel what you must."

Teek lowered her eyes, and felt herself lowering her guard as well. She had not wept for many seasons, would not weep to mourn her parents even when she most wanted to. She had rechanneled her sorrow to rage, channeled that rage to training herself to meet Vultross in one-on-one combat. One of them would die, and either way the pain in her heart would be placated.

Now, things were changing.

"It's okay," the unicorn assured. "I will not tell anyone."

Teek slowly straightened her legs out, then just as slowly she shifted how she was sitting and pulled her legs back to her, keeping them flat against the rock this time. Tears were welling up in her eyes for the first time since she was a little girl. Long ago, to prove to her father she was a strong girl, she would not cry, refused to cry, and had not done so since she was only about six seasons old. Now it was forcing its way through her.

Shahly moved a little closer and brought her shoulder against the elf girl's.

Her jaw quivering, Teek felt her little body racked by quakes even as she fought hard to suppress her tears one more time. Something about being so close to this unicorn was defeating her and she wanted to spring up and run away, and yet she wanted to stay, to release these emotions and memories once and for all.

A tear escaped and rolled down her cheek, and as she closed her eyes, even more poured forth. She shuddered, sobbing for the first time in so many seasons, more than half her lifetime. Breaths entered and left her in short, broken gasps and finally she could take no more. Turning to the unicorn, she wrapped her arms around her neck and buried her face in the unicorn's soft mane. And for the first time in more than ten seasons, she cried.

Shahly could feel the sorrow pouring from the girl and turned her head, brushing Teek's arm gently with her cheek and offering a soothing whicker, and ever so gently she touched the girl with her essence.

Neither would know how long they stayed there by the river, how long the girl wept and finally mourned her lost parents, her lost love, her lost life. Such contact with a unicorn was forbidden, but in this moment she did not care. For the first time, nothing mattered but the moment.

Finally, Teek found herself huddled up against the unicorn and staring over the water, into the forest on the other side, not really seeing anything, just staring. She felt drained inside and had her head leaning against the unicorn's shoulder, her arms crossed over her belly and her legs drawn tightly to her. A strange peace she had never known had settled into her and she could feel the essence of the unicorn within her. Her emotions were heightened and she felt loved by this creature she had always dreamt of but had never known.

Shadows were growing long across the water, shadows of the trees behind them and the castle just beyond the trees.

Shahly turned her eyes to the elf girl, meeting her gaze, and she observed, "Night is coming."

Teek nodded.

The unicorn blinked, then informed, "I'm hungry, and so is the little foal I carry."

This coaxed a smile from the elf girl and she patted her chest, then touched her lips.

With a little effort, Shahly stood, stretched, and as the elf girl backed away from her to do the same, she shook her head and neck, her mane flailing in every direction until she was still again, then it fell evenly to the sides of her neck.

"That felt good," the unicorn sighed. Turning, she bade, "Well, let's go see what there is to eat. I'm sure…" She raised her head and gave a hard stare forward.

Teek also looked that way, seeing the big bay unicorn standing on the path to the stone outcropping. He was motionless and staring back at the white unicorn and Teek could not read his expression, but he was clearly watchful of his little mare.

Shahly paced right to him and nuzzled him, asking, "And how long have you been back here?"

"I followed you when you went looking for Teek," he replied. "You two seemed to need some time to yourselves so I didn't want to disturb you."

With a smile and a soft whicker, the white unicorn commended, "You are the best stallion any mare could ever hope for."

Watching them, Teek could not help but smile, and yet there was a heaviness to her heart now as she remembered her lost prince. She looked away as those sweet and bitter memories whirled within her, and in that moment she realized that there was very little left for her. Even a budding friendship with a unicorn could not fill the emptiness within her. So lost in her thoughts was she that she did not notice the unicorns approach her until the white mare nuzzled her.

"Come on," Shahly ordered. "We need to get back to the palace and see what nonsense they've concocted without us."

Staring at the ground before her, Teek simply nodded.

Vinton whickered to the elf girl and drew her attention, and he assured, "Everything will get better, I promise. Once this dragon has been dealt with you will be able to get back to your life."

The girl absently nodded again.

"Vinton," the white unicorn started, "I know we've gotten her home and I know… I don't want to go back yet." She turned her head and touched the stallion's spiral with her own. "I think we should see this through."

He stared back into her eyes for long seconds, then he looked to the elf girl and agreed, "I think we should as well, and I think this is what Ralligor was counting on." His eyes narrowed. "When that dragon returns he will have all of us waiting for him, and he won't expect us. If he can't be driven away, he will be dealt with otherwise."

Shahly smiled. With a glance at the little elf, she turned and paced down the trail, saying, "It's starting to get dark and I'm getting really hungry. Come on, you two."

**

Vultross did not return before dark as he was expected to, as the Dragonslayer was hoping he would.

The main gate into the castle would be closed for the night soon and Sir Rayce stood outside of it, his eyes panning back and forth over the treetops across the grain field in the waning light. That was where the dragon always seemed to come from, according to the elves, and surely that was where he would approach from again.

Dosslar and the silver unicorn paced to his sides, also staring up at the treetops in the distance. Teek and Shahly stopped behind them and glanced at each other.

The silver announced his presence with a whicker, then narrowed his eyes and grumbled, "I wish he would come back and get this nonsense over with."

With a nod, Rayce agreed, "So do I. The Elvan Council is meeting with King Arlo and that wizard. Apparently our coming here was not exactly a welcome event by all."

"I could sense that," Dosslar confirmed. "I could also sense self-serving motives and corruption among them, that and those who are genuinely concerned with the welfare of their people. They are a strange lot to watch."

The Dragonslayer huffed a laugh. "Not too far departed from mankind, I think. It sounded like they meant to have a vote on our part in this matter. I don't personally see where there is even the need. Show me the beast and I'll attend to him, and that will be that."

"He may not be so easily attended," Dosslar pointed out. "The Elvan Army has stood against him a few times now and has been sorely defeated."

"They don't know how to fight dragons," Rayce pointed out. "I've killed four already, four about that size, and I intend for this to be my fifth."

The silver turned his eyes to the Dragonslayer. "And final?"

Heaving a hard breath, the Dragonslayer nodded and confirmed, "I've no need to continue this life, I think. I'm certain that a soldier of fortune like myself can find other means of employment."

"Glad to hear you coming around about that," the silver unicorn assured. "I'd heard your talk of confronting the Tyrant, and believe me that was unsettling. Thousands, perhaps tens of thousands have charged to their deaths against him and it would be a shame for a human of your character to be among those he kills every month."

Sir Rayce looked to the silver unicorn, nodding as he met his eyes. "You honor me."

A guard approached them and informed, "The Council has summoned you, human Dragonslayer. They would speak with you." His eyes shifted to the elf girl and he added, "And Miss Brebor as well."

Turning fully, the knight folded his arms and observed, "It would seem their deliberations are at an end. Now we will find out what they've concluded."

**

The council chamber had a feeling of mixed emotions when Teek and Rayce entered. All of the council members were in their seats, the King was in his, and the chair to the King's left was conspicuously empty, the very seat that should have been occupied by Prince Wazend. His goblet was still there, and a fresh cut, white rose lay on the table with it.

While the knight strode confidently into the chamber and stopped at the corner of the table near the Prince's empty chair, Teek entered as quietly as she could, approaching the King and gently grasping his shoulder.

King Arlo did not look back at her, instead reaching up to grasp her hand. He stared down at his half full goblet of wine and from the look of him had not stopped drinking for some time or slept for at least as long. His head bobbled subtly and his eyes did not seem to be able to focus on one spot for long. There was also an odor about him, as if he had lost interest in bathing and keeping himself clean.

Leedon had been pacing on the other side of the room, and he also did not seem to be in good spirits as his eyes met the elf girl's with a mix of anxiety and frustration.

Gisan was, of course, in her chair with her hands folded on the table as she stared at Teek. There was that authoritative look about her and something—smug. This was a look Teek had seen on her before, a look that meant to tell everyone that she had won and she would make no secret about it.

An older councilman, sitting on King Arlo's right side of the table and four chairs down, sat there with his eyes on his hands, which were folded on the table, and he was the first to speak, grimly informing, "Sir Rayce of the humans, it has been decided that your services will not be required by the Elf Kingdom. You may stay the night, but you must leave at first sun tomorrow." He drew a breath and released it forcefully from his nose as if venting his frustration. "And you must never return here."

Rayce set his jaw and took a step toward the table. "I would kill this dragon for you, and I would ask nothing in return but his head. Keep your gold and your treasures, but let me have this kill."

"The decision is made," Gisan informed with harsh words. "Your kind does not belong here. If the dragon is to be killed, then it will be an Elf champion who will do the deed. You have been offered the hospitality of the Elf Kingdom. Do not put us in the position of having to repeal that."

The Dragonslayer eyed her for long seconds, then he hesitantly nodded and agreed, "I'll go as you wish, just know that you haven't the tools to deal with dragons like I do."

She did not acknowledge him further and turned her gaze on Teek. "Miss Brebor, you were banished to be hunted by the dragon, to save the lives of many elves. You returned here and it has cost the lives of scores. As far as I am concerned, your act of cowardice borders on murder and you will be attended to accordingly. Let the record show you were arrested this night and remanded to the dungeon until the dragon returns. It has been decided that you are to be condemned to death by the hand of Vultross himself as should already have happened." Her eyes shifted behind the girl and she ordered, "Guards."

Fear took the girl's features and she frantically shook her head, tugging on the King's arm in hopes of reviving him from whatever drunken stupor he had descended in to. The guards advanced on her from the door and she looked over her shoulder, shaking her head again as one reached for her.

They stopped before they could take her, their eyes on the big bay unicorn who strode right between the guards and elf girl. Vinton snorted and they knew to back away from him.

Turning to Gisan, the stallion informed, "She did not return here of her own accord. She was brought here by the unicorns of Abtont to see about this dragon that plagues you." He motioned to Sir Rayce with his head. "This Dragonslayer means to rid you of the dragon once and for all, and you would turn him away?"

"What if he fails?" Gisan questioned. "The dragon would be worse than ever! He could demand more tributes of elvan blood."

"We don't dare risk it," another councilman added. "We've sacrificed well enough."

Vinton snorted, his gaze sweeping the Elvan Council. "So now you would surrender your freedom to him. I had always heard that elves were fierce warriors, that you would defend the Elf Kingdom and those in your favor to the last. I can see now that those were the elves of long ago, and the elves of now simply cower before the first real threat that comes your way." His eyes narrowed and focused on Gisan again. "You sicken me." Looking to the elf girl, he added, "If she will not be welcomed here and protected as you should, then she will return with us."

"I'm afraid that is not possible," Gisan informed. She stood and raised her chin, clearly meaning to hold her ground as she added, "The Elvan Council has decided. She shall be given to Vultross when next he returns."

King Arlo finally raised his head, his brow low between his eyes as he growled, "She will not be given to him. She will meet him in battle." He pushed himself up, standing with some difficulty as he bored into Gisan with his eyes. "And she'll not be treated as a common prisoner. She'll return to her home to await him and she will be comfortable."

Gisan's tone was a condescending one as she started, "King Arlo, the council has decided what—"

He shouted back, "I have spoken!" He slammed his palm on the table and repeated, "I have spoken!"

A deafening silence gripped the council room.

Arlo turned and looked up at the human knight who stood behind him. "Sir Rayce. Your offer is appreciated, but I am afraid the council had a rare moment of clarity and accuracy when they decided you should leave. While I wish I could extend the hospitality of my people, I must ask you to leave the castle before Vultross returns." He raised his brow. "He should not see you riding against him from the castle. He might think that we hired you to kill him."

Hesitantly, the knight nodded. "I understand, your Majesty. Perhaps I'll go ahead and depart." A little smile touched his mouth and he informed, "I'm no stranger to a camp in the forest, and if I'm about a league away he'll not know I was ever here." He bowed his head to the King and finished, "I shall take my leave of you, your Majesty." With a glance toward the other council members, he turned and strode to the door.

And Teek watched with despair in her eyes as he left, and her eyes widened as he looked over his shoulder to her and winked.

Leedon strode to the King as well, bowing his head as he said, "I should go as well, King Arlo. Thank you for the wine your people are legendary for and for your company."

Arlo reached up and took the wizard's shoulder. "Do visit again soon, my friend. Perhaps when you return we will no longer be plagued by such misery as this and we can speak of times past."

With a nod, Leedon assured, "I shall return indeed, your Majesty, and at your convenience. Just know that my services are yours should you ever need me." With a glance at Vinton, he also strode for the door.

The stallion whickered, seemingly in acknowledgment of the wizard, then he also turned his attention to the King, raising his head as he informed, "I have no wish to stay, either." His eyes slid to Gisan again and narrowed. "I shall take my people back to the forest. There are those here who are unworthy of our company." Looking back to Arlo, he assured, "I find you to be, and Teek, but most of the rest of the elves I have encountered do not please me and I'll have my herd here no longer. Be well, King of the Elves." He looked to Teek and nuzzled her. "And you take care. A great darkness would cross my heart if you were lost." And he thought to her, *So you mustn't be.*

**

The King had ordered that Teek be taken back to her suite, the very one she had lived alone in since her parents had been killed. There, a meal was brought to her and she was kept under heavy guard, but in comfort.

After eating, Teek busied herself with preparations to meet Vultross, as he would clearly be back the next day, and if she was to be taken to him for him to kill, she intended to die fighting. Only one of her father's enchanted arrows remained, and that one would have to count. It would have to kill him.

Hours later she had laid her archer's outfit out on the dining table, an outfit which consisted of a forest green jerkin, green leggings, light leather shoes that she could maneuver easily in and a white shirt that was really more ceremonial of the Elvan archers than anything. This she picked up, looked over, and tossed aside. Her weapons were also there including her favorite bow, given to her by a close friend of her father, and the quiver she had made herself out of dyed dark green leather with a brass ring that held the top open and a cork disk at the bottom that would easily hold the sharp points in place. There was but one arrow in it and she pulled it slowly from the quiver and held it in both hands, staring down at it with blank eyes. This time, it had to work. It had to. Her eyes shifted to the table where the second lay—in two pieces. Perhaps it could be repaired. Perhaps it would work.

A light rain began to fall outside as was not so unusual in the deep of the Abtont forest and her eyes strayed to the open window, seeing glints of silver against the blackness of the night beyond. Almost ceremonially, she returned the arrow to the quiver and then laid it back in its place on the table with her other weapons, shifting her eyes from it to her father's sword. This was a sword with spells on it, what her father had called spells of victory. They would enable the blade to slice through the most stubborn armor, and should the arrow fail she would test this sword against the armor of the viper dragon, and secretly she hoped she would not have to.

Turning quickly, she strode to the bedroom and began to strip off her clothing as she walked that way.

This would be a time she would savor. She bathed with slow movements, enjoying such a simple chore for the first time in many days. Her movements were slow and she cleaned herself thoroughly for the coming day. Should she not succeed, at least she would make a clean and pretty corpse.

Some subtle movement in the living area caught her sensitive ears and she turned her head, growing perfectly still as she listened for it to happen again. With the window open and the rain outside, she tried to convince herself that it was the wind entering and finding something to blow over, but instinct told her not to listen to that.

Slowly, silently, she stood and stepped from the marble bathtub, her eyes on the partly open door of her room as she padded to her bed and retrieved her thin white robe. She continued to watch the door as she slipped her arms into it and closed the front, tying it off with the sash. The thin material of the robe stuck to her wet skin but she barely took notice of this. Her eyes flitted to the sword that hung on the wall near her door, more of a ceremonial piece that she would wear when her father was being honored for something, but it was still made of fine steel, though it was not sharpened. With its rounded edges, it would be little more than an arm length metal club. Still, with all of her other weapons out there where she expected the intruders to be, it would have to do.

Knowing that the door hinges would creak ever so slightly, she pressed her back to the wall where the door stood open about two hand widths and peered out, scanning the room carefully.

There was the shuffle of soft soled shoes out there somewhere. Someone was moving about and trying to be very quiet about it.

Turning her head the other way, she saw her dresser, and a hairbrush that sat ready for her. Taking it with her left hand, she looked back out into the living area, her eyes narrowing as she scanned the room once more. Near the open door to her parent's bedroom was a small table that held a vase that her mother had always kept flowers in. It was about seven paces from her bedroom, big and blue, and it was in her sights. Throwing the brush underhand with a true aim, she watched as it struck the vase and tipped it over.

There was a crash as it shattered on the floor.

A long few seconds of absolute silence followed.

A voice out there harshly whispered, "Quiet!"

"It wasn't me!" another whispered back.

That shuffling of soft soled footwear again reached the girl and her heart thundered as a shadow fell over her doorway, then a black clad figure moved across her line of vision.

Training and instinct were fed by her fear and she slipped out of her room behind the figure that approached the shattered vase. With both hands grasping the hilt, she poised her weapon over her right shoulder for a decisive strike.

The black clad figure stopped and turned around, but it was too late.

Teek slammed her weapon into the side of his head with all her adrenaline-driven strength and he collapsed limply to the floor.

One down.

Swinging around, she poised her weapon as she would her sword, over her right shoulder and gripping it tightly with both hands as her eyes fixed on the second intruder.

Also dressed in all black, he appeared to be a big elf. All she could see of him were his blue eyes as his head was wrapped in lightly made black cloth to conceal who he was. His black attire fit him loosely, adding to the appearance of his size, and was clearly meant for camouflage and freedom of movement, very quiet movement. On the belt he wore was a dagger that was dangerously close to his right hand and in his left was a short wooden club. Also hanging from his belt were two coils of thin gray rope, and these gave her an ominous crawl in the pit of her stomach.

He held the club ready and pulled his dagger from its black leather sheath, poising himself to meet her.

"Come now," he warned. "Let's not have no problems out of you tonight."

Clenching her jaw, Teek's eyes narrowed and her lips drew away from her teeth ever so slightly.

His eyes shifted to his fallen colleague, then back to his target.

Slowly, she directed her left palm toward him and her blade directed tip down behind her back. Many seasons of unused training was boiling up in her, eager to be called upon and this could be seen in her emerald green eyes, eyes that were fixed on his and seemed to be unblinking.

Her stance gave him pause, but his superior size, age and experience were able to override his uneasiness and he poised his own blade before him, holding his club defensively as he warned, "If ye mean to do this then you'd be assured that I'll offer no quarter."

Teek spun all the way around and her sword was a blur as it swung at him. Wide eyed, he backed away, watching as she spun again and brought the sword across him at chest level, and this time he caught it on his club and was nearly disarmed. The girl set her feet and pulled the hilt to her side, then stepped into him and thrust the tip of the sword at his belly and he dodged away again, hitting the sword with his dagger as he retreated. As she pulled the sword back again, she stepped into it and then spun herself around once again. The sword cut the air with a loud sound this time and he flinched away, stumbling into the wall behind him.

Training was now instinct and Teek's attack ceased as quickly as it had begun. As the big, shaking elf stood with his back to the wall and both of his weapons held defensively before him, she grasped the hilt of her sword with both hands and held it over her shoulder as she had before. Her brow lowered between her eyes and she held her left palm toward him again, but this time she turned her hand around and made a fist, then she beckoned to him with her finger.

The intruder set his jaw and pushed himself off of the wall behind him, taking a step toward the girl as he held his blade ready. "Okay, little mouse. I guess I'll have to bleed ye after all." His confidence wavered once again as she raised her chin and winked at him.

With a mighty yell, he raised his club and charged at her, thrusting his dagger as he did. His nimble opponent spun as she had before, but this time she sidestepped and brought the sword down low, striking him hard across the shin with it, and his yell became a pain inspired scream as he staggered and fell.

Teek was aware that something blunt struck the back of her head. There was a bright flash of light as it hit her, then darkness.

**

Apparently, there had been a third intruder.

She was aware of rain falling on her and slowly her eyes opened. She was lying on her back in the middle of a patch of trampled down grass. The sky above her was still dark but for those little silver glints that streaked toward her, silver glints she knew to be rain. Blinking her eyes, she rolled her head one way, realizing that her head hurt terribly and this pain seemed related to her fleeing wits. Her body felt drained, her stomach sour and she was very sleepy. Looking around her, she realized that she was surrounded by three people, all dressed in black with black wrappings over their heads that concealed everything but their eyes. In the darkness, they were ominous shadows against the oil lamps that two of them carried.

One of them crouched down beside her and whispered, "You couldn't just stay away. You had to come back and spoil everything I worked so hard for."

This was a woman's whisper, and Teek was sure she knew who it was.

"It comes to this," the woman in black continued in a whisper. "You'll hear the horns right before sunup, and by the time anyone realizes that you are here, you'll be under the dragon's attention, and before anyone can act, you'll be dead and gone forever." Her eyes narrowed. "Like your parents."

Teek's heart jumped and she felt fear and anger roused at once.

The woman stood and produced the last of Leumas' enchanted arrows, the very arrow Teek hand intended to kill Vultross with. Holding it in the middle of the shaft with both hands and where the elf girl could easily see what she was doing, she strained a little as she bent the arrow's shaft, and with a sharp crack the arrow broke in half. She dropped it and allowed it to fall beside the girl, then she turned and strode toward the castle.

One of the others had Teek's ceremonial sword in his hand and closed the distance to the elf girl with two steps, and he said, "I think I owe you something." He swung the sword hard and slammed it into her shin.

A breath exploded from Teek that would have been a scream had she a voice and she rolled to her side, curling up as she reached to her stricken leg with both hands. As the other two departed, she clutched her knee, tightly closing her eyes as horrible pain surged from her broken leg. This was the worst pain she had ever felt and it was all consuming. For the second time in so long, she wept. Pain ripped through her, hope was lost, and she would spend the rest of the night in the cold rain with only her thin, soaked bathrobe to cover her, exposed and helpless, unable to call for help or even crawl to safety.

And in the morning, she would meet her end.

Somehow, only a moment after her attackers left her, a strange, peaceful sleep washed over her.

CHAPTER 12

Teek found herself standing in the middle of a sun bathed meadow. Flowers bloomed everywhere, a warm breeze blew which caused the tall grass and yellow flowers to undulate like waves on water and the trees all around were filled with song birds. She looked around her, seeing that this was the most beautiful place in the world. It had to be. In the distance, she could see a lake. Deer wandered about, songbirds flew overhead and she found herself in a yellow spring dress that was silky and comfortable. She was barefoot and the grass beneath her feet was very soft, almost like a cloud.

She turned many times to see her surroundings, and finally stopped as she saw the white unicorn standing only a pace away. Recent memories found their way back to her and the smile that had curled her lips up faded from her. Her heart sank and she shook her head, saying to the unicorn, "It's only a dream."

Shahly smiled and countered, "Well, it is better than where you were."

"But it isn't real," the elf girl whimpered. "I can't talk in real life, only when I dream, and when I awaken…" She turned away, closing her eyes as she bowed her head. "When I awaken, the pain will still be there, the cold, the rain…" She drew a broken breath. "Vultross will be there."

The unicorn butted her with her nose and added, "So will I."

"You all left," Teek countered in a slight voice. "I'm alone. I'll be alone when I awaken, and hurt."

"Will you?"

Teek felt a coldness in her leg and reached for it. Warmth swept through it and she looked down to her shin, shaking her head as she breathed, "I don't want it to hurt anymore."

"It doesn't hurt now, does it?" the unicorn asked.

"It will when I awaken," was the elf girl's reply.

Shahly butted her with her nose again and suggested, "Just enjoy your dream, then. Don't give into despair here in your twilight mind, just do what you wish."

"I used to dream about Prince Wazend," Teek said softly. A little smile touched her lips. "We were very much in love. He was there for me when we were children, and much more so after Vultross killed my parents."

Tears spilled from her eyes as she struggled to say, "Vultross killed him, too. He's taken everything from me. Everything! Everyone I loved."

Shahly paced around her, looking into her face as she insisted, "He hasn't taken everything, Teek. You aren't finished yet. You have lost those closest to you, but you've found others who would be close to you as well. A chapter of your life has tragically closed, but another has opened and is awaiting you."

Teek looked to the unicorn, into those deep brown eyes, and slowly she shook her head. "That next chapter is my death." She shrugged slightly, then closed her eyes. "At least it will be the end of my pain."

"A heart as beautiful as yours cannot be allowed to be taken by such a foul beast," Shahly insisted. "It is time for you to awaken and face that new chapter, and know that you will not face it alone." She whickered gently and ordered, "Open your eyes"

"I don't want to wake up," Teek whimpered.

"It is time," the unicorn said with gentle words. "Awaken, Teek."

Teek sat up and tried to scream "No!" but there was no voice. She blinked and looked around her, to the castle to her right. An early morning glow illuminated it from the back and the sun would rise right over it. All around her the light was just bright enough to illuminate what was around her, the trees in the distance to the left and in front of her and the tall grass and grains that waved ever so gently on the cool morning breeze, sparkling as the dim light reflected off of the small droplets of rain water that clung to them. Her bathrobe was still damp and the air was chilly and she drew her legs to her, wrapping her arms around them as she fixed her eyes on the castle. Inside, she wished she could return there, but…

A gasp whispered into her and she looked down to her leg, straightening it out to see her shin. It did not hurt anymore and was not even bruised. Her head no longer hurt and she raised a hand to touch the back of it where she had been struck.

"Good to see you are feeling better," Shahly teased from behind.

Teek half turned, her wide eyes finding the white unicorn lying on her belly behind her.

"As I said," the unicorn reminded, "you'll not face this alone."

Horns trumpeted from somewhere in the forest in deep notes that rumbled through the morning air, the same sounds Teek had heard before, the horns that would summon the viper dragon.

Shahly casually looked that way, then to the elf girl, and she almost smiled as she said, "Sounds like it is about time. She stood and turned toward the forest, toward the west where Vultross usually approached from. "He is not far, not quite a moment, I think."

Teek took the unicorn's side, also looking that way. She was fearful of the approach of the dragon, but now was even more fearful about what could happen to the unicorn should she remain. Patting Shahly's back, she looked to her eyes when she had her attention, patted her again, then pointed to the forest.

"You want me to go," the white unicorn guessed with an amused tone, "but we both know I won't. Don't worry over me. I'm a big mare and I can take care of myself." She looked back to the treetops over the forest. "Besides. I want to be… Oh, here he comes."

As the sun rose behind them, they found themselves standing in the long shadow of the castle, looking to the forest as a bright orange light illuminated the treetops of the forest beyond. The treetops appeared to be ablaze, and right over them, right where Teek was looking, soared the ominous form of the viper dragon.

Panic began to set in as the dragon looked right at her, focusing on her even from so far away, and as he turned fully and angled himself downward, Teek retreated a step, her heart thundering as she watched the approach of her death.

"Be still," the unicorn whickered to her.

Teek felt something wash over her, an unseen wave of warmth and safety as Shahly folded her essence around them both. In that instant, as the dragon closed half the distance to them, he swept his wings forward and lowered his feet, his eyes darting about as he seemed to become confused.

As Vultross landed only fifty paces away, Teek felt panic quickly taking control of her. Breathing in quick, deep gasps, she had her eyes locked on the creature that was there to kill her.

Don't move, the unicorn ordered in a thought, *and calm yourself. He can't see us. Just don't make a sound.*

To the elf girl's amazement, the dragon glanced about, and a growl rolled from him as his brow lowered over his eyes. Confusion had him and he took a step back, his eyes sweeping the grassy field where he was sure he had seen her.

Lowering his head, Vultross sniffed loudly. He drew his head back and growled again. He could smell her, but he could not see her. Another growl rolled from him and his eyes narrowed as he lowered his head again and looked around the area he had last seen the elf he hunted. Taking a couple of steps back, he gaped his jaws and roared through bared teeth.

Feeling the elf girl grow uneasy, Shahly urged in a thought, *Steady. Dragons do this to frighten and flush out prey that is hiding from them. He wants you to run so that he will know where you are. Just remain still.*

Vultross growled again. His eyes darted about and his frustration was growing more and more evident.

His eyes cut to one side and narrowed, then his lips slid away from his teeth and he wheeled around, lowering his body to bring it parallel to the ground and half spreading his wings.

Teek looked that way and only then did she make out the galloping hoof beats. Her mouth dropping open, she felt her heart slamming away within her as her gaze filled with the image of Sir Rayce charging from the forest on his big war horse, fully armored with his face plate down and his sword in his hand, the blade trailing blue flames as he rode. He held his shield at the ready and clearly meant for this to be an epic battle against his fifth dragon.

Vultross snarled and turned fully to face his new opponent. With long strides, he went to meet his much smaller challenger and roared as the distance between them rapidly closed.

About fifty paces away, the Dragonslayer swung his sword and sent a burst of blue flames to the dragon with a true aim. The dragon rose up slightly and tried to twist away but the sword's power caught him high on the chest, right at the shoulder and exploded. The dragon shrieked as the blast spun him around and he stumbled and fell to his side, crashing onto the field hard and kicking up mud and brown water as he slid to a stop. Regaining his wits quickly, he raised his head and belched fire back at the human, who stopped his horse and took the deadly flames on his shield.

When the knight hesitated to defend himself, the viper dragon took the opportunity he needed to roll to his belly and rise up on all fours.

Rayce swung his sword again, but this time the quick and nimble dragon dodged aside and backed away. He was learning quickly and seemed to be favoring his left arm. Smoke rose from his chest and shoulder where he had been struck and he seemed reluctant to approach his much smaller foe.

A quiet fell over the field as the two seemed to size each other up.

His tail thrashing behind him, the dragon growled and backed away a step, then he sidestepped a few times, studying his opponent.

The Dragonslayer pulled on the reins and his horse responded by pivoting. Sir Rayce would not allow the dragon to flank him and the fire that engulfed his sword burned brighter and brighter against the morning sunlight as he readied himself for another strike. This time, he was waiting for the dragon to make a move.

With another growl rolling from him, Vultross snaked his neck around, drawing his head back as he slowly opened his jaws.

Teek knew right away what that meant and patted the unicorn's back frantically as if to warn someone, anyone as to what was coming.

His jaws gaping again, the dragon lowered his fangs, then drew them back half way as he took two quick steps forward, and even as the knight raised his shield, he unleashed a burst of his venom in a fine mist.

Expecting fire, Rayce simply raised his shield to defend himself, but the cloud of venom found his horse's eyes. Whinnying in pain and terror, the horse backed away, shaking his head frantically as the venom burned his eyes, and he wheeled around, stumbled, reared up and finally launched himself into a blind gallop away from the dragon. The knight hit the ground rather hard on his back but did not lose his grip on his weapons.

With his enemy down, Vultross acted quickly, lunging with open jaws and his fangs in the perfect position to strike! They would plunge right through the knight's plate armor, and when he was well within striking range, less than a height from the Dragonslayer, he gaped and prepared to sink his fangs into this new victim and fill him with venom.

Rayce responded quickly and plunged his sword right into the dragon's mouth, into the roof of his mouth through to the inside of his nose.

Once again, Vultross shrieked and drew away, his eyes closed as he shook his head and stumbled backward. Blood began to trickle out of his left nostril and drip out of his mouth as he roared a high pitched, pain driven roar.

His big foe now on the defensive and backing away, Sir Rayce struggled to his feet and held his weapons ready, and as the dragon stood fully and grasped the end of his nose with one hand, he swung the sword and sent another burst of deadly blue flame at his chest, and this time he connected with a terrible purpose.

The explosion blew Vultross from his feet and about twenty paces backward and he slammed onto the ground again, this time flat on his back. His head struck last and blood spewed from that stricken nostril on impact.

Sir Rayce advanced a few steps and held his shield and flaming sword at the ready as he watched his downed foe gasp for breath. It was time for his death strike, time to end this.

Teek looked to the ground where the broken arrow lay at her feet. The killing of this foul beast was not for the Dragonslayer to do, it was for her. It was her right! Revenge called to her, rage spoke louder than reason and she picked up the front of the arrow, held the shaft tightly in her hand with the enchanted crystal arrowhead down like she would the point of a dagger and turned to the dragon that lay forty paces away. She saw the Dragonslayer, the human, closing in on her quarry and in an instant found herself running toward the downed viper dragon, the arrow in her grip and ready to plunge into the dragon's heart.

"Teek!" Shahly whinnied in a futile effort to stop her. In a panic, she hurled herself in pursuit of the elf girl, knowing that she would likely not reach her before she reached the dragon.

Rayce strode forward and had his weapon poised to give the dragon one more good burst, then he stopped as the elf girl ran right at the dragon, and nearly in a panic he raised his face shield and shouted, "Lass, what are you doing? Get away from that thing!"

Teek did not listen, could not listen. Vultross had to die and he had to die by her hand!

The Dragonslayer could not strike his downed enemy so long as the elf girl was so close and he watched in horror as she jumped up onto the dragon's chest and knelt down.

Vultross' armor had been burnt and blasted open in places by the knight's powerful sword and she laid her left hand down right beside where the armor looked the weakest, and she looked down at the burnt flesh that was exposed, blackened and pink. The skin was cracked and bled and somewhere beneath was the beast's heart. Slowly, she raised the arrow above her head, her eyes locked on that point that she meant to plunge the enchanted crystal arrowhead into, and for a second she hesitated, but did not know why.

The dragon rolled suddenly, brutally over and Teek found herself thrown from him, controlling her fall to the grass and mud beneath as best she could but still coming to rest on her side.

Pushing herself back up, Teek drew a gasp as she realized that she had lost her grip on the arrow and it had disappeared into the tall grass somewhere. Her eyes dance frantically as she dug through overturned stalks and those still standing in a desperate attempt to find it, then she froze, and slowly looked to her side and up, to the dragon that had righted himself and stared back at her with anger in his serpentine eyes.

Scaly lips drew away from thin, sharp teeth and the viper dragon growled, then his attention was abruptly ripped away from the elf girl. Hissing through bared teeth, he lowered his body and backed away on all fours, his eyes fixed on something behind the elf girl.

Teek swung her axe at the dragon and looked over her shoulder, seeing Sir Rayce stalking toward the beast with his weapon ready, the big bay unicorn with his horn engulfed in ruby colored flames approaching from beside and just behind the knight, and the silver unicorn, his horn encased in a bright, silver-blue glow, pacing toward the dragon from the knight's other side.

Vultross' eyes darted from one to the next and he backed away further. Clearly unwilling to do battle with all three, he hissed again before snaking his entire body around almost as a retreating serpent would and scurried with quick steps toward the castle. With one leap he was atop the wall, and before the Dragonslayer could strike with his enchanted sword again he opened his wings and took to the sky, stroking his wings in air grabbing sweeps as he sped south just over the treetops.

Slow to rise, Teek watched the retreating dragon with anger in her eyes. She had finally been in a position to kill him, and once again the opportunity had been ripped from her grasp. Hearing the knight and unicorns stop behind her, she could not bring herself to turn around and only watched after the dragon even after he was out of eyeshot.

Sir Rayce gently grasped her shoulder and in just as gentle a voice he scolded, "What were you thinking, Lass? That thing could..." He trailed off as she pulled her shoulder from his grasp and walked away from him and the unicorns.

Her hands were clenched into tight fists as she stormed to the castle's main gate, her brow low over green eyes that betrayed nothing but rage.

The castle gate opened before her and she did not break stride as she stormed to it, through it, and approached the palace with her gaze fixed on the tall timber doors that now stood open.

Gisan emerged from these doors with two guards behind her and she strode right at the elf girl with that smug, condescending look about her. At only ten paces away, she began, "You were supposed to stay in your suite, young lady, but I suppose even King Arlo's generosity means nothing to you. So if you'll not—"

Teek's fist was a blur and drove hard into the councilwoman's jaw, and she never broke stride.

Spinning half around, Gisan collapsed unceremoniously to the muddy ground where her white shirt absorbed a fair amount of muddy, brown water and her face splashed into a small puddle. The guards simply backed away as she went down, then they watched the slight elf girl storm into the palace. Looking to each other, they raised their brows, then looked down to the councilwoman who was slowly pushing herself back up.

Vinton paced by her, giving her a hard look and an amused whicker as he did so. Shahly was right behind him and also stared down at the elf woman who finally looked up at them with mud all over her face, in her hair and all over the front of her. Shaking her head, the white unicorn simply turned her attention forward again as she paced on.

Finally reaching her suite, Teek slammed the door and stormed into it, pausing to look around her at the mess that had been created the night before. Her clothes for the battle with the viper dragon were still laid out on the table and she gave them a long stare before she spun around to go to her room.

A knock at the door stopped her and she turned toward it. She did not want company and just stared at the door even as a second knock beckoned. Huffing a loud breath, she stormed that way, turned the handle and jerked it open, and she drew a gasp as her eyes met the white unicorn's.

Shahly stared back for long seconds and finally informed, "It's been decided that one of us will remain with you." She paced into the room as the elf girl moved aside. "They figure they can keep watch over both of us at once if we're together."

Teek looked out the door, peered down the hall way one way, then the other, then she closed the door and turned back toward the unicorn.

Looking around her, Shahly nodded and complimented, "This is nice." She looked over her shoulder at the elf girl and informed, "I think you wanted to bathe and change clothes. Don't worry over me. I'll just admire the artwork you have here, perhaps see the view from the window."

And stare out the window is what the unicorn did as Teek went about the ritual of bathing and dressing. She still felt a bit modest about doing this in front of someone she did not know well, even a unicorn, so she had taken her clothes with her into her bedroom. As she emerged, dressed in her archer's attire with forest green leggings, a white shirt and a brown jerkin over it, she dropped her boots by the bedroom door and looked to the white unicorn who stared out over the forest from the high window, she leaned against the wall near the door to her room and just watched, allowing herself to be lost in the presence of this magical beast for a while.

Shahly knew she was there, knew she was staring at her, and just allowed it. She did not mind.

Long, silent moments passed between them.

Finally looking over her shoulder, Shahly suggested, "Perhaps you should find some food. I'm sure you are hungry."

Teek looked to the floor and just shrugged.

"Do you know who they were?" the unicorn asked.

The elf girl's eyes slid to the unicorn.

"The people who attacked you and took you to the field," Shahly went on. "I watched from a distance, crouched down in the grass, then I summoned Vinton when they left you there. I'm sorry they hurt you. I did not know they were going to do that or I would have done something more."

Teek shook her head, placed a hand over her chest, then extended that hand to the unicorn.

Shahly turned and paced to the girl, her hooves making subtle clops on the stone tile floor as she approached. "I have a feeling you suspect who one of them is. I kind of suspect the same. Should we..." Her ears swiveled to the front door and she looked that way.

Someone knocked.

Also looking to the door, Teek glanced at the unicorn as she turned fully and approached. Grasping the door handle, she pulled it open confidently, feeling safe in the presence of the unicorn, and her eyes met the King's.

He was still in his clothing from the day before, smelled of ale and wine and sweat and clearly had not slept nor stopped drinking. He could not stand steadily, his eyes were bloodshot and he was a little pale, and looked exhausted.

After staring back at the elf girl for a moment, he shook his head and admitted, "I wish I knew what else I could do. I don't want to give you to that beast. I don't want... He took my son, my close friend your father, your mother..." A little snarl took his mouth. "He can't have you, too. He won't have you." As she stepped aside, he strode into the suite with unsteady steps and looked hard at the unicorn who stared back at him. "I could only think of one thing. The council will never allow us to do what must happen, so you must take Teek far from here." He bowed his head and his eyes slid to the girl as she took his side and looked up at him. "So long as this menace plagues us, you must leave, and you cannot come home."

Shahly approached a couple of steps, raising her head as she asked with a harsh tone, "You are banishing her again?"

"It's the only way I can protect her," he confessed shamefully.

Teek took his hand, squeezing it tightly, and when his eyes finally shifted to her, she slowly shook her head.

He clenched his jaw and insisted, "I'll not allow you to throw yourself against this monster like Wazend did, like your father did, like so many have."

"And Sir Rayce?" Shahly asked. "He is a Dragonslayer and wishes to deal with this dragon his way."

"The council has spoken," King Arlo informed, "and their decision is final."

Shahly leaned her head. "Their decision. Are you not the king here?"

Arlo found himself unable to look her way and hesitantly, shamefully explained, "The power lies with the council now."

Raising her head, the unicorn insisted, "Surely you still wield power of your own."

He turned away from her, toward the door. "I have arranged for Teek to be taken from the castle after dark. Please see to it she gets to safety."

"Stop!" Shahly ordered. When he hesitated, she paced to him, sniffed his back, then his neck, then she drew away and snorted. "It's no wonder you feel so... How long have you been poisoning yourself so?" He turned and looked to her and all she could see were his defeated eyes. "Your people need you, King Arlo, now more than ever." An emerald glow emanated from her horn and she leaned her head forward, and she gently touched the tip of her spiral to his forehead, touched him with her essence.

That glow enveloped him and he drew a deep breath, his eyes widening as he stared back at the unicorn. He felt the unicorn's essence surround him, absorb into him, and for the first time in many seasons he felt cleansed. The ache he had felt for so long, the pain from his body and the penned up emotions felt washed away. Somehow, he felt twenty seasons younger, no longer feeling like an elf who had seen nearly fifty seasons, but a young man who was in his prime.

The glow faded and Shahly backed away, looking into his eyes as she said, "That should do it. I've purged what that stuff was doing to you and you should feel better now." She raised her head, holding her ears straight up as she ordered, "Go and reclaim your kingdom, King Arlo. But first, go and bathe and change your clothes. You stink a little."

He smiled slightly, and nodded. "Lady Unicorn, I shall be in your debt." He looked to Teek. "If you two will excuse me, I've a few things to attend to."

**

The Elvan council was reconvened and all sat in their places. There was an uneasy buzzing among them and all looked to the door as the guards opened it, and silence gripped them as Teek entered with the Dragonslayer and Shahly behind her. King Arlo still was not present, but Hes of the gnomes was, him and two other gnomes who were burly men who wore clean leather coveralls, heavy boots, and long sleeved white shirts. As with Hes, they wore long beards and had long hair, one brown and one black. They stood there with a chest between them near the King's chair and had their hands folded before them, and neither spoke. The chest itself was reinforced with thick, black iron straps that were riveted onto the sheet steel at the sides and corners. The lid was rounded at the top and held in place by heavy iron hinges and a big hasp that was locked shut with a big padlock. About half a pace long and half of that deep and high, it was made up of dark metals and was clearly built for strength rather than to be ornate.

As the doors were about to close, Leedon pressed his hand to one and pushed it open again, offering a smile to the guard on that side as he announced, "One more, my good soldier." He strode in and his eyes found Shahly immediately, and she got a little nod from him. "Why Ralligor would want you to come here is more than evident, my dear. I think only you could have seen such a huge issue looming so small, and I think only you could find the wisdom to fix it."

Shahly leaned her head.

Leedon approached and scratched her under one ear. "King Arlo is feeling much better and his mind is as clear as I can remember."

Arlo banged his way into the Council Chamber, forcing both doors to open wide ahead of him as he shouted, "I heard your insults, wizard, and don't think I'll not answer them."

All looked that way.

He stopped just inside, his clothes clean and pressed, his white shirt almost glowing under the torch light, and his attention on the wizard. While he wore no smile on his lips, it could be seen easily in his eyes. His gaze shifted to the white unicorn as he was slow to approach, and he dared to reach to her with both hands and grasp her gently under the jaw. He bent slightly and kissed her nose, then he stroked the side of her neck and whispered, "I shall be in your debt forever, Lady Unicorn."

"Call me Shahly," she whispered back, "and I hold no one in my debt."

He smiled. "Just know that a king is your servant." He released her and turned to the Dragonslayer, setting his fists on his hips as he looked up at him and loudly announced, "So you would come for the head of Vultross, would you?"

"I would," Sir Rayce confirmed, "if you'll allow me the honor of taking it."

The King's eyes shifted to Hes and he gave an important command in one subtle nod.

The Gnome representative slid from his chair and turned toward the chest that was guarded by two of his men, and as he reached it he removed a key from his pocket, bent down and unlocked the chest. This done, he turned to the King and backed away a step.

Arlo strode to the chest and kicked the lid open to reveal sparkling jewels of many colors and sizes, and many had been cut and fashioned and left to be set into whatever precious metal one would decide to put them in.

All eyes found the chest, and all but the eyes of the unicorns and wizard widened.

"Enough to make you a king among your people," King Arlo announced, "and it will stay here at the Elf Kingdom so long as Vultross lives." He locked his eyes on the knight and held a finger up. "But, it will leave with the brave soul who would kill that foul beast. What say you, Dragonslayer?"

With a slow nod, Sir Rayce confirmed, "It seems quite a handsome bounty, your Majesty. Quite a handsome bounty. Would I have your blessing to smite down this beast?"

Councilwoman Gisan stood and slammed her hands onto the table, barking, "Absolutely not!"

King Arlo swung around and pointed a finger at her as he shouted, "You will be silent!"

That silence consumed the entire room.

Arlo strode to his chair and kicked it aside, his eyes shifting from one of the council to the next as he yelled, "This Elvan Council has become about as toothless as a newborn elf! Our people are dying by the hundreds and you seek to give us all over to this beast without even a fight. I say no!" He slammed his fist down onto the table. "No more! We have stepped aside and allowed this madness for too long, and if the council will not rise to the defense of the elves then the council will be dissolved." His eyes found Gisan and narrowed, and he snarled, "Starting with you."

That young councilman who had always advocated fighting the dragon to the end stood and shouted, "It is about time! King Arlo, you have my backing and my full support!"

An older councilman raised his fist and barked, "Here here!"

"But the Council has spoken!" Gisan reminded with desperate words.

"And now your King has," Arlo growled back. His eyes scanned the Elvan Council and he shouted, "Would any of you here dare oppose your King?" He looked from one to the next.

Some met his eyes proudly, and some simply looked away.

Watching this, Teek tugged on the knight's arm, and when he looked down at her and she met his eyes, she had a big smile on her lips and gave him a satisfied nod.

**

This now seemed more than a dislike for Gisan. Teek could feel in her belly that something was very amiss with the councilwoman who seemed determined to undermine the King at every turn. She had begun swaying members of the council to her side even before the death of Leumas Brebor and this had not gone unnoticed by many.

Teek had retired to her suite to change into darker clothing and a very dark green cloak and hood, so dark as to appear black in the shadows. She had traded her short top boots for moccasins that were very light, very quiet to walk on. Her archer's belt held her dagger and her combat sword, a weapon that had always been well cared for but had never before been used. She also had that axe shoved into the belt on the side where her dagger hung, feeling just a little too attached to it to leave it behind.

After changing, she met Shahly outside of the Elvan Council Chamber to await the end of the session, and they waited halfway down the hallway, listening as voices were raised from time to time and Teek would smile each time she heard King Arlo's. Leaning against the wall, she kept her arms folded and just watched the door.

Shahly also watched the door, and some time later she butted the girl with her nose and whispered, "I can't help but feel your instincts are right. I sense that the King has swayed two members of the council to support him, but the others are still seeking to remain in Gisan's favor, and they are afraid to lose it."

Looking to the unicorn, Teek had her brow low over her eyes as she thought, *That can only mean that she means to overthrow King Arlo and she sees the dragon as a tool to do so.*

"You also said she has been interested in your family's lands," Shahly whispered. "What has been happening cannot be just a coincidence, especially since you are sure she put the charm in your pack that would lead the dragon to you. The question is where would she get such a thing?"

Teek shrugged and looked back to the door.

The door opened and the elf girl and unicorn raised their chins as the council began to emerge. Teek felt that wave of safety she had experienced before fold around her and the unicorn as Shahly folded her essence around them both and they watched unnoticed as the council and those who served them strode down the corridor. All looked strained, a couple looked frazzled, and it appeared that this was merely a recess, and that the debate would continue.

Finally, Gisan exited, right behind King Arlo, and still she was arguing her case.

"Your Majesty," she urged, "I can assure you I don't mean to challenge your wisdom, but we've spilled so much blood over this thing as it is. I beg you, don't allow the people or the council to lose confidence in you."

He snarled and growled back, "I lost that confidence seasons ago when my wife died. Now it is time to rebuild it." He was not looking toward the councilwoman as he stormed down the corridor. "You would be wise not to oppose me further, Gisan. I've grown tired of your so called well meaning rhetoric that does little more than undermine the very foundation of everything the elves have built over the centuries."

"But King Arlo, times are changing. We must change with them."

He finally stopped and turned toward her. "That does not mean abandoning all that we are and giving the future of this kingdom over to some monster! Everything you've said and done in there has favored our enemy and you'd better know that it has not gone unnoticed." He poked her hard in the chest with his finger, hard enough to make her take a step back. "Be very careful where your loyalties lie, Councilwoman Gisan. Very careful. I'm sure you would not want to be the next sacrifice to that beast you insist we should not try to kill."

Teek could not help the big grin that overpowered her lips as the King strode by her, then she looked back to Gisan, and her eyes narrowed. There was no fear on the woman's face, only defiance, anger. That should not have been there.

As the councilwoman strode on to leave the corridor and go straight to her suite on the third level, Shahly and Teek waited for her at the end of the hall to her suite near the stairs. Only moments later she emerged, now wearing a forest green traveler's cloak with a hood, carrying a black suede sack that looked big enough to hold a small melon, and it was burdened with something that looked heavy.

They followed as she mounted a horse at the stable, stuffing the black sack into the saddlebag behind her, and she rode alone toward the forest behind the castle, not acknowledging any of the elves who milled around the marketplace around her, not acknowledging the guards who met her at the gate behind the castle wall that led out to the lake and waterfall. She simply rode in silence, veering to a trail there that was only rarely traveled by anyone, a trail that would lead her into the deep of the forest itself.

"On my back," Shahly ordered in a low whicker. "We'll be able to keep up with her easier with only four feet following her."

Teek complied and they followed the councilwoman at a discreet distance into the forest. Teek was afraid they would lose her a number of times, but the unicorn seemed to be able to feel where she was going, and even when there was a fork in the trail she knew which way to go.

This path followed the river behind the castle and eventually crossed it where it became shallow enough. They wound around again, coming back to the river and eventually to a creek that fed into it, and up ahead, where the water was a little swifter, Gisan stopped her horse and dismounted, allowing the animal to drink as she looked about her for unwanted eyes. Shahly and Teek had stopped among the trees and quietly crawled into the underbrush, watching the councilwoman from the safety of the thick leaves there. Still, Shahly kept her essence folded around them both so they would be nearly impossible to find.

Nearly.

As Gisan looked like she was going to mount her horse again, Shahly crawled backward from the underbrush and watched as the elf girl emerged, then she half turned and drew a start, sidestepping as her eyes met the blue eyed white unicorn. Teek also spun around and she and Shahly stared back at the older mare like two children who awaited a good scolding.

The elf girl got but a glance before the blue eyed unicorn's attention turned back on the pregnant mare, and she started in a low voice, "Shahly, we talked about this. Do you remember our talk?"

"This is important!" Shahly hissed. "We are sure she is—"

Shawri snorted and took a step closer to the younger mare, her eyes narrowing as she reminded, "You are not to put yourself at risk like this!" She raised her head and looked to the departing councilwoman, then back to her daughter and ordered, "Go and find Vinton and Dosslar and tell them where you have been, and go quickly."

In one last defiant act, Shahly snorted, then turned and trotted away on very silent hooves.

When the unicorn looked to her, Teek turned her eyes away and closed the cloak tighter around herself.

"Stop worrying," Shawri insisted as she looked back to the departing elf woman. "I feel as you and Shahly do. She should be watched. On my back, now."

This was not what the elf girl expected and the bewilderment in her wide eyes was easy to read.

Shawri offered her a little smile and assured, "She got that adventurous side from me, I hear. Now come on and let's see where that elf woman goes."

They did just that for another half hour or so. Teek did not feel the unicorn wrap her protective essence around them but she was confident nonetheless. Both were very quiet as they stalked toward the seemingly oblivious councilwoman, and suddenly the unicorn stopped, her eyes locked forward as she lowered her body slightly.

"There is a large field ahead," Shawri whispered. She scanned the area with her eyes and essence, then she moved noiselessly toward the trees, ordering in a whisper, "Jump down and follow closely."

They made almost no sound as they crept among the trees, the elf girl following the unicorn, and they came upon a huge opening in the forest. Gisan had left her horse near the edge of the tree line that surrounded the field and the reins were tied to a low branch there, and she walked slowly out toward the center of the vast field. This was a field covered with tall, amber grass and grain that was dotted by dark leaved bushes.

Shawri lay down to her belly, her eyes narrowing as she whispered, "What is she doing?"

Crouching beside her, Teek slipped an arm over the unicorn's neck as she watched the elf woman. She felt Shawri's essence fold around them both and sat all the way to the ground, pressing herself against the mare's side and trying to make herself as small as possible.

"Don't move," Shawri ordered in a whisper as she turned her eyes skyward.

Gisan stopped only fifty or so paces from the trees and looked upward herself.

Vultross soared in over the treetops, his eyes quickly finding the councilwoman and he turned hard toward her and lowered his feet to land.

Slowly shaking her head, Teek tensed up as she watched the viper dragon land only about ten paces beyond the councilwoman, and she was certain that this would not end well for Gisan. Instead, things did not go as anyone would expect.

Kneeling down, Gisan bowed her head and greeted, "Lord Vultross."

Unicorn and elf girl exchanged looks of bewilderment.

The viper dragon nodded to the councilwoman and demanded, "Telling why Vultross attacked by human and unicorns! Vultross wounding and hurts and demands to know why betrayed!"

With her head still bowed, Gisan explained, "I opposed any involvement of the Dragonslayer and I had the council send even the unicorns away, but—"

"Did not go away," the dragon roared, his dorsal scales growing erect. "Vultross attacked by treacherous human and demanding to know why!"

"He had gone," Gisan replied with a shaky voice, "but clearly he was anxious to kill another dragon." She finally looked up at him. "He is an enemy of your kind and has convinced the King and Council to employ him to kill you."

Vultross scaly lips drew away from his teeth and he looked away. "And bringing unicorns with. Vultross not pleased. Vultross not knowing how to fight human's magic."

"I can help you," she assured. "Once he has been killed and the unicorns driven off then we can resume our plan and you can be the ruler of Abtont."

"Helping before," the dragon scoffed. "Now Vultross wounding and defeated by treacherous human."

"I can give you the means to defeat him," she assured, "and I can make you invulnerable to unicorns."

"No," Shawri whispered. "She can't!"

They had not noticed Gisan remove the black suede sack from her saddle bag, had not noticed her carry it with her, but now she laid it in front of her, opened it, and reached inside.

"This is bad," the unicorn mumbled. A breeze caught part of her mane and whipped it around into her eyes, and her attention cut that way as she hissed, "This is worse! Teek! Stand up and move slowly with me!"

The elf girl did not understand at first, and then she saw the unicorn's mane caught on the breeze again, and that breeze was blowing directly toward the dragon. Standing as the mare did, she slowly backed away with her, keeping her eyes on the dragon and the council woman as they slowly retreated deeper into the trees.

Vultross snarled, "What is this?"

"It is a shard of the Heart of Abtont," Gisan explained. "Merged with it, you would control great power and have immunity against anything that could harm you, even the power of unicorns."

That treacherous wretch! Teek thought angrily, her brow low over her eyes.

"Treacherous, yes," the unicorn agreed. "He cannot be allowed to merge himself with the Heart of Abtont. Stay here, Teek."

Teek simply did not know what to do as she watched the unicorn stalk forward. Shawri held her head low, her ears flat against her head and a sapphire blue glow enveloped her horn.

"Merging with it how?" the dragon asked, his words laced with suspicion. He abruptly raised his head and tested the air in loud sniffs, then he lowered his nose and sniffed. Lifting his head again, he glanced about, a low growl rumbling from him as he mumbled, "Unicorn."

Gisan swung around, her eyes darting about as she barked, "Where?"

Vultross' gaze swept the forest and field before him and he growled again, then his jaws gaped and he roared.

Dropping to her knees, Gisan fell back onto her calves, bent over her legs and covered her ears.

Shawri was nearly within striking range when the dragon swept his wings and sprang backward. He retreated a few steps more, then his jaws gaped and he belched fire in front of him, setting the top of the tall grass in front of him ablaze. The unicorn's essence faltered as she leapt from the flames and bolted around the dragon's side, keeping her attention locked on him. He could see her now and pivoted to keep her in front of him. The timeless battle between dragon and unicorn was at hand again, but this dragon found himself facing a unicorn whose power was not so vast, nor was her experience against his kind. Still, he half opened his wings and stalked sideways, circling to keep her from outflanking him. The white unicorn kept her attention locked on him, her eyes boring into him and glowing the same sapphire blue her horn did as the two sized each other up. Shawri clearly did not intend to allow this dragon to merge with the Heart of Abtont, nor was she sure how to stop him.

This confrontation of enemies would not remain idle long.

The dragon's jaws swung open and he roared a mighty challenge, and the unicorn flinched backward only a step before rearing up and lunging toward him. He shied away, then he belched fire at her, setting more of the grass ablaze as she leapt easily aside to avoid it. Snorting and kicking at the ground beneath her, Shawri lunged at him again, and when he shied away she charged fully and her horn seemed to trail blue flames as she did.

Vultross retreated, shrieking at the surprise move, but with a quick sidestep he easily thwarted the unicorn's aim on him. Shawri turned sharply and thrust her horn at him, knowing that he was too far away, but her feint had the desired effect as he retreated straight back, allowing her to square up on him and charge again.

Teek watched with desperate, hopeful eyes as the seemingly outmatched unicorn kept the deadly viper dragon on the defensive and backing away from her. Still, she reached to her belt and took her axe from her belt and held it ready, and she found herself in a hesitant pursuit of the combatants.

Shawri pressed her attack and kept the dragon backing away from her. Despite her age and all she had experienced in her long life, fighting dragons had not been among those experiences, and overconfidence would conspire against her.

Dropping to all fours, the viper dragon snaked himself around, seemingly to outflank his much smaller foe, but again she turned to thwart his attempt. This time, his jaws opened and he sprayed a misty shower of his venom at the white unicorn. Shawri tried to shy away but too slowly closed her eyes and the venom found them both, burning her eyes and effectively blinding her. As she whinnied and shook her head, backing away from her larger foe, the dragon swiped hard, his clawed hand finding her shoulder and spinning her around as two of his claws ripped through skin and muscle, almost to the bone and she was thrown from her hooves and slammed onto the ground on her side.

With a deep, silent gasp, Teek acted quickly, throwing her axe with a true aim and hitting the dragon on the side of the head, but not penetrating his armor. She did not expect it to. She only wanted to distract him, to draw him away from the wounded unicorn, and she did just that.

Vultross' head swung around, his lips sliding away from his teeth as he looked down on the little elf once again, and he slowly turned that way, advancing on his tiny quarry with anger in his steps.

"No!" Gisan cried, drawing the dragon's attention. "Kill the unicorn! I'll attend to this little brat!"

The dragon stared at her for long seconds and watched as the council woman produced a long dagger and turned to advance on the elf girl who turned to face her.

Apparently, Gisan had forgotten about this girl's lineage, who her father was, and she clearly did not realize how extensively trained the daughter of Leumas Brebor was in the art of combat. This is what Teek had waited a long time for, the opportunity to have at the woman she hated most in the world. Drawing her own dagger, she held it ready as she closed the twenty paces between herself and her foe with purposeful strides.

Shawri gasped for breath, still holding her eyes closed against the burning venom and the horrific pain that tore through her shoulder, her ribs. She dared to open her eyes, blinking rapidly against the pain. Her vision was very blurry, but she could make out the dragon turning on her once again. He was less than thirty paces from her and now held his body low as he strode toward her on his hind legs, closing the distance with hesitant, savoring steps.

The tip of a walking staff plunged through the grass and solidly met the ground beneath, right in front of the unicorn, and the dragon stopped.

Leedon's robes took ferociously to the breeze as he fearlessly held his ground only two paces from the unicorn, keeping himself between her and the dragon. His bushy white eyebrows were low and his gaze locked on the viper dragon as he announced in a loud voice, "You'll be killing no unicorns today." He raised his arms, his staff held firmly in his fist. "Leave here forever and leave the Elf Kingdom in peace."

Vultross could sense the power of this human and he gaped his jaws again, hissing loudly through bared teeth.

Sweeping his staff, the wizard shouted, "Away with you! Leave this land forever!"

His fangs dropping half way down again, the dragon sprayed a storm of his venom at the wizard, who responded by sweeping his staff the other way. The venom exploded into hot flames halfway to the wizard and those flames erupted all the way back into the viper dragon's mouth.

Vultross shied away and retreated. With a low growl, he looked back to the wizard, his lips sliding away from his teeth again, and this time he struck with fire, and this time the wizard waved his hand and the flames thinned and became a cool mist about halfway to their target.

Leedon's eyes narrowed as he watched the dragon take a step back, then he thrust his staff, lightning lancing from the end of it with an ear splitting crack. The dragon was struck square on the chest and was blown from his feet and thrown backward another thirty paces. As he hit the ground and rolled to all fours, he was quick to force his wits back to him and look to the wizard, who thrust his staff and hit him with another that rolled him over again.

The viper dragon had had enough and stumbled to all fours again, this time retreating from the wizard. He looked to his one ally on the field, who also retreated from a smaller foe, back to the wizard, then he scrambled toward the councilwoman, scooped her up with both hands and stroked his wings hard to lift himself into the sky.

Teek watched as both of her enemies escaped, and she clenched her teeth, her brow low over her eyes as she shoved her dagger back into its sheath and kept her attention on the dragon until he flew out of sight. Looking to the wizard, she saw him turn and kneel down beside the stricken unicorn, and she ran that way as panic surged into her.

Dropping to her knees as she reached the unicorn, the elf girl slid another pace or so and almost into the bleeding unicorn but brought herself to a stop right beside the wizard.

Leedon had his hand placed gently on Shawri's wounded shoulder and there was a cool blue light spraying from between his fingers. He drew a deep breath, then assured, "I can ease your pain, but I think it is best to await the arrival of your comrades to heal you." He placed his other hand over her eye and the same blue glow sprayed from beneath it.

Shawri's labored breathing slowed as her pain subsided and she offered in a deep breath, "Thank you."

Many hoof beats from behind drew Teek's attention and she looked over her shoulder to see three unicorns running from the trees. Dosslar led the way with Shahly and Vinton right behind him. She kept her eyes on them as they arrived and she watched Dosslar circle around and lie down to his belly and press his body to Shawri's back. That glow overtook his horn and he lowered it to her wounded shoulder, and the wizard withdrew his hand as the big unicorn worked.

Vinton whickered and Dosslar replied with, "No worries. I can attend to this easily."

Leedon looked over his shoulder to Vinton and reported, "She took a spray of that dragon's venom to the eyes. I think I have purged most of it but I would not get my feelings hurt if you were to be sure."

"My eyes are fine," Shawri assured. "Thank you." She drew a deep breath and stared ahead of her, her head lying flat on the ground. "I suppose I should have waited for you, but I could not allow him to merge with the Heart of Abtont." She closed her eyes. "Now he has escaped with the shard."

Leedon stroked her neck and assured, "We'll figure out how to counter it."

"He'll be invulnerable to unicorns now," Shawri said softly. "I'm sorry. I failed."

"You did not fail," Vinton insisted. "Now we know what to expect. Now we can plan for it."

"Just lie still, Ammi," Shahly ordered.

Teek watched with blank eyes as Dosslar slowly healed the white unicorn's wounds. There was a heaviness to her heart, a certain sense of guilt. Slowly, she got to her feet, stared down at the wounded unicorn for long seconds, then she turned and strode toward the forest.

Nearly to the trees, she looked over her shoulder as she heard someone following, but even as she saw the pregnant white mare and the big stallion pacing toward her, she did not stop. She looked forward again and quickened her pace.

Shahly trotted to catch up and took her side, looking to her as she said, "I can feel what is in your heart and there is no reason for you to feel guilt for what happened. My mother is a big mare and makes her own decisions and none of this was your fault."

Teek finally stopped, and she bowed her head and lowered her eyes as she thought, *It is too my fault. All of this was. I should have just let that dragon kill me in the desert. If only I had... She would not be hurt, many of my people would not have been killed...*

"And we would be no closer to stopping him," Vinton added as he caught up to them. "Perhaps if we had all gotten here much sooner then we could have put a stop to him, but we didn't get here sooner and brooding about it now is pointless. It will change nothing. Shawri will be fine and now at least we know that Vultross has made an ally among your people."

Teek clenched her hands into tight fists.

Butting the elf girl with her nose, Shahly assured, "We will stop him."

How? Teek thought.

Shahly looked to Vinton and his only response was to look back at her.

He is impervious to you now, the elf girl pointed out. *You cannot hurt him. You cannot stop him.*

"He is not invulnerable," Vinton countered. "Even if he is one with the Heart of Abtont there is a way to bring him down. The Elf Kingdom will be free of him somehow."

I wish I was as confident as you, she thought grimly.

**

King Arlo and the council were informed that Gisan would not be joining them for the afternoon session. They were also told why, and that news was not well received.

Despite the unicorns wanting to keep watch on her, Teck slipped away and wandered the marketplace of the Elf Kingdom's south courtyard. Still in her dark green traveler's cloak, she had the hood over her head to try not to be noticed. Part of her craved company, but she truly wanted to just be alone.

Never before had she paid such attention to the marketplace. She had attended with her parents and the sights the sounds and the smells brought back many a pleasant memory. Her father so loved to indulge her, buying her sugary treats and little flowers and ornaments to wear, just as he always indulged her mother. Different foods cooking in different little storefronts along the wide pathway mingled on the scant breeze that snaked its way through and the sounds of music and merriment were everywhere.

Somewhere about the middle of this huge marketplace was an older center, a part of the market that seemed a little run down despite the best efforts of those who sold their goods there to keep it maintained. Some of the store fronts sported new paint, others were of vine covered stonework, and some were little more than tents with wooden structures making up the backs.

Standing alone here with no other shops touching it was a tent that looked to be four paces square. It was a patchwork of many different colors of heavy canvas and there were carved wooden pillars flanking the entrance flaps, one of which was red and the other blue. Hanging on each of these ancient looking pillars was an oil lamp with multicolored glass, and both lamps were burning to let a passerby know that the establishment was open for business. Hanging on a chain that spanned the top of the pillars was a wooden shingle, painted bright yellow with the name *Madame Miscree* in black letters.

Teek had seen this tent before and had even passed it by a couple of times since losing her parents, but for some reason this day she paused. This old elf woman was a fortune teller, supposedly a clairvoyant who claimed to be able to see people's futures and could read destinies of those who were willing to give her a piece of silver. Leumas had always scoffed and was known to make a crude joke or two at the soothsayer's expense, but he paid her no mind otherwise. And, with a dismissive shake of her head, his daughter turned to pass the tent by yet again.

"Stop!" a small elf man ordered from behind.

She spun around, seeing a rather thin elf who was bent over at the back and had thinning black hair that was streaked with silver, limping toward her with his big blue eyes locked on hers. He wore a green and yellow jerkin over his slight frame and loosely fitting yellow trousers with black vertical stripes down them, trousers that were only just below his knees. He was barefoot and wore a variety of cheaply made rings, one on each of his fingers and thumbs, a long chained necklace with an amulet that was a red eye made of copper, and an anklet above his foot that appeared to be made of silver. His appearance made her uneasy, but she held her ground. He was taller than she, slightly heavier made, but she was sure she could defeat him should he be foolish enough to attack her.

Instead, his intentions were far from assaulting this attractive young elf girl he approached. Reaching into his pocket, he removed a stiff parchment card the size of his hand, a yellow and red card with an eye right in the center that was in the middle of the image of a glowing pyramid. He stopped about a pace away and held it to her, and he explained, "I was instructed by Madame Miscree to deliver this to one who would come this way, one whose aura is far stronger than one would suspect." His eyes widened. "Your aura is most strong, daughter of Brebor. His spirit dwells around you, his destiny to be assumed by his bloodline." He offered the card to her again, pushing it closer to her. "Take this. It was always yours." When she hesitantly took it from his hand, he bowed his head and backed away from her, holding his palms to her as he assured, "Madame Miscree is expecting you, Lady Brebor. I bid you welcome." He turned to the tent and strode to the entrance, turning back to the elf girl as he pulled a flap open to invite her inside.

Teek raised her chin and stared back at him. She looked down at the card he had given her, then turned her eyes back to him with a blink. With a hesitant first step, she strode toward the tent, pausing right before she entered to give him another look.

Inside, the tent was very colorful, but for the gray wooden floor. Tapestries divided it in half and concealed the back of it. There were shelves of powders, skulls, crystals and other charms cluttering each shelf. There were also books on these shelves, old books that were bound in leather. Right in the middle was a small table with a chair on each side, left and right, and in the center of the table was a crystal pyramid. More cards were stacked up in front of the chair to the left, right on the edge of the table and both chairs had red pillows on the seats.

The elf girl stopped halfway from the entrance to the table, glancing around her. Light was offered by more of those old oil lamps that hung from the framework of the tent with the fire contained inside of the glass chimneys, and two hung at the entrance, though those burned low. Looking back to the table, she saw a thick bodied candle on the far side, on the other side of the crystal pyramid, and a cold wave swept through her as she realized it had not been there the first time she looked to the table. Glancing about again, she noticed that the tapestry wall did not go all the way to the walls of the tents on both sides, and more light burned behind it.

Drawing a nervous breath, she looked down to the card she had been given again, holding it with both hands as she gazed at the eye that stared up at her.

"Finished the day you were born," an ancient woman's voice informed from beyond the tapestries.

Teek's breath caught and she froze where she stood, but for her wide eyes that slid to the unseen other side of the tent. Footsteps could be heard beyond the tapestries and she followed them to the left. A tapping joined them, like a walking stick on the wooden floor.

A very old woman emerged, a plump elf with white hair and a pale and wrinkled face. She seemed to walk with some difficulty and leaned heavily on a walking stick that was half of her height, one carried in a crooked left hand. She also wore many rings with many huge jewels and stones in them. Her snow white hair was worn long to her mid back. She also wore a long, heavy looking dress that appeared to be a colorful patchwork of many fabrics sewn together in such a way that the edges of the patches stood up. She had a shawl around her shoulders, one that was made of every color yarn imaginable and ended in many tassels, no two the same color.

The old woman stopped as she turned into the front room and turned ancient eyes on the elf girl, not looking her up and down in a study of a new guest, but meeting her eyes as if she had known her for many seasons, perhaps a lifetime. "No voice to summon me from the back, but then you did not have need of one today, did you? I have been expecting you."

Teek lowered her arms and swallowed hard, her eyes widening slightly despite her best efforts not to show any fear.

Extending a wrinkled and crooked hand to the far chair at the table, she bade, "Sit and be comfortable, Miss Brebor. You have much to learn today."

Once again, Teek's steps were hesitant, but she complied and strode slowly to the table, taking the back of the chair and pulling it out as she watched the old woman do the same.

They both sat and Miscree leaned her walking stick absently onto the heavy tapestry beside the table.

Slowly, the old woman raised her hands to the crystal pyramid, sliding her fingertips from the tip to the base, and then doing this again. Hers was an unblinking stare as she gazed into the pyramid for a long, tense moment.

Teek also looked to the pyramid but could not see what might interest the old woman so much about it.

Sucking a hard breath from between her teeth, Miscree's eyes widened and she turned a horrified look to the elf girl, just staring at her for many horrifying seconds. She shook her head in slight motions and hissed, "It was written from the night your parents laid together that first time, the very night you were conceived by them. Your destiny is why Leumas Brebor never made a son. Were you a son, you would be dead already, and had you a brother, he would have taken the battle training meant for you and thrown himself against the dragon and would have perished a season ago. The same vengeance that drives you would have driven him to a quick end against Vultross. Only the daughter of the elves' greatest hero can save the elf kingdom." She shook her head again. "You cannot kill him, but you can placate him. Your flesh can end his interest in conquest of the elves once and for all. The end of your line was always his destiny, and your sacrifice to save the elf kingdom was always yours. Your destinies are intertwined and inseparable. You must become part of him. Your flesh must meld with his through his belly. Battle him if you must, but only your sacrifice will save us all."

Teek stared back at her for a few seconds, then her eyes shifted away as that nervous crawl began in the pit of her stomach again.

"Keep that card with you," Madame Miscree continued. "Go alone to that place in the forest that you hold dear. Go there and make your peace with this world. When Vultross has joined with the Heart of Abtont and you have joined with his flesh, then he will not be a conqueror, but a defender of our people through you. The Brebor line complete inside of him will make him so. Cast away notions of vengeance and join your family within him, and together you will sway his heart and defeat the beast from within, and you will make the dragon defend the elves for a thousand seasons."

With a deep breath, Teek nodded. She stood and reached for a pouch were she kept her money, only to stop when the old woman grasped her hand.

Miscree shook her head and insisted, "Your service to the elves is more than payment enough, Miss Brebor. Go forth and fulfill the destiny that was written in the stars ten thousand seasons before your birth."

Teek stared back at her for long seconds, then she turned and left the tent.

Madame Miscree's eyes narrowed slightly as she watched the girl leave, then a slight smile curled her lips, and she said when she was sure the girl had passed beyond earshot, "Convincing enough for you?"

Gisan, still wearing that black traveler's cloak, peered around the side of the tapestry wall, her eyes wide on the tent flaps that the girl had disappeared through.

CHAPTER 13

Teek did not sleep that night.

She sat huddled on that flat stone by the river. She was alone, and sat there all night. There was much to think about, too much to think about.

That familiar early morning glow illuminated the clouds over the east horizon and that began the stirring of that nervous crawl in her stomach. A whole night of thinking had resolved nothing, only the same conclusion that kept popping up in her mind: Vultross would kill her, and he would arrive just after sunup to do so.

She lowered her eyes to her hands, knowing that she feared the pain of her death more than her death itself. Perhaps it would be quick despite his threats.

So lost in her thoughts was she that she did not notice the approach of the white unicorn until a gentle whicker alerted her, and she looked over her shoulder into motherly blue eyes.

Shawri stared back and leaned her head. "Did you find the answers you sought?"

Teek looked to the horizon again and shook her head.

"Dosslar has taken Shahly and Relshee deep into the forest," the unicorn informed. "None of us wanted them anywhere close to the coming battle. I'll be joining them before this dragon arrives." She whickered a laughed. "I have no intention of sparring with him again, so I'll be waiting with the other mares. All of us wanted to extend an invitation to you to come with us."

Teek half turned at the waist, planting a hand behind her to steady herself as she looked with wide eyes.

A little smile touched the unicorn's mouth and she admitted, "I didn't think you would come with us. It is too much in you to face such adversity rather than hide from it. While I wish you would reconsider and come with me, I know you will not." She paced forward, closing the distance with only a few steps, and she nuzzled the girl's neck and whispered to her, "I hope you will take care, and trust that your destiny with this beast is not set. Be well, Teek, and I will see you again when this is at its end."

As the white unicorn turned and strode back down the path, Teek just sat there and watched her until she disappeared beyond the greenery. The mystic she had spoken to had made her destiny clear. The unicorn now brought that into question. She looked back to the treetops across the river and watched as that orange glow became brighter and brighter. A new resolve found her. If she was to die, she would die fighting like her father, like her mother.

She pushed herself up and brushed off her backside, then she spun around, her hair flailing as she stormed back toward the castle.

Her father still had one weapon that might be of use to her.

**

Most of the Elvan army was mobilized, armored and armed and standing in columns and square formations all over the western courtyard. Many of them on horseback lined the cobblestone road that led to the main gate, awaiting the order to turn and charge out. Archers and pikemen lined the walls, and all eyes there were on the skies. All were quiet and at attention as King Arlo, also in his highly polished battle armor with his sword at his side, inspected the troops about the middle of the formations. This fight would be decisive, and all knew that if the Dragonslayer should fail, it would fall to the elvan troops to swarm onto their enemy and kill him at all cost.

All eyes turned to the castle and a buzzing began as a small figure strode out of the palace.

Teek would not look to the troops that awaited Vultross. Her eyes were on the open gate. She wore her form fitting battle armor, commissioned for her by her father a season before his death. Shoulder plates were padded and gave the illusion of size to her, as did the plates worn on the outsides of her arms. The chest plate covered her ribs and was also padded, and accommodated all of the feminine parts of her, as did the back plate. Chain mail covered her midriff and plate her thighs and wrapped around the outsides of her legs. Greaves were strapped tightly over her boots and extended up over her knees. A thick leather belt was worn tightly around her waist and her sword hung on her left side, her dagger on the left, and that axe she had found was shoved into the belt in front of her dagger. A quiver hung from her shoulder, one with only two arrows in it, and her bow was held tightly in her left hand. Her long black hair flowed from behind and beneath the polished helmet that covered her head and the sides of her face, a helmet that had a metal ridge over the top for additional protection.

How she strode with purpose, how she carried her bow and wore her armor told all present that she did not intend to just give herself to the dragon. She intended to fight him to the death.

King Arlo turned that way as he saw her, and he hurried to the road to the gate to head her off.

When the Elf King stopped right in front of her, Teek stopped and looked up at him, defiance in her eyes as she stared back at him. Taking one step back, she bowed her head to him, then drew her sword and held the hilt at her waist and the blade across her body to the opposite shoulder, a salute to her king.

He set his hands on his hips and said, "I suppose trying to talk you out of this would be breath wasted."

She nodded.

"I won't even try, then," he assured. "Should things go badly for you and the Dragonslayer the army will charge forth and swarm him. Either way this ends today, even if he can channel the Heart of Abtont now. Every soldier not out looking for Gisan is ready for battle." He nodded to her. "We'll be ready, Teek Brebor. The kingdom is in your debt and we all rally to you." He stepped aside, clearing the way for her and ordered in as loud a voice as he could muster, "Present arms and salute!"

The whole army drew their weapons and turned toward the road, and in one voice over five thousand elves shouted, "To battle!"

Confidence surged into the little elf girl as the army cheered her as they had cheered her father in seasons past and she strode toward the gate, still not looking to them but one could see in her eyes how her resolve had strengthened.

With long, quick steps, she strode out of the castle gate and toward her destiny. Nobody else was in the field. The Dragonslayer and unicorn stallions were not to be found. She was sure they would show themselves, but for the moment she intended to face her enemy alone.

A distant roar alerted her and she looked to the trees to the southwest. Slowly, she reached over her shoulder, her hand finding the last of the crystal tipped arrows. Gisan had broken the shaft, but she had other arrows and one of them had been retipped with that crystal point. She hoped it would still work, was confident that it would, and it would be the first weapon that Vultross would face.

Expecting to see the black, winged form any second, her whole body tensed, and a whicker from behind made her draw a hushed start and spin around.

Vinton flinched back. He was half a pace behind her and staring at her with a familiar disapproving look. "Teek, what are you doing? You are supposed to be in the forest with the other mares."

Her lips drew to a thin slit and her brow lowered over her eyes, and defiantly she shook her head and held her bow at the ready in front of her.

With an annoyed snort, the stallion shook his head and grumbled, "You are even more stubborn and reckless than Shahly." His eyes shifted to her weapon and a ruby glow overtook his horn, and as the elf girl watched through wide eyes, he touched the tip of his horn to the arrowhead. With a bright flash, the point burst into bright red flames. "I've given the point some of my essence," the bay unicorn explained. "The spells in the arrowhead had weakened, but they've accepted my essence well and this should be much more powerful than it was."

Teek looked to the arrow, then she reached behind her for the second one and held it to him with her brow held hopefully high.

Whickering a laugh, Vinton shook his head and looked to the big iron point on this one, a point that looked as if it was forged to kill dragons and monsters. "There are spells on this one as well," he observed. Lowering the point of his horn once again, he touched it to the arrowhead with the same bright flash, but this point seemed to glow from within as if it was heated steel. "It looks hot," he informed, "but it will only burn dragons. I would use it first." Something serious took his eyes as he met hers. "If he has truly merged with the Heart of Abtont then my essence will be useless and these will not work. If that has happened I want you to get to safety, and don't fight me on this!"

Her eyes shifted away from him and that familiar annoyance and defiance was clear in them.

"I mean it, Teek. If we cannot stop him then I don't want you throwing yourself at him in futility."

Sir Rayce kicked his horse forward and from the protection of Dosslar's essence and suddenly became visible, suddenly made them both visible. He was fully armored as he had been before, but his face shield was up and his attention was skyward, over the trees to the southwest as he exclaimed, "Another dragon? We don't need this right now!"

All turned and looked that way as a scarlet winged form with an ocher breast and belly and wing webbing glided in toward them.

The knight drew his sword and it instantly burst into bright blue flames as he growled, "We'll need to make this quick!"

Vinton looked over his shoulder and calmly assured, "Just calm down. She's one of us."

At a hundred paces away, Falloah swept her wings forward and lowered her feet, settling to the ground almost noiselessly and trotting off the rest of her speed, folding her wings to her as her eyes found Vinton.

The stallion strode to the dragoness, looking up at her as he asked, "What are you doing here? And where is dung-head?"

Falloah drew her head back. "I came to see how you are all fairing here."

"We think the viper may have merged himself with the Heart of Abtont," Vinton reported. "If that has truly happened then he'll be a problem to deal with. We may need Ralligor's power to deal with him."

"Hence, I've come to check…" She craned her neck around, looking behind her with her jaws held slightly agape and the tips of her teeth showing.

Even before anyone heard the roar of the approaching viper dragon, Vinton ordered, "Falloah! Get behind us!"

The scarlet dragoness turned fully, lowering her brow as she countered, "It's a vipera. I'll not cower from one of his kind."

Vultross' black form soared over the treetops and his eyes found the dragoness immediately, and as he descended toward the ground his jaws swung open and he roared a challenge.

Falloah lowering her body almost parallel to the ground as she roared back at him, her tail thrashing over the heads of those behind her.

Sir Rayce steered his horse around the dragoness, grumbling, "So much for the element of surprise."

"Don't worry about it," Vinton ordered as he took the knight's side, watching the viper land a hundred paces away. "We only need to keep him on the ground this time.

Dosslar took the dragoness' other side, raising his head as his eyes locked on the emerald jewel that was set into the viper dragon's head behind and between his eyes. "Vinton, his forehead! He possesses the power of Heart of Abtont!"

"Not good," the bay grumbled.

Teek would not be dissuaded and stormed forward as the viper dragon advanced. Bow in hand, she readied the first arrow, the one with the big iron point that still glowed as if it was red hot, and she took careful aim as he stood and half spread his wings. Her brow was low over her eyes and she squinted slightly as he stood fully erect. He had advanced to about forty paces, way too close for the scarlet dragon who hissed and retreated a step, still holding her head low and her lips curled away from her teeth.

Vultross seemed a little too confident, but this was lost on a vengeful elf girl who adjusted her aim ever so slightly, and she loosed the arrow and willed her hate along with it.

It seemed to take forever to fly to him and he did not seem to notice as his attention was consumed by the scarlet dragoness before him, but when it struck it exploded with a terrible purpose and the sharp crack of lightning, followed by a thunderous boom. The dragon roared angrily and staggered back only two steps. When the fire and smoke cleared, it revealed him unmarked, uninjured.

Teek's eyes widened and she slowly lowered her bow.

Silence consumed the whole Elf Kingdom, the vast grassy field around it, and even the surrounding forest.

Vultross' eyes met the elf girl's and were brimming with confidence and conceit, and he seemed to be smiling.

As her enemy advanced on her again, she pulled the other arrow from the quiver, her last, and took aim at him, this time loosing it when he was only twenty paces away. The enchanted crystal tip exploded with all of the fury of the spells it contained and the power of the bay unicorn's essence, and the crack of the explosion was twice as loud, and the boom that followed shook the very air all around. A shockwave radiated outward and the dragon staggered back another step, but the smoke and fire cleared again to reveal the same results, and the dragon casually set himself to receive another.

With his sword hand, Sir Rayce reached up and lowered his face shield, announcing, "Stand aside, my friends. It is time this beast tasted *my* wrath." With a loud yell, he kicked his horse forward, swinging his sword to send the terrible power against the dragon, and at less than twenty paces he connected with all of his sword's fury.

The burst hit the dragon's chest as the arrows had, but the power of the blue flames simply shattered against his black armor and did not cause him harm. As the knight veered his horse to the side and made ready to strike again, the viper dragon retaliated with fire. Rayce expertly caught the fire on his shield and loosed his sword's power again, this time striking the dragon's side, but to no avail.

Vultross thrust a hand at the knight and a lime green light lanced from his palm and struck the knight's shield with horrible force, blasting the Dragonslayer from his saddle and toppling the horse.

Both unicorns charged forward, stopping halfway to the dragon as they directed their horns to him, and at the same time they loosed their essence toward him in brilliant red and light blue light that lanced forth and hit the dragon's side. He seemed to just absorb the essence and it was only enough to distract him.

Slowly, the dragon turned on the unicorns, a snarl on his mouth as he directed his full attention on them with a low brow and bared teeth.

Sir Rayce stirred and quickly reclaimed his wits, groped for his sword and finally had it in his hand as the viper advanced on the retreating unicorns. The blade exploded into those blue flames and he yelled a mighty challenge from where he sat and swung the sword to blast the dragon with his power again, and again his power shattered against the dragon.

Vultross lurched sideways, then wheeled around to face the knight who struggled to stand.

Nothing was working against him. Even unicorn essence failed to do more than irritate him.

Teek took the axe from her belt, then she turned her attention to the scarlet dragoness who lowered her body and charged the seemingly invulnerable viper.

She did not roar to announce herself and instead collided with him at a run, clamping her jaws shut around the middle of his slender neck. Even as she raked at him to tear open his armor and skin, he had enough of his neck free to turn his jaws on her, and he sank his fangs deep into her shoulder. Falloah cried out as the burn of the venom overwhelmed her with pain and she tried to retreat but only stumbled a couple of steps before he released her and struck again as she twisted away, this time connecting fully with her side. Falloah shrieked and bit back, but the venom was already taking its toll on her.

Vultross threw the dragoness from him and watched her collapse to the ground, and watched longer as she gasped for each breath, as her body was racked by tremors. His own neck and throat bled from many points where her teeth had penetrated him, but he did not seem bothered by it.

Teek hurled her axe at him with all her strength, aiming for his eye, but he moved ever so slightly to avoid it and turned fully on her. Drawing her sword, she was determined that her last stand would be one that would give the scarlet dragon a chance to escape or recover, or give someone the opportunity of a lucky strike that would bring this beast down.

Thrusting a hand at the elf, that lime green light lanced from his palm and she backpedaled barely out of the way. The burst hit the ground and exploded with enough force to throw the girl a man's height into the air and about five paces back where she slammed awkwardly onto the ground and rolled to a stop. She heard him growl, heard and felt his heavy footsteps and forced her wits to clear, forced herself up and struggled to stand and face him as he closed in on her.

Rayce struck again, and this time his power connected with the dragon's head.

With an angry roar, the viper dragon wheeled around and thrust his hand toward the knight. Once again, the Dragonslayer took the burst on his shield, but it was powerful enough to blow him from his feet and knock him about three paces backward where he hit the ground flat on his back, and the wind exploded from him. Dazed, he raised his head, then looked to his shield, through the smoking holes that peppered it. Turning his attention to the dragon, he knew that his enchanted shield would take perhaps one more burst like that before it was reduced to useless scrap, and he was not even sure it would stop the dragon's next attack completely.

And Vultross was moving in to kill him.

Vinton galloped to the dragon and rammed his horn into Vultross calf, and despite holding the power of the Heart of Abtont, the horn plunged through his hide and scales and sank about halfway in.

With a surprised screech, the viper dragon wheeled around and limped sideways and turned a half circle as he looked down to his leg to see what had gotten him. By that time the unicorn had charged away and folded his essence around himself and was concealed from view.

Though already horribly sick from the venom, Falloah sluggishly raised her head and looked to the viper. She realized that he was only about fifty paces away and well within range of her fire, and her eyes narrowed as she opened her jaws, squeezed her crop as hard as she could and loosed a hellish burst of flames at him, and she connected with neck and head.

Vultross shrieked and retreated from the dragoness as he turned away from the flames and stumbled away.

Sir Rayce took the opportunity to strike again, connecting with the dragon's belly but still not doing any damage. When the dragon turned on him, Falloah blasted him with fire again, drawing his attention back to her.

Opening his jaws, the viper dragon roared at her through bared teeth, and as the dragoness watched helplessly, he lowered his fangs and advanced on her with quick steps to deliver another venomous bite.

Teek drew her sword and ran toward him. Rayce hit him with another burst of fire and both unicorns charged.

And all of them stopped as Vultross' roar was answered by the deep, nightmarish roar of another dragon.

The viper wheeled to his right, to the south and as he retreated he roared a warning.

Ralligor turned hard as he descended and slammed into the ground only eighty paces away. He ran into his momentum, roaring loudly through bared teeth as his wings stroked backward and finally folded to his back and sides. Holding his body almost parallel to the ground, he charged his much smaller foe with a clear intent and opened his jaws to that end.

Vultross roared back as he retreated and he dodged aside and narrowly avoided the big black dragon's jaws which slammed shut half a pace from his head.

The Desert Lord pressed his attack, turning as sharply as his bulk would allow and lunging again with open jaws and bared teeth. When the viper spat venom, he finally veered away, but held his ground between the viper and the scarlet.

Vultross backed away a few more steps before he stopped. Now only thirty paces away from the bigger dragon, he faced an enemy that put doubt into him. Even with his new found power, he was hesitant to attack.

His eyes glowing red, Ralligor backed away a few steps, toward the injured scarlet dragoness, and a deep growl rolled from his throat as he lowered his body, stepped over her and finally stood over her. With his eyes still on the viper, he lowered a hand to his injured mate. An emerald glow sprayed from between his fingers and in seconds completely enveloped her.

The viper dragon watched curiously as the glow covered the scarlet, then retreated back into the black dragon's hand.

It faded from her and she was healed and cured of the venom and strength surged back into her.

As the scarlet dragoness raised her head, the Desert Lord strode toward his smaller foe with slow, heavy steps, and another growl rumbled from his throat. Clearly, injuring his mate had made this a personal issue, and it was time to settle.

Vultross retreated again, his eyes locked wide on his big, advancing enemy. He half opened his jaws and hissed, curling his lips away from his sharp, slender teeth.

The rest of the combatants backed away as they watched the two black dragons size each other up once again and the whole Kingdom watched from wherever they could. The assembled troops slowly filed out of the gate, spreading out along the wall to watch what they hoped would be an epic battle.

Vultross' confidence was shaken, but he knew he was too close to what he wanted to withdraw again. His eyes narrowed, his brow lowered as he crouched slightly and he held his hands ready with his claws curled and ready for combat. His slow retreat stopped and his dorsal scales stood erect from between his eyes to the end of his long, thrashing tail.

Ralligor stood, half opening his wings as he towered over the smaller dragon who was ready for him only thirty paces away. His jaws swung open and he roared an ear splitting roar, a challenge to deadly battle.

The viper dragon thrust both his hands at his foe and lime green light lanced from both palms.

The burst impacted the Desert Lord's chest with enough force to knock him from his feet and forty paces to the castle wall where he slammed back first into the unyielding stone. Stunned, the black dragon crumpled to the ground. His head struck the ground last, landing flat on his jaw and he lay there for long seconds as his wits slowly returned to him.

Sir Rayce struck with his sword again, and when the dragon turned on him Dosslar struck from somewhere to his left, drawing him that way.

Ralligor slowly opened his eyes, growling deeply as he blinked to bring his world back into focus. To his annoyance, the first thing he saw was the big bay unicorn standing right in front of him. With an irritated grunt, he raised his head slightly and said, "You could have told me he could do that."

"I could have," the unicorn admitted, "but you finding out this way was much more amusing."

"Get fleas and die," the black dragon snarled. With a groaning growl, he pushed himself up to all fours, and he turned an angry look to the viper dragon who seemed to struggle to focus on one opponent.

"Can you defeat him?" Vinton asked hopefully.

"He's awfully powerful," Ralligor grumbled.

"Surely you can match his power," the unicorn insisted.

"He's channeling the Heart of Abtont, Plow Mule. I have to find a way past that to get at him."

"Just merge with the Heart!" Vinton barked as he watched the dragon stand. "That may be the only way!"

"You're talking madness," Ralligor growled. "He already has the Heart of Abtont."

Vinton drew his head back and watched in clear bewilderment as the dragon strode by him to resume the battle. "What do you mean he has the Heart? That doesn't make sense!"

Ralligor strode to within about thirty paces of the viper and barked a short roar at him, and when his foe turned he raised his hand and blasted his smaller foe with an emerald burst of his own. Vultross instinctively raised his hands before him and the Heart of Abtont responded and met the black dragon's attack with a lime green wall before the viper's arms, stopping it in a brilliant flash of white light.

This surprised the black dragon and he raised his head slightly, watching as the viper lowered his arms. Another growl rolled from the Desert Lord's throat as he balled his hands into tight fists. An emerald light that grew brighter in his eyes burst into emerald colored flames and as he opened his fingers his claws also were engulfed in emerald flames. Clouds rolled in unnaturally fast from somewhere behind the castle and began to fill the sky, darkening the forest and kingdom as they blocked out the sun.

All eyes went skyward as thunder began to roll through the sky, and even Vultross cringed as lightning flashed, lancing from the clouds that built over the castle to those that began to boil up seemingly out of thin air over the forest. Wind began to swirl around the entire field, laying over grass and causing the trees to sway and creak.

With his teeth bared, Ralligor snarled, "Let's see how you fair against the forces of nature itself." He thrust a hand at the viper and the clouds responded with lightning that lanced down to strike the viper dragon many times in ear splitting cracks before he could respond.

The barrage was over in seconds. Vultross' body just absorbed the lightning and he simply stood there and looked as bewildered as everyone else did.

The glow in the Desert Lord's eyes faded and he grumbled, "Well this can't be good."

Vinton watched another lime green burst slam into Ralligor and he danced aside as he watched the big dragon slam into the castle wall again. As the black dragon collapsed much as he had before, Vinton cantered to his head and stared down at him, and he almost seemed to have amusement in his eyes.

Ralligor snorted and pushed himself up, turning furious eyes to the black viper as the Dragonslayer and other unicorn engaged him to draw his attention. He looked down to the bay unicorn and snarled at him, grumbling, "I assume you are still enjoying this."

With a shrug, Vinton admitted, "Well, of course I am, but sooner or later you are going to—"

"I don't need combat advice from a grazer," the black dragon interrupted as he stood. "He has the Heart of Abtont but he does not have a clear understanding of how to use it."

"Looks to me like he understands how to use it just fine," the bay unicorn countered. "You need to understand that the only way to fight the power of the Heart of Abtont is to merge with it."

"I'll take that under advisement," the dragon growled as he strode with heavy steps toward his foe again.

Vinton watched the third round of this battle take place as the Desert Lord struck with his own power again. Bright flashes of emerald green light enveloped the unicorn and all around him as the cracks and booms of discharging power reached him, then again. The lime green light flashed, the blinding blue-white burst of lightning with sharp cracks that split the air all around, and in a bright flash of lime green light and a loud bang, the unicorn sidestepped and turned as the Desert Lord was hurled into the wall a third time. Once the dragon had settled to the ground, the unicorn cantered to him again and asked, "Are you ready for that advice you don't need yet?"

"Merge with the Heart," Ralligor grumbled. He pushed himself up a little slower this time, his eyes finding his enemy again. "You still haven't told me how I'm supposed to do that when he has the Heart and is currently using it."

"He doesn't have the Heart!" Vinton whinnied. "Don't you understand? *Nobody* can have the Heart!"

"He was given the Heart!" the dragon roared as he looked to his foe again, watching as the viper turned to face the knight who had attacked him from behind.

"He can't be given the Heart," the bay stallion insisted, "he can only give himself *to* the heart. Don't you understand? He may wield the power of the Heart, but he cannot possess it."

"Would you make sense?" Ralligor growled.

"I am making perfect sense! He was only given the means to channel the Heart, but he has not merged with it!"

The Desert Lord finally turned his eyes down to the unicorn and demanded, "Then where is the Heart?"

"You're here!" Vinton shouted.

Ralligor drew his head back, his eyes locked on the stallion for long seconds. He glanced about, then turned and looked to the castle, his eyes fixing on the stone that was formed from beneath the ground, and the words of the ancient dragon returned to him. "Too small to be seen," he said absently, "or too vast. The Heart of Abtont is not an object at all, not like..." He closed the distance to the castle wall with two slow strides, reaching out to touch the stone, and as he did the entire castle, every stone that made it up, began to glow with an emerald light from within.

Vinton backed away, raising his head as he almost smiled. "You finally seem to understand," he observed. "You finally know the Heart of Abtont."

Teek took the stallion's side, also staring up at the dragon as he raised his other hand to place onto the glowing stone of the castle wall. She looked over her shoulder as she heard Vultross roar and saw him facing away from her, looking around him as if trying to find something, someone. His attention was easily taken and this was working to their advantage, though it was only a matter of time before he would turn back on the Desert Lord to finish off this greatest threat to him.

Looking back to the big black dragon, she saw him press his hands against the castle wall. Her eyes widened as ripples radiated out along the stone as if it had turned to liquid. As he pressed his hands harder, they penetrated into the stone, and he hesitantly took a step toward the wall, then into it!

Slowly shaking her head, she backed away a step as the dragon disappeared into the castle wall of the Elf Kingdom.

The glow about the stone that made up the castle slowly dimmed until all that remained was the stone, and the dragon was gone.

"I did not expect that," Vinton admitted grimly. Looking to Teek, he ordered, "Go into the castle and tell King Arlo not to advance on the viper. Keep the elves inside the safety of the castle walls. Vultross cannot bring them harm so long as the castle protects them. And get Falloah to go in there with you. Go!"

She watched, feeling dismayed, disheartened as the big unicorn charged toward the viper dragon again. She turned and saw the scarlet dragoness staring at that spot that Ralligor had entered, the last place he had been seen, and the dragoness' eyes were wide with shock and filling with tears as her jaws parted slowly.

Teek dared to stride up to the scarlet dragon and waved her arms to draw her attention, but Falloah could not be distracted. A silence on the battlefield was like a beacon and the elf girl looked that way, seeing Vultross staring at the castle. He looked confused and no longer interested in the knight and unicorns who by now had backed away from him.

The viper dragon slowly lowered his head, his eyes fixed on the last place he had seen the bigger dragon. He glanced about, then up to the higher parts of the castle, the towers and turrets. A smug, self satisfied expression took his features and he almost seemed to smile, and ominously, he turned his attention to the scarlet dragoness, the only other dragon on the battlefield.

Slowly, Falloah's eyes slid to the viper, and she hesitantly turned toward him.

His brow lowered and his lips slid away from his teeth.

Falloah took a step back, realizing that she was now under the viper dragon's full attention, and Ralligor was not on his way to aid her.

There was a pulse, a low vibration through the air and ground as the entire castle lit up with that emerald light as it had before, brightest from between the seams between stones, small fissures and cracks. It seemed at long last the castle of the Elf Kingdom had returned to life. The light intensified and a low rumble caused tremors to radiate from its very foundation and along the ground in every direction. Ripples formed in the stone right where Ralligor had entered, making the wall look like it had transformed into liquid and the light that emanated from the castle pulsed a little brighter.

A thump was heard from the castle, like a huge foot fall, then another. Falloah and Teek backed away.

Ripples radiated from that point in the wall again, then the stone seemed to boil, and from within that boiling stone a brighter light shined, one that was eclipsed by a shadow from within. The boiling stone parted as the shadow drew closer.

Ralligor emerged from the boiling stone of the castle with slow, purposeful steps. He held his head down, his eyes half closed and his arms just dangled. With his body also low, his tail dragging the ground and his shoulders slouched, he looked drained as he simply walked from the wall and finally stopped thirty paces from the castle.

Slowly, the stone of the castle went dark.

All eyes were fixed on the black dragon as he just stood there, hunched over and staring at the ground before him.

Teek leaned her head, squinting slightly as she looked to the black dragon's head. There was a glint of light, some kind of flash from his head. She trotted toward him to get a better look, veering toward the front of him, and she stopped suddenly as she saw the glint again when his head moved ever so slightly.

There, imbedded in his forehead between the brows of his eyes was an emerald jewel that looked to be the diameter of her head. A smaller one was just down from it, and both glistened in the sunlight.

Ralligor's eyes slid to the elf girl and he wore no recognizable expression.

Staring back up at him, she did not know what to think or feel. He had returned from the Heart of Abtont, and something was vastly different about him.

The frustrated roar of the viper dragon drew the Desert Lord's attention and he fixed his eyes on his smaller foe, and his brow slowly lowered over them. Slowly raising his head, his lips drew away from his teeth, and before the dragon could find his next target and strike, Ralligor opened his jaws and roared a mighty challenge.

Vultross swung around and found the big dragon standing only twenty paces from the castle, and he found himself under his full attention. Still, he had felled him three times and was confident that a fourth would not be a problem. With a snarl on his snout, he thrust his hands at the Desert Lord and sent yet another burst of that lime green light at him, connecting solidly as he had before. Both beams hit the black dragon's chest with ripples of green light radiating outward, and this time he simply absorbed them.

A tense, silent moment hushed the entire kingdom and the surrounding forest.

Wide eyed, the viper dragon tried again, pouring everything he had into the attack that he sent at his foe, and when the big dragon simply absorbed it as he had before, he took a step back, his jaws falling open as he stared dumbly at the bigger dragon.

Just staring back, Ralligor raised a brow slightly.

Vultross lowered his body, keeping his eyes locked on his big opponent as he tried to figure out what to do next.

The black dragon's eyes narrowed as he began to slowly stride toward the smaller dragon with steps that sounded heavy on the ground.

Cooing nervously, the viper backed away, and he thrust his hands and sent another burst of that lime green light at his advancing enemy, a burst that was simply absorbed as the others had been.

"You have little understanding of that power," Ralligor informed. "Allow me to enlighten you." His eyes flashed emerald, and when they did, an emerald blast hit the viper from seemingly nowhere and blew him from his feet and halfway across the clearing.

Vultross landed awkwardly and rolled to a stop, quickly pushing himself back up and looking toward the big dragon that continued to stalk toward him like some prehistoric monster from long ago. It was clear to him that even with the power he had, there was no way he could hope to match the Desert Lord. There was a nervousness to the growl that escaped him as he opened his wings and ran toward the south, stroking them hard to fill them with the wind and get himself airborne.

Ralligor watched his smaller foe take flight to escape once again and he snarled, "Not this time." That emerald glow overtook his eyes and the jewels that were imbedded in his head and he raised a hand to the departing viper, then he closed his fingers and thrust that hand sideways, toward the castle.

Vultross shrieked as some unseen force grabbed onto him and stopped him in mid flight, then he was hurled into the castle wall where he hit with brutal force and bounced back about ten paces, coming to rest on the muddy field.

Turning fully, the black dragon strode toward the stunned viper, walking almost casually as the smaller dragon struggled to get his wits about him and stagger to his feet. "Well, now," Ralligor started as he closed to within twenty paces and stopped. "It would seem that the advantage you were given is not so great after all." That emerald glow overtook his eyes, and this time it also enveloped the viper. There, on the viper's chest, he could see the shape of a stone in his crop among all of the others that were used to grind down brimstone to enable him to breathe fire. "Perfect hiding place," he observed as he slowly raised his hand to the smaller dragon again.

Throwing his head back, Vultross roared toward the sky as he was enveloped in an emerald green fire, and as he staggered back toward the wall, a lime green light spat from his chest and something enveloped in the same light green light erupted from him at great speed and flew toward the Desert Lord.

The stone given to the viper by Gisan slammed into the black dragon's hand, and in that instant the fire enveloping the viper ceased. Turning his palm up, Ralligor looked down to the stone that lay harmlessly in his hand, and he leaned his head. When he turned his eyes to his bewildered foe, he found a dragon that held a hand over his chest, though there was no wound to be found there. The stone was simply no longer within him.

"So this is what's causing all of my grief," Ralligor grumbled. "Looks like an original stone from the formation of the castle, from its very foundation. That's how you were able to channel the Heart of Abtont. That's why you had such little understanding of its power." He tossed the stone toward the castle and it hit the wall and plunged into it, producing ripples in the stone as if it had gone into water. Taking a step forward, Ralligor bared his sword sized teeth and declared, "Now we can fight as dragons, vipera."

Vultross sank to all fours and raised his nose, cooing submissively as the big black dragon neared.

Leedon shouted down from the castle wall, "This is a perfect time to apply the teachings of the Heart of Abtont!"

Ralligor stopped and looked up at him, his brow lowering somewhat between his eyes as he declared, "There you are! Why weren't you down here in the fray with the rest of us?"

Standing among elvan archers and pikemen, the old wizard smiled as he leaned on the stone of the battlement and shook his head. "I am no warrior, Mighty Friend, I am but a teacher, and the power I wield would have been as useless as any other against the Heart of Abtont. Besides, the Heart is protection and wisdom and knowledge and was never meant for such nonsense as warfare. That is why the castle itself did not strike out against the viper before you."

"It also did not protect the elves," Ralligor pointed out.

"It surely did," the old wizard corrected. "Every elf within its walls had its protection, but not those who ventured without. The elves, like so many before them, have lost touch with the ancient power of their ancestors, but it is not lost. Their heritage remains strong and awaits rediscovery."

The black dragon looked to the viper that cringed at his feet. "Okay, so what do we do with him? I'm all for killing him."

Vultross crooned again and lowered his head nearly to the ground.

"There is a truth within you, Ralligor," Leedon informed, "one that will answer your question in ways you'd never imagined before.

The Desert Lord stared down at the defeated, cringing serpentine dragon for a long moment as he pondered what to do with him. Turning to look behind and slightly beside him, he noticed Teek standing there with her gaze locked on the viper. When she looked up at him, Ralligor asked, "There are worse fates than death, aren't there?"

She stared up at the big black dragon for long seconds, and finally she nodded.

There was something mischievous about the black dragon's eyes as he looked back down to the viper, and he stood fully and folded his arms, looming over his vanquished foe as he said, "I agree. I won't kill you today, Vultross, but tomorrow I will hunt you, and I will hunt you every day, search for you every day, and on the day I find you we'll see just how many pieces of you I can tear from your body before you die."

The viper, now almost flat on his belly, slithered and scurried backward toward the castle wall until the wall itself stopped him.

"I'll sense you no matter where you are," Ralligor continued, "no matter how far you run or where you go, I'll know where to find you. My hunt begins at sunup tomorrow, so you'll have an ample head start."

Vultross nodded.

Ralligor stared down at him for a moment, then informed, "That was your cue to leave." He bared his teeth and added, "As fast as you can!"

With a frightened shriek, the viper dragon scurried on his belly past the big black dragon, then he stood to all fours to run faster, opened his wings, and took to the sky with all haste.

Ralligor watched him until he flew out of sight, then he grunted and looked down to the elf girl with narrow eyes. "He'll spend the rest of his days looking over his shoulder, looking behind him, and looking into every shadow. From today forward he'll know only fear and any power he thought he had over another will be gone. His nightmare begins today." His eyes swept the elves who looked on anxiously and he announced, "The Elf Kingdom is free."

All at once, the entire Elf Kingdom exploded into cheers and shouts of joy. Their season long nightmare was finally over and all of the elves of the kingdom celebrated the hard fought victory of their newest hero.

As her people cheered the Desert Lord, a defeated heaviness took her heart and she slipped away once again to seek solitude. It was time to visit someone.

CHAPTER 14

A festival was at hand, one that was long overdue. The celebration had begun shortly after the viper dragon's withdrawl and even the unicorns enjoyed themselves among the many thousands of elves who reveled in their new found freedom, a freedom from the dragon that had plagued them for over a season.

A shrine was what she sought, one that was built of stone and carved by the skill of the gnomes who called the Elf Kingdom home. Two busts were there, one of Leumas and the other of his wife Werhess. Their family crest was between the busts and the name Brebor right over it. Below the crest were the words *Of elvan heroes, remember the greatest of those who gave their lives to defend the Elf Kingdom.*

Teek did not know how long she stood in front of the shrine to her parents. The sounds of the celebration were all around her and seemingly very distant, but she paid them no mind. Her people had been freed, but her heart remained very heavy, a burden within her.

She sank to her knees, looking up at the well made white marble carving of her father's face. Tears rolled freely from her eyes as she stared up at him, at all that was left of him. She was ashamed, and did not feel worthy of her name, her heritage. Bowing her head, she thought to him, *I'm sorry, Papa. I'm sorry. I meant to be a great hero like you, but I'm... I couldn't do it. I am too small and weak and despite everything you taught me I could not save our people. Please forgive me.*

"I think he would be proud of you," Shawri corrected from behind the elf girl.

Wiping the tears from her eyes, Teek slowly raised her head and looked back up at her father's bust, and slowly she shook her head.

"You saved your people," the unicorn insisted.

The Desert Lord saved my people, the elf girl corrected. *Sir Rayce, that wizard... You and the other unicorns. Nothing I did made any difference. I failed everyone.*

"Would all of those involved even known of the plight of the Elf Kingdom but for you?" Shawri asked.

Teek looked to the ground in front of her. *I fought that dragon as best I could. I was nothing to him, even with my father's enchanted weapons I was nothing. I could not do it.*

"Did your father fight alone every time?" the unicorn asked as she paced noiselessly toward the girl. "I've heard the stories people tell about him. He was a man of great courage, but also great wisdom, and he knew when he needed help. You could have run from this, Teek. You could have hidden from him or you could have allowed that dragon to kill you and that would have been the end of it all. You did not. Like it or not, you brought us here to help your people. This was all your doing."

Teek finally looked over her shoulder to the unicorn who was now only a pace behind her.

"Nobody expected you to prevail against such a beast," Shawri continued. "I would say that any adversary you would face that is your own size or even twice as big would have their hands full dealing with you. I fought him and lost. Rayce tried, Falloah… We are all much larger than you and in our own ways more powerful, and once he had the Heart of Abtont with him then even the Desert Lord had difficulty with him. You brought us all together to defeat this threat to your people."

The elf girl just stared back for long seconds, then she looked back to the shrine and thought, *It just isn't the same.*

Shawri took two more steps toward the girl and butted her shoulder with her nose. "Did you do all of this to save your people or to be a hero to them?"

The words penetrated the girl, stung, and made her feel even worse. Tears welled up in her eyes again and she bowed her head. *I wanted Papa and King Arlo to be proud of me. I wanted to get even for the deaths of my parents, for Wazend's death. I wanted revenge.* She wiped away a tear that rolled down her cheek. *I wanted to be the hero my father was.*

"Then be that hero now," Shawri insisted.

Teek looked back at her, then her eyes shifted to Sir Rayce who stood beside the unicorn with a pitcher of ale in his hand.

A little smile touched the knight's lips and he said, "Been looking for you, Lass. There's a celebration to be had." When her eyes turned down and she looked back to the shrine, he also looked to it, taking a drink before he spoke again. "I never had the honor of meeting him, but I've sure been hearing about him. He's a bit of a legend in these parts, and I can see where you might pick up that torch." He took another drink, keeping his gaze fixed on the bust of Leumas. "Wish I'd known him. Sounds like a fellow that I could trade stories with over a few mugs of ale."

Drawing a deep breath, Teek finally stood and turned to the knight, pointing to him, then she touched her temples and moved her hands evenly away from her head before turning to point at the bust of her father.

A smile touched Rayce's face. "I remind you of him?" When she nodded, he nodded back. "That is something I can only take as a great compliment, lass." Something more serious hardened his features and he advised, "Don't let bitterness and mourning take hold on you as I did. I'm no hero, Teek, just a soldier of fortune with a score to settle." His eyes found the bust of her father again and he went on, "A dragon attacked my village many, many seasons ago. Everyone fled to the village meeting hall and..." His gaze turned down to his mug. "I was off at the castle serving a king who was indifferent to those he considered beneath him. The dragon killed my whole family, most of my comrades... Almost everyone in the village died. I wasn't there to protect them, or my family."

Shawri turned fully and butted him in the chest with her nose. "You've carried that heavy heart for so long, Rayce, and still you would use your burden to help another. That is a quality that any unicorn would hold in high esteem."

He forced a smile and softly offered, "Thank you, Lady Unicorn." His eyes turned to Teek and he advised, "If you'd be a hero, then you'd better learn how. A hero is not necessarily one who would win all of the battles against all of his foes. A hero is most often one who can serve better as a rallying point, that point of light that would give his people hope. Or her people."

Teek's eyes locked on his and she heard his words, and felt them all the way to her heart.

Rayce closed the distance between them with two steps and took her little shoulder. "Teek Brebor, it is time your people saw their hero, the very one who would bring the downfall of the viper dragon, even if her own weapons did not vanquish him." He smiled and offered her a nod. "Come along, warrior. I've told my own stories enough. Time to tell yours."

The elf girl turned hopeless eyes to the unicorn and thought to her, *But I didn't do anything.*

Shawri smiled and shook her head. "You brought together unicorns and a human Dragonslayer and dragons and united your people against this threat. That is an undertaking that none of your people were able to do. Are great tasks not the mark of a hero?"

Teek considered, then looked up to the knight.

"A hero is known more for his deeds than the monsters and enemies he can smite down with enchanted weapons, Lass. Your people see this. It is time you allowed them to rally around you as a hero should."

Reluctantly, she allowed them to lead her back to the Western courtyard where most of the Kingdom was celebrating. They got there to find the gates still open, and just beyond them she could see part of the big black dragon lying on his belly. That was a dragon she was anxious to see again and she quickened her pace ahead of the knight and unicorn, her eyes on him as she was seemingly oblivious to everything around her, until the crowd of thousands of elves exploded into cheers and shouts when they saw her, and she paused and looked about as the deafening accolades shook her to her core.

Teek looked nervously about her, surprise on her young features as elves all around her cheered for her, shouted to her, and all waved. She turned as Shawri nudged her shoulder, and she found the unicorn smiling at her.

"As I said," Shawri reminded, "you are no less a hero for bringing us here. Your best weapons were your abilities to communicate, and especially your ability to win the hearts of those around you."

Her mouth tightening, a little smile curled the elf girl's lips.

King Arlo found his way to her, and for the first time he celebrated without a drink in his hand. Taking her still armored shoulder, he could only smile and he offered her a nod.

The other unicorns also found their way to her and did not seem to be bothered by the deafening cheers and accolades that roared from all around them. This was a proud moment for them and they would relish it.

Her eyes found the black dragon again, and found him staring down at her.

"You have a celebration to attend to," Ralligor informed. "I'm going home before that castle swallows me again." He winked. "I have this merging with the Heart of Abtont to come to grips with." He pushed himself up and stood, looking toward the castle and the crowds that gathered around them, and with a mighty roar, he silenced them. His eyes sweeping the elves, a growl rolled from his throat and he informed, "I'll be back before winter to discuss a few matters with you. In the meantime, I believe you have those in your midst you would like to thank for disrupting my life and bringing me here." His attention found Teek again and he snarled. "See if you can keep watch on your people on your own. I'll come again if I have to, but I'd rather not be disturbed again." He reached to her and touched her chest ever so slightly with the tip of his claw.

An emerald light flashed from that point where he touched her high on her chest and two strings of light snaked their way upward and met behind her neck. When he removed his claw she looked down to see a golden amulet in the shape of a dragon's talons and holding a perfect emerald sphere dangling from a gold chain, and she hesitantly reached to it. Amazement in her eyes, she looked to Shahly, realizing that the same amulet hung from her neck, and when the unicorn smiled at her, she smiled back and looked back up to the dragon, touched her lips, then extended her hand to him.

"You're welcome," he replied. "Don't waste your life living in this moment. Use that life in the service of the elves."

"As your father did," Vinton added.

Leedon appeared behind her and patted the armor of her shoulder, and he smiled when her attention turned up to him. "Get out of that battle armor, dearest Teek. You should be comfortable for the celebration in your honor." He looked up to the black dragon and shouted up to him, "I'll be staying on for a few days, Mighty Friend." Turning to the Elf King, he raised his brow and added, "With your permission, of course, King Arlo."

Arlo laughed a jolly laugh and reached up to slap the wizard's shoulder. "Permission? You know you are always welcome here, my friend!" He looked around him, his eyes meeting those of the unicorns, then to Sir Rayce. "You are all welcome!"

Cheers erupted from the elves anew.

Shahly stepped toward the elf girl and bumped her with her nose, ordering, "Come on. You need to get changed, then we will celebrate."

Ralligor growled, "I'll be leaving now." His eyes narrowed as he looked to Teek again and he pointed a clawed finger at her, snarling, "Stay out of trouble."

Teek watched as the black and scarlet dragons took flight and she waved to them as they disappeared over the horizon. In the company of the unicorns, she finally felt that a new and brighter chapter had opened in her life. Closing her eyes, she bowed her head and thought to her father, *I'll make you proud of me, Papa. I'll make you proud of me.*

CHAPTER 15

Madame Miscree stared blankly at the violet glowing pyramid in the center of her table, and there was a strain behind her eyes as she whispered, "But I did all I was instructed. Is there no other way?"

A surge of light was the answer, then the violet light faded quickly from the pyramid, leaving just the crystal and the lights it reflected from the candles. Her eyes stayed on it as she heard the flap to her tent open and she just sat silent and unmoving as the hooded figure sat down in the chair across from her.

Gisan pushed the hood from her head and locked her gaze on the fortune teller. Her eyes were hollow, her skin pale from strain and no sleep and her hands shook in uncontrollable tremors. She cleared her throat and hissed, "We've a bigger problem." She sounded like she could not muster her voice.

"I know we do," Miscree confirmed. Her eyes finally shifted to the councilwoman with a blink and she raised her chin ever so slightly. "It would seem you have failed in your given task."

"It was that little girl," Gisan snarled. "But for her we would be in control of the Elf Kingdom! She must be dealt with."

"Agreed," the fortune teller said in a wisp of a voice. Finally pushing herself up, she ordered, "Wait here," then she turned and strode around the tapestries that divided her tent.

Watching nervously, Gisan could hear her rummaging around back there, and when she saw the colorful soothsayer return with a long, thin dagger, she slowly stood, her wide eyes locked on the weapon.

Miscree reached her and hissed, "This will attend to our problems and cover our tracks. No one will ever know nor suspect what has really transpired here." She turned it in her hands and offered Gisan the hilt. "Take it tightly in your hands."

Though hesitant, Gisan did as she was instructed, looking down at her hands as they tightly wrapped around the hilt of the dagger, then she looked to the fortuneteller's eyes as if looking for approval. "Like this?"

Nodding, Miscree confirmed, "Like this." She wrapped her own hands tightly around Gisan's and met the other woman's eyes. "With this weapon and my help, you'll end our involvement in this matter."

"And the little girl's life?" Gisan asked hopefully.

With a wicked smile, Miscree corrected, "Not hers." She pulled the dagger and councilwoman to her with all her might, plunging the sharp blade into her chest. Her eyes flared wide, her mouth opening as fully as it could, and as Gisan looked on in horror, the fortune teller screamed with all of the horrible intent of an attacking mountain cat. With her last bit of strength she pushed Gisan away from her and allowed the blood from her ruptured heart to spray onto the councilwoman, then she fell to the planks of the tent floor with a loud thump.

Her eyes still locked wide on the soothsayer as her blood poured from her and she took her last breaths, Gisan slowly shook her head. Her attention whipped to the tent flaps as several elves and a palace guard brushed them aside and entered only a few paces, and their attention went from the dead fortune teller to the fugitive councilwoman who still held the long dagger.

Gisan glanced about at them, down to the dagger she still held and she winced and dropped it. Backing away, she looked to the growing number of people in the tent, and shook her head in quick, terrified movements.

CHAPTER 16

Good to her unspoken word, Teek would not remain at the Elf Kingdom. After the five day celebration, things around the castle began to return to normal, a quiet routine resumed and she took her leave of the King and Elvan Council to seek her destiny among the elves who lived elsewhere.

Elvan villages were not easy for any but elves to find, but one that lay a little over ten leagues northwest of the castle was known to all elves. This was a thriving community, though at times it was one that did not know if it wanted to remain as a part of the Elf Kingdom proper. Farms surrounded it, plantations of nut and fruit trees and the village served the needs of the gnomes who mined jewels and metals from hidden places beneath the forest and in the green covered, rocky hills that surrounded the village.

The journey to this village took Teek ten days as she was in no hurry and traveling with her unicorn friends and Sir Rayce. The unicorns had parted ways with her seven days into her trek to take the knight to a castle in Northern Abtont that they knew. With her assurance that she would make her way that direction before winter, she bade farewell to her new friends and traveled alone after that, camping in the deep of the forest as she was accustomed to, but traveling alone to collect her thoughts was, well, lonely.

With evening falling and her traveler's cloak over her shoulders and the hood over her head, she guided her pony down the main road that led into and through the village, which was only about a half a league in any direction from its center, and did not make eye contact with those who paused to stare at the small, strange traveler who visited.

Hoping to find a room where she could spend a night or two and maybe get a bath, she stopped her pony with many others in front of what appeared to be the only tavern in the village, one made of stone that was covered with vines. It was one of the larger structures in town, two stories and had a big doorway flanked by big windows that had the shutters open. The top level had many windows which told her that there was lodging to be found here. Weary from her journey, she tied her pony among the others, took her pack and her bow and quiver from the saddle and strode toward the door.

Entering, she found it rather busy inside and paused to scan the spacious room where many patrons sat at many wooden tables, and she was barely noticed as she negotiated her way through the tables and found one near the back of the tavern. A long bar was to her left where those who waited the tables picked up food and drink for those who had come to eat, drink, and share stories. The small table she selected had only two chairs and she took one and put her pack in the other, hanging her bow over the back of it before she sat down in the other.

She just stared at the table for a moment as she awaited someone to come and ask her what she wanted, then her eyes shifted to the bow. The buzzing of many conversations reached her, but one caught her ear, a conversation at the next table, a larger table that was surrounded by four elf men and two women, and they all seemed excited about what one rather plump elf in the overalls and boots of a farmer was saying.

"I'm telling you," he insisted, "the whole Elvan army could not repel this thing for more than a season. Killed and ate Leumas Brebor himself, him and his wife, and nothin' could stop it. Got a stone from the Heart of Abtont and that gave it unlimited power from the Heart itself. They thought nothin' could bring it down."

A woman added, "I heard that what brought it down was the child of Brebor, a daughter he trained since her birth."

"She didn't just smite the beast down," the first man insisted. "She took on a quest to find those of great power, came back to the Elf Kingdom with a human Dragonslayer, she did. Even convinced the Desert Lord himself to awaken from his long slumber to come and fight the thing. Came back with the favor of unicorns, a whole herd of them! Hundreds of them!"

Teek's eyes slid that way, her brow arched as she listened on in disbelief.

"She knew she couldn't bring it down by herself, so she brought in all manner of wizards and dragons and unicorns to fight at her side. She united enemies and convinced them to fight at her side. Took the battlefield at dawn and led the fight against it. It's said that when the Desert Lord himself was felled, well she took him to the castle and helped him merge with the Heart of Abtont to heal him. In his gratitude he took the power of the Heart and turned it on the beast that would see all elves dead. At her side he helped to bring it down, he did, and it is said she commanded an army of unicorns to stand watch over the castle should another such dragon come to bring our people down."

Shaking his head, another man, a thinner elf with graying hair who sat on the opposite side of the table, clutching a mug of ale, said almost proudly, "That Leumas. Raised himself something of a spitfire, he did.

That serpent dragon knew not who he was tangling with."

Teek smiled and shook her head as she looked down to her table. She had not expected the exaggeration of such tales to happen so quickly and enjoyed a hushed laugh over it.

"Hasn't a voice, I hear," another informed. "Talks with gestures, with her hands, and I hear she can look ye in the eye and you'll know what she says in her gaze. That's how she persuaded the Desert Lord himself to come to our aid at the castle. Hell, I hear unicorns sought her favor while she journeyed to find him."

They could not hear, but Teek covered her mouth and giggled a hushed giggle.

"Lost our greatest hero," the first elf observed, "but he's left us with one who will fight with her wits as he did. He's maybe left us with one as great as him."

"I'd buy her a glass of wine," the woman assured, "Ale, if she'd prefer."

"I heard she was in the village," the man with the cup of ale said, "came in secret. Heard tell she's on her next quest for King Arlo. Think she'd help us against the goblins that plague us from time to time?"

Teek's eyes slid that way again.

"We'd have to find her first," the first elf informed grimly. "Besides, how would she lead us against a hundred of them elf eating goblins? We have numbers, but they're goblins! The castle wouldn't even send us troops to send against 'em."

"The moon's right for 'em tonight," the elf woman observed. "I'd not want to be outside after dark on this night or the next. They'll be about for sure and lookin' to make off with whoever is foolish enough to be found outside."

The elf man who still clutched his cup of ale turned and looked outside, shaking his head as he grumbled, "Almost dark now, and with a chill finding the air at night, they'll be in the village for sure tonight."

Looking fully that way, Teek finally stood and took her bow and quiver from the back of the chair as she strode by, hanging her quiver over her shoulder.

Someone on the other side of the table saw her, and his eyes widened, his mouth dropping open as she reached up and swept the hood from her head.

Others saw him and swung around, and all grew silent as they saw her, and they all looked into those big, emerald green eyes of hers.

Her eyes met one then the next, and when she had looked to all of them, she looked up to the man who had spoken the most.

"Miss..." he stammered, "Miss Brebor?"

She raised her brow and nodded.

"So it's true," the woman drawled as she stood. "You're on a quest for King Arlo."

"Could ye be persuaded to stay a day or two?" a man at the table asked as he also stood.

Teek looked to him and shrugged.

"I'll see to a room," one of the women assured. "You'll have whatever you need if you'll just..." She looked to the tavern doors as a commotion was heard.

Someone ran into the tavern, a young man who also wore the dirty attire of a farmer, and he was quick to slam the doors and shove the bolt home to lock them. Swinging around as all looked that way, he shouted, "Bar the windows! Goblins are coming this way! Ten of 'em! Maybe twenty!"

A nervous hush fell over the tavern.

Her eyes narrowing, Teek patted the chest of the elf who had spoken the most, then looked around to the other men and gestured with her head for them to follow.

Outside the tavern, darkness was settling in and torches were lit on many of the structures, including the wooden columns of the tavern that held up the roof overhang over the front door. With sunlight fading fast, they provided most of the light.

Teek reached over her shoulder and took an arrow, looking down at her bow as she positioned it to shoot, then she looked to the score of men who hesitantly exited behind her. All had either found weapons of some kind or already had them. Five of them, including two of the women who had joined them, had bows and held them ready to pull. Striding to the middle of the forty pace wide street, she turned to face the shadowy figures that approached from just outside of the torchlight.

The men from the tavern fanned out behind her, forming an almost shoulder to shoulder line nearly all the way across the street.

There was a mumbling coming from the mob of goblins, not anything that any elf could understand, just a mumbling. The largest one, brandishing a rather large, double bladed battle axe, was in the lead and covered in leather armor and a battered metal helmet that looked like it had been taken off of a soldier he no doubt killed. They were short and stocky, heavier built than the elves, but no taller. Gray skin and stringy black hair gave them a frightening look, and their big eyes found the elves before them quickly. About a dozen in number, they realized they were outnumbered, but did not seem to care. They knew their quarry would panic, break and run as soon as they charged, so they just lumbered forward, readying their axes, their short swords and their spears. Half of them had nets in their free hands, no doubt to capture fleeing prey.

Teek's eyes narrowed and fixed on that largest one, the one that was clearly the leader.

Seeing the elves who were formed up before them, the goblin leader stopped and raised his hand to stop those behind him.

One on one, goblins were difficult to defeat. They were slightly larger, stronger, and better able to absorb battle damage than any elf. Teek had listened to her father's stories her entire life, and many of them were about his dealings with goblins. While she was afraid, she knew what to do, knew not to show even a hint of her fear. She beamed only confidence as she slowly raised her bow, pulling the string back and taking careful aim down the shaft of the arrow.

The goblin leader's big, almost fully black eyes narrowed to a squint and he sneered as he saw the elves standing their ground. With a defiant yell, he raised his axe to spur his fellow goblins forward and advanced ahead of them, only to stop abruptly as Teek's first arrow plunged into his head, almost perfectly between his eyes.

All of the Goblins watched the leader fall backward to the ground with the momentum of the arrow. He lay there unmoving with the arrow sticking straight up from his forehead and they stared at him for long seconds before turning their attention back to the elves.

Teek already had another arrow ready to shoot, and when the goblins looked her way, she took aim at another. The elves behind her raised their weapons and shouted in frenzied battle cries, and in that instant the goblins knew things had unexpectedly changed.

And as the daughter of the Elf Kingdom's greatest hero loosed her second arrow and began to advance with her elvan brethren behind her, the ten remaining goblins began to retreat from them for the first time.

The legend of Teek Brebor had only begun to grow among her people and those known by the elves. Stories would be told, fanciful tales would be exaggerated, and all would speak of a young elf who was not quite a woman, a small but savage warrior who had boundless courage, but no voice to tell her own story.